SURPRISE PARTY

The Sea Cobra had to plow along through the thick canyon air the old-fashioned way: by disturbing it, briefly. Norton's fingers were already going numb, his grip was so tight on the controls.

"How long do we have to do this?" Norton yelled up to Delaney. "Just two or three minutes, right?"

This made Delaney laugh. "Try more than ninety minutes," he said. "Maybe I'll take my nap now . . . the exciting part is over."

No sooner were those words out of Delaney's mouth than a shrill ringing began blaring in Norton's headphones. Suddenly the cockpit was vibrating with warning buzzers. Norton's control panel lit up like a Christmas tree. Delaney's did too.

"Talk to me, Slick!" Norton yelled ahead. "What's this all about?"

"If I'm reading these things right," Delaney reported. "Someone is hot-painting us . . ."

Norton couldn't believe what Delaney was telling him: They were being tracked on radar, probably one hooked up to some kind of antiaircraft system, probably one that was very close by and pointing down at them.

"Who the hell has a look-down radar set out here?" Norton shot back.

They were still twisting and turning through the canyon, following the contours of the river, sometimes coming as close as twenty feet to the top of the raging icy water. This was already inhospitable terrain. The cliffs seemed to become taller and more jagged the faster they went.

So it was a good question. Who *would* have such a hot-shit radar set way out here?

A moment later, they went around the next bend—and found out . . .

Berkley Books by Mack Maloney

CHOPPER OPS
CHOPPER OPS 2: ZERO RED
CHOPPER OPS 3: SHUTTLE DOWN

CHOPPER OPS

SHUTTLE DOWN

Mack Maloney

B

BERKLEY BOOKS, NEW YORK

This is a work of fiction. Names, characters, places, and incidents are either the product of the author's imagination or are used fictitiously, and any resemblance to actual persons, living or dead, business establishments, events, or locales is entirely coincidental.

CHOPPER OPS: SHUTTLE DOWN

A Berkley Book / published by arrangement with
the author

PRINTING HISTORY
Berkley edition / December 2000

The Penguin Putnam Inc. World Wide Web site address is
http://www.penguinputnam.com

ISBN: 0-425-17774-2

BERKLEY®
Berkley Books are published by The Berkley Publishing Group,
a division of Penguin Putnam Inc.,
375 Hudson Street, New York, New York 10014.
BERKLEY and the ''B'' design
are trademarks belonging to Penguin Putnam Inc.

PRINTED IN THE UNITED STATES OF AMERICA

10 9 8 7 6 5 4 3 2 1

For Bro

1

Trixxi was late for work.

She had driven back from Las Vegas earlier that day, her boyfriend Vince at the wheel. But for some reason the trip had taken much longer than usual. When he dropped her home in San Luis Obispo, it was already getting dark. By the time she took a bath, got dressed, and left for the club, it was almost eight o'clock—and she had already missed her first show.

Her bosses, the men who owned the strip joint called the Dollhouse, weren't exactly sweethearts. She was scheduled to do a private show at nine. If she was late for that, they would dock her at least a week's pay. Or maybe even fire her for good.

She arrived with a screech of brakes at the back of the club, hastily parked her Jeep, and dashed through the rear entrance to the dressing room. Krystal was at the makeup table, tossing her hair. Trixxi leaned over, gave her a quick kiss on the lips, then sat down next to her, out of breath.

"Tough night in Vegas, sweetie?" Krystal asked her.

Trixxi lit a cigarette and began digging deep into her makeup bag.

"It was the weirdest thing," she said. "Me and Vince left Caesar's, you know, like we always do, right after the early breakfast."

"Sure, the free midnight buffet."

"Right—but we didn't get back here until, like, really late afternoon. There wasn't any traffic. We didn't even stop to eat. It usually takes us about seven hours—but today it took twice that long. Isn't that strange?"

Krystal smiled. She was petite, gorgeous, small-busted, and a blonde this week. Trixxi, on the other hand, was tall, gorgeous, brunette, with 38DDs. They were both "twenty-nine," and almost best friends.

"You don't have to lay a story out for me," Krystal told Trixxi. "If you and Vince stopped on the way home for a quickie someplace, that's okay with me. I'm not the boss."

"But I'm not BS-ing you," Trixxi protested, applying eyeliner with an applicator the size of a Magic Marker. "I told Vince I thought his speedometer was wrong or something."

"I've seen the way Vince drives," Krystal said. "If the needle fell below a hundred, then I'd begin to worry."

"That's what I mean," Trixxi said with a long drag of her cigarette. "It was just very weird."

Krystal stood up and began taking her clothes off. "I hope you weren't kidnapped by aliens or something," she said.

Trixxi froze in the middle of an eyelash squeeze. She looked up at Krystal.

"Why did you say that?"

Krystal folded her blouse and began undoing her bra.

"Well, I know for a fact that there is always strange stuff flying around out in the desert. And you've heard of people being abducted by aliens, haven't you? They lose a few hours of their lives and . . ."

Krystal stopped in midsentence and looked down at Trixxi. Her friend was about to cry.

"Oh, my God, what's the matter, honey?"

Trixxi began to shiver. "We *did* see something strange this morning," she said sniffling. "I just *knew* it had something to do with it."

Krystal was quickly at her side. She passed her a box of Kleenex.

"What are you talking about?"

Trixxi blew her nose. "Just after we came over the mountains from Nevada. It was still dark and this weird light thing . . . it went right over our heads. It was going so freaking fast, we could hardly see it. And then, it, like, went straight up into the sky and disappeared. . . ."

Krystal looked deep into Trixxi's eyes. They weren't glassy or overly bloodshot, the telltales signs of coke or speed. She seemed legitimately upset.

"I'm sure it was just an airplane, honey," Krystal told her. "You know the Air Force has a big base out in Vegas, just like the one down the highway at Vandenberg. Like I said, plenty of weird things fly out of that Vegas base. Believe me, I know."

"But this didn't look like an airplane," Trixxi insisted. "It looked more like a pancake with wings. And it went way too fast, and it was turning and twisting real crazy, almost like it was out of control or something. I don't think any airplane can do what that thing did."

She began crying again. Krystal handed her some more tissues. Krystal wished she had never brought up the subject. For many reasons, "strange flying things" was not a topic she was comfortable talking about.

Trixxi blew her nose again. "Do you really think that's what happened? That we were picked up by alien freaks and, like, probed and stuff?"

Krystal hugged her and kissed her cheek.

"Honey, look at it this way: I can see someone wanting to kidnap you—some spaceman from somewheres. But Vince? I mean, come on! They would have zapped him on the spot."

Trixxi thought about this seriously for a few moments. Then she wiped her eyes again and said: "Yeah, you're right."

She crushed out her cigarette and went back to putting on her makeup. Krystal was now stripped bare.

"Besides," Krystal said, teasing her hair one last time. "It's just about a given now that all UFO sightings are actually due to either ball lightning or seismic ghosts. They're these strange electrical thingies that come out of the ground and can travel long distances as collections of positively charged electrons. It's like slow-motion lightning, which means really fast. Of course, they can't move at the speed of regular lightning because, well, it's against just about everything Einstein stood for. To go beyond the speed of light is impossible. Or much beyond it anyway."

But Trixxi wasn't listening anymore. She finished her makeup and began taking off her halter top and jeans.

"Did I tell you I'm thinking of changing my name to Angel?"

Krystal looked over at her friend again. The smile left her face.

"Really? Why? What's the matter with Trixxi? I thought you liked it."

Trixxi shrugged. "I'm just getting sick of it, I guess."

Krystal stared into the mirror for what seemed like a long time.

"I used to use 'Angel'," she said wistfully. "It was a very long time ago. And I had nothing but bad luck with it."

The two dancers finished slipping into their costumes for the night. Both were dressed in very skimpy cheerleader outfits, complete with bobby socks and saddle shoes.

"Who is this party for anyway?" Trixxi asked Krystal.

"Guys from down at Vandenberg—they might be pilots, I think. It's either a bachelor party or a divorce party. One or the other."

Trixxi began spinning her hair into pigtails, all thoughts of their previous conversation long gone by now.

"I just hope they tip a whole lot better than the usual crowd," she said with a sigh. "I really need the money."

Both girls selected a set of pom-poms from the club's prop bin, then cued their music and pranced out onto the stage. They were surprised though to see the club was empty except for four men in casual clothes sitting at the center table.

"Just four guys?" Trixxi stage-whispered to Krystal. "I should have stayed in Vegas. . . ."

The show began. Trixxi and Krystal went into their usual act—taking turns twirling around the chrome pole located in the middle of the stage, removing an article of clothing every thirty seconds or so. Once they were nude, the two dancers would do an erotic dance together; then they would work over the four customers individually.

But just as the music was changing from a pulsating

dance mix to a slow track, the front door to the club flew open and six men in dark uniforms rushed in.

They looked like cops, but their uniforms had no badges or emblems. They were armed, but their guns were holstered, at least for the moment. One of the club's bouncers appeared, but he was quickly pushed aside. It took a moment for the intruders' eyes to adjust to the low lights of the club. But once they spotted the four men sitting near the front of the stage, they headed straight for them.

One man seemed in charge of the black-uniformed squad. He had a hushed conversation with the men at the table. Then came a round of frantic hand-gesturing and watch-checking. There was no mistaking the expressions on the faces of the four men. It was clear they were being told some shocking news.

The four customers quickly got to their feet and left the club. One of the uniformed men pulled a wad of bills from his pocket, counted out a handful, and threw them up on stage.

"They were never here," he said to the dancers with a grim smile.

Then he too left quickly.

And just like that, the club was empty again.

"Now what the hell was that all about?" Trixxi asked.

Krystal just shrugged, sat down on the edge of the stage, and began counting the money.

"Like I said, those guys were all military," she said. "And if there's one thing I've learned from working this part of the world, when someone in the military does something strange around here, it's best that you don't ask why. . . ."

Less than an hour later, the four men hustled from the strip club were sitting in an expansive, dimly lit flight compartment. They were strapped tightly into heavily padded seats, thick helmets on their heads, feet up, their eyes pointing skyward.

"Okay, what's our launch status?" the man in the pilot's seat asked.

"Not good," the man sitting in the copilot's seat replied. "We've got less than forty-five percent of critical systems on-line."

"Which ones are at one hundred percent?" the pilot asked as he began tapping a row of flat-panel screens to life.

"Environmental support and propulsion are the only systems at peak," the copilot replied, the tone of his voice growing tense. "This thing doesn't tune up like the old ones."

"No matter, we'll have to go with it," the pilot said.

"That's impossible, Donny," the copilot told him. "I don't think the computer will kick in with bare minimums like that."

The pilot never looked up from his control panel.

"So we go to the manual override," he said. "It's time we tried that thing out."

The copilot just stared back at him. Not an hour ago, he'd been looking at two beautiful girls taking their clothes off. Now he was seconds away from being blown to smithereens. Some party this turned out to be.

"Doing this without the computer involves a very high risk factor," he told the pilot as calmly as possible. "Hypothetically, we might not even make it off the pad."

The pilot just scoffed at this. They were in a hurry.

"Is there a chance we can get to where we want to go, alive, with the systems we have on-line now?" he asked.

"Well, yes," the copilot replied. "But . . ."

"No buts," the pilot interrupted. "If it can happen, then let's make it happen."

"But . . . there's also a very good chance we'll be killed," the copilot said anyway. The two other men, strapped into seats right behind them, were listening very intently to the conversation.

"Look, this is what we're trained to do," the pilot told them all. "We've done a million hot launches in the simulator. We should know the drill by heart. Now, we got a job to do up there and we've got to get to it 'toot sweet' before the shit really hits."

He pulled down his helmet's green eye visor.

"Besides," he added, "we're not going to get killed. I'm certain of it."

"How can you be so sure?" the copilot asked him.

"Because," the pilot replied. " 'Getting killed' just ain't in our orders."

Ten minutes later, the sky around the Santa Lucia Mountains lit up as bright as day.

The ground rumbled; the mountains themselves began to shake. The initial glow could be seen for miles. But as it turned out, very few people living near Vandenberg Air Force Base paid much attention to the bright orange fire rising slowly into the deep night sky. Strange things were always flying out of Vandy, especially at night. This one seemed no different.

Two minutes later any sign that a space shuttle had been launched were gone—all except for the long trail of smoke and icy exhaust curving out over the ocean.

It would take another ten minutes for that to finally blow away.

2

On the border of Kyrgyzstan and China
Twenty-four hours later

Zatuk Yazek was at the beginning of a very long day.

He was a shepherd. His herd of three hundred goats was spread out over one side of a mountain called Repek Ca. This snowy, mile-high peak was perpetually shrouded in fog, as was the deep crater on its eastern side. Thin air. Little sunlight. A haunting, howling wind. Not surprising weather for this strange location, known to be one of the most isolated places on Earth.

Zatuk's goal for the day was to collect his herd, cull any pregnant females from the pack, and count them. Then he would select the biggest kid and bring it home for his family's evening meal. Depending on how scattered the herd was, these tasks might take up to fourteen hours or more. He would need all his strength and endurance to make it a successful day.

The problem was, Zatuk felt a bit out of sync this morning. He blamed this on a strange dream he'd had the night before. In the dream, he looked out his window and saw something floating very slowly above his house. It was so huge, it took up most of the sky. It was colored bright red, and the edges were sparkling, as if somehow charged with electricity. Strangest of all was its shape: It looked like an enormous can of soda pop.

Restless upon waking, Zatuk decided to set out for the mountain long before the sun came up.

If he worked fast and got lucky during the day, he might be back home before nightfall.

He found the first batch of dead goats about thirty minutes into his hike up Repek Ca.

There were five of them strewn about a tiny streambed. Nothing seemed amiss from the condition of their bodies— not at first anyway. But Zatuk knew immediately what had killed them. The bloodshot eyes. The pink ooze running from the mouth. He'd seen this before. His goats had died of fright.

He found four more dead kids another five hundred feet up the mountain path, just before the snow line. Like the goats down below, these animals had died of fright as well.

Zatuk was very puzzled. What had frightened his goats so? A family of mountain cats? A pack of wolves? No— not up this high. And besides, where was the blood? And why weren't at least some of the animals eaten?

A chilling thought came to him. Could it have been a yeti? He reached into his day pack, took out his rifle, and checked his ammunition clip. It was full.

He took a deep breath of the frigid morning air and continued up the path. This time he moved a little slower, a little more carefully. By now he would have expected to see some of his herd, or at least hear them braying at his approach. But the mountain was silent this morning.

No wind. No crows calling. Nothing . . .

He climbed up another one thousand feet and came upon a third pile of goats. There were at least twenty of them, his finest females among them. They were all dead too.

Baffled by all this, Zatuk finally reached the top of the mountain path. The interior of the great crater lay before him. At that moment a wind came up, and began sweeping the fog from the bottom of the deep crevice. And for just a few seconds in the dim morning light, Zatuk saw the crater's floor.

There was something down there. Something big and white. A piece of a wing, a large tail. Other things sticking out of the snow. The fog rolled back in an instant later, but the vision stayed burned into Zatuk's eyes.

What in God's name was that? he thought.

3

Osh Kya Air Base
Eastern Kyrgyzstan

No one was really sure where the two elderly helicopters
had come from.

They were of U.S. manufacture, at least that was certain.
But exactly how they'd made their way from America to
the tiny air base at Osh Kya was a little hazy, especially
since it had taken more than fifty years and several dozen
stops along to way to make the journey.

Their serial numbers were 981645-23 and 312099-99,
respectively, and back when the pair were built in 1948,
their model's official designation was the HRP-1. They
were long, slender, with a cranked rear end supporting one
of two rotors, the other one being located up front above
the glassy, bug-eyed cockpit.

As far as choppers went, the HRPs were slow. Very
slow. Like molasses-slow. Neither aircraft could break a

hundred miles an hour in a stiff wind. They could barely carry a ton of cargo—eight passengers was the maximum load, along with the crew of two. And it took more than five minutes for the chopper to reach a piddling two thousand feet in altitude.

The HRP design had acquired several nicknames during its long service life. The first was Rescuer, this because the aircraft was originally designed for search and rescue duties. A later variant built for the U.S. Air Force was called the Shawnee, but was also known simply as the Work Horse. The name that stuck with the HRP-1 for more than a half century, however, was the least glamorous, yet most apt. With its oddly angled, upturned rear end, the appellation Flying Banana was probably inevitable.

These two particular Bananas first saw squadron duty in the early 1950's, flying supplies up to Air Force radar bases in deep-freeze northern Alaska. By the mid-'50's, the two copters had been shipped to Europe for duty in the Berlin Crisis. Returning to the U.S. in late 1959, the choppers' squadron was transferred to Nevada and used to transport scientists monitoring atomic bomb testing. Then in 1962, both aircraft were shipped to Southeast Asia, where they served as troop carriers in the early days of the Vietnam War.

After that, their history got fuzzy.

It was believed that both copters were captured by Communist troops late in 1963. Supposedly, they were disassembled and shipped to Russia, where they sat in a warehouse near Rostov-on-Don for nearly twenty years before being stolen, still in their crates. They were eventually reassembled and bounced around Africa for a while, winding up in Angola, where they were used by UNITA as flying ambulances. Captured by South African forces in 1987, they went into storage once again—until the government of Kyrgyzstan secretly bought them in 1998.

It was one of the first major purchases the new nation had made for its fledgling armed forces. Prior to this, all of its equipment had been hand-me-downs, leftovers from the Russian military when Krygyzstan was still part of the old Soviet Union. And while there was little doubt that Kyrgyzstan had gotten royally screwed on the purchase price of the two Flying Bananas, the tiny nation, nestled in the rugged terrain between northwest China and Tajikistan, and close to many other alphabet-soup countries, was proud of its oddly shaped helicopters, simply because they hadn't been forced on them by Mother Russia, now so far away.

In other words, they were their own.

By any measurement, the operational armed forces of Kyrgyzstan were tiny.

Lack of money and the confusion after the breakdown of the Soviet Union had led to some challenging times over the last decade. At any given moment, less than a quarter of the nation's military could be considered ready to fight. Its air force was nonexistent, its border units stationed in such far-flung posts that even simple radio contact between them was impossible at times.

But there was one unit of the Kyrgyzstani armed forces that was in a constant state of readiness, eager to do combat on a moment's notice. Established in 1997, it had selected its members from the best of the country's depleted ground forces and put them through rigorous training based on old U.S. Green Berets instruction manuals found on the Internet. Envisioned as an aerial assault team, this unit became complete when Kyrgyzstan purchased the pair of Flying Bananas. Just forty-four-men strong, it was Kyrgyzstan's version of a special-ops unit, a rapid-deployment force, and a hostage-recovery team, all wrapped into one.

It was known simply as Company X. Its home base was Osh Kyr.

The commander of Company X was a young Army captain named Shakpak Azzur.

Though his family had grown up in Kyrgyzstan, Azzur was actually of Mongolian blood. As such, he was a proud soldier and a fierce warrior. He had two nicknames among his men: Krxystzni, which loosely translated in local Kyrgyzstani slang meant "Big Brain"; and Krznistnygx, which, in no uncertain terms, meant "Crazy Man."

Azzur was known for his brain because he was one of the few people in the armed forces who had actually graduated college. He had attended schools in Moscow, Berlin, and Ankara, eventually accumulating enough classes to cop a bachelor's degree in military science.

Azzur was known to be crazy because he was absolutely ferocious when it came to combat. Several years before, the Kyrgyzstani army had been involved in a tiny, almost-secret war against drug smugglers operating on the western edge of the country. Azzur was a lieutenant at the time, and he commanded an advance unit of recon troops sent to seek out the drug lords. In several pitched battles with the smugglers, Azzur showed an intensity that even frightened his own men. He was equally adept at firing his machine gun as he was in lopping off heads with his ever-present *krysttky,* a long, razor-sharp sword traditionally given to Kyrgyzstani officers upon receiving their commissions.

Azzur had been awakened just after dawn this day by a loud pounding on the front door of his officer's billet. It was a sergeant sent from the High Staff office at Osh Kyr. A secret message carried by the man informed Azzur that Company X was being activated immediately. Azzur had to report to the base at once.

Thirty minutes later, Azzur was standing beside Osh Kyr's main runway, shivering in the bitter morning cold, watching as the base ground crew rolled out Company X's pair of Flying Bananas and frantically began to get them ready for flight. The men of Company X were already on hand. They were lined up in two rows on the edge of the runway, checking over their gear and anticipating their first call to battle.

Azzur knew nothing about where they were going or why—he'd yet to get a final briefing from his superiors. But he'd been assured of one thing: This was not a drill. Company X was being sent on a legitimate, real-life mission. Because of this, the excitement Azzur felt in his chest was nearly overwhelming.

Azzur's best guess was that he and his men were being sent to battle the western drug lords again.

There had been rumors lately that the heroin gangs, finally recovered from their war against national forces two years before, were building up their operations again, supposedly with money supplied by a mysterious billionaire/terrorist who'd once lived somewhere in the north of Iraq.

But Azzur was in for a surprise. No sooner had the ground crew declared both HRPs "adequate" for flight than a staff car drove up to where Azzur and his men were waiting. One of Kyrgyzstan's two full-time staff intelligence officers—a colonel named Tzen—was in the backseat of the car. Tzen indicated that Azzur should get in.

Climbing into the back of the battered Benz, Azzur welcomed the blast of warm air pouring out of the car's noisy heater. He did not know Colonel Tzen very well. However, they had something in common: Both were of Mongolian descent.

Tzen handed him the mission packet, essentially an envelope containing details of his orders along with operations maps and a code list. Azzur would have wagered a gallon of goat's milk at that moment that his destination was Tash Kumyr, the scene of the bloodiest fighting against the drug lords two years before. But one look at the first page of his orders told him he would have lost that bet.

Company X was being deployed in the opposite direction, to the far east, to a place very close to the Chinese border.

A place called the Paswar.

Not many things could send a chill through Azzur's veins, but any mention of the Paswar usually did the trick.

Azzur had never been there, had never *wanted* to go there. But he'd heard about the place ever since he was a child. The Paswar was literally a no-man's-land, a tiny piece of isolated, rugged mountainous country located on the southeastern edge of Kyrgyzstan. The terrain of the Paswar was so treacherous—high mountains surrounding one incredibly deep valley—that no nearby country had ever laid claim to it. China, Tajikstan, Afghanistan, as well as Kyrgyzstan itself, all probably had rights to take over this forgotten piece of Earth, yet none had, simply because the place was so remote, so forbidding, it would do little good for any country to absorb it into its borders.

When Azzur was a child, his father used to scare him shitless by telling ghost stories about the Paswar. "Souls go in, but souls don't come out," were words that stuck with Azzur even today. Few people actually lived there; those that did were mostly backward goat herders. The mountains of the Paswar were sheer ice, prone to avalanche and supposedly thick with yeti. Criminals who managed to escape from Kyrgyzstan's notorious prisons and were desperate to remain un-captured, would traditionally head for the Paswar, usually to die there soon afterward. Legend had it that hundreds of years before, after China decided it would annex the small territory, it sent one thousand of its best men marching into the Paswar to stake their claim. Not one came back out.

"What is so important inside the Paswar?" Azzur now asked Colonel Tzen.

Tzen retrieved a small notebook sealed tight with dozens of rubber bands. He opened it to reveal another, smaller map of the Paswar, this one drawn on top of an old satellite image.

There was a series of red arrows connecting the edge of Kyrgyzstani territory to the absolute center of the Paswar. Here was the deep valley that was actually the burnt-out crater of an ancient volcano. It was ringed by mountains that ran more than two miles high in some places and were perpetually covered with thick mist and snow. In the middle of this crater, at the place where the red arrows were pointing, someone had drawn a large black star.

"Last night, an aircraft of some kind overflew our territory," Tzen began. "Many of our western border guards saw it, as did the crews of two cargo planes. This aircraft seemed to be on fire, yet it was flying as if it was under control.

"Our radar people acquired it just as it was leaving our airspace. They determined that the aircraft either crashed— or crash-landed—twenty minutes later."

Tzen pointed to the big black star.

"They believe it came down right here."

Azzur looked at the map and then up at Tzen. He was clearly puzzled. "Are they saying of all the places in this world, this thing came down in that little piece of hell?"

"That's the thinking," Tzen replied.

"But my colonel," Azzur said, studying the map again,

"what kind of an aircraft could be on fire yet still under control?"

Tzen just shook his head. "We don't know. It was of substantial size and created many sonic booms as it went over, they said. That indicates an aircraft of some speed and sophistication."

Tzen turned the page and read a summary of Azzur's orders.

"Therefore, your unit will transit to the Paswar, attempt to locate this unidentified aircraft, determine whether it is of extraterrestrial origin or not, and report your findings back to our President himself."

Azzur shook his head. *Did he just hear that right?*

" 'Extraterrestrial origin?' " he asked Tzen. "Doesn't that mean a 'flying saucer'?"

The intelligence officer frowned. "It's probably unwise to use that particular term," he said. "Let's just say our president is a man interested in the edges of science—plus he is a big fan of American movies and TV. Put two and two together."

Azzur was astonished. "We are being sent into the Paswar to see if a UFO has crashed there?"

Again, Tzen frowned. "It's really best that we stick with the term 'unidentified aircraft,' Captain Azzur."

Azzur lost his veneer of military protocol at that moment.

"This is madness, Tzen," he said defiantly. "The Paswar is hardly territory suited for my men or our equipment. Indeed, I can't think of *any* force who would want to be deployed to such a place."

Tzen waved away his protests. "You have been given orders by our commander in chief. He is entrusting this very special mission to you and your men, and he expects nothing less than your best effort."

"But there is a good chance we will not return," Azzur

insisted. He was thinking of his men now and the flying conditions in and around the Paswar. It was the last place he wanted them to go on their first real mission, especially in the antique Bananas.

"I must repeat to you the words our president himself said to me not two hours ago," Tzen said. "Imagine what prestige it would bring to our country, our people . . . if we were the first ones to recover an . . . 'unusual aircraft.' "

Azzur's temper was rising. "You cannot even say it yourself, Colonel," he told Tzen. "You cannot even say the words 'flying saucer.' "

Tzen put his finger to Azzur's lips for a moment. His eyes said it all: He knew this was nonsense, a fool's errand. But orders were orders—and these were right from the top.

"We are wasting time discussing this," Tzen told him. "The president feels that we might not be the only ones looking for this aircraft—so time is our enemy now."

He pressed the operational plans into Azzur's hands and then saluted the junior officer.

"So, good luck, my brave friend," he said, opening the car door as a signal that their meeting was over. "I'm afraid no matter what happens, you will need it."

Xianganga Air Base
Sinkiang Region
Northwest China

The flag brigade was late.

It was midmorning. The five helicopters of the 17th Aerial Rotary Squadron of the Zhongkuo Shenmin Taifang Tsunputai, or Air Force of the People's Army, were warmed up and ready for takeoff. An honor guard consisting of one hundred soldiers was lined up along the main runway of the air base, shivering in the cold early morning weather, waiting to cheer their comrades aloft.

But the flag brigade was late. And the five helicopters could not take off until it arrived.

This made the ground commander of the helicopter squadron absolutely furious. He was Major Li Shit-zu, and he knew just about everything there was to know about the 17th Aerial Rotary, a unit that made up a substantial portion of China's military helicopter resources in this remote part of the country.

The squadron's choppers were Aerospatiale Dauphins of French design. They had been assembled from kits bought by the Zhongkuo Shenmin Taifang Tsunputai two years before. They were impeccably maintained and serviced, highly polished in dark camo green, hand-washed and buffed every night. The aircraft were armed with Giat M621 20-mm cannon pods as well as HOT wire-guided antitank missiles. In addition, each copter was carrying ten members of the Quang Fung, a highly secret special-operations force devoted to service in the far western provinces of China. This would be their first real operation— which was why Major Shit-zu was growing more incensed with every minute the flag brigade was late.

Shit-zu had not been made privy to the circumstances that had led to his unit being dispatched this morning. But the People's Army was a big barrel, and thus, not without some holes. From his sources inside the far western military region command, Shit-zu had learned that an aircraft of some kind had reportedly crashed in rugged terrain about 150 miles to the west. Witnesses said this aircraft had lit up the skies the night before as it made a fiery plunge to earth. As to what kind of aircraft it was, his sources did not know. Only that it was a "flying machine of great sophistication," and that recovering it would be considered an enormous coup for the People's Army. Vague as this was,

Shit-zu took it all to mean an American military craft had crashed somewhere out west—and he was guessing the airplane was a B-2 Stealth bomber.

Whatever the case, these were big doings for Shit-zu's unit. A gaggle of high-level officers was on hand just to watch them take off. So it was imperative that everything went right with the mission. There was one sticky part, though: According to their top-secret orders, this mission would actually take them beyond the borders of China. This was a very unusual thing to do for any unit of the People's Army, which only served to heighten the anxiety. With the stakes growing by the minute, Shit-zu wanted his men to leave before their stress levels grew more acute. Yet, already their takeoff was behind schedule by fifteen minutes.

Finally, the truck bearing the flag brigade rolled onto the airfield. Knowing they would be severely punished for their tardiness, the dozen soldiers frantically jumped from the truck and assembled in front of the honor guard, about two hundred feet away from the waiting helicopters.

Although the combined racket of the five rotors twirling made hearing anything else just about impossible, a loudspeaker was set up on the side of the flag brigade truck and some truly awful scratchy music was turned on. The flag soldiers began waving their long red banners, rippling in the early morning wind. The scratchy music reached painful decibels for those close by. The honor guard stood rigid, their rifles held out far in front of them.

A few moments of ceremony was all that was required. On a signal from Major Shit-zu himself, the five Dauphin helicopters lifted off, one after another, and began circling the air base. Once all five were at the same altitude, the lead copter broke out of the orbit and began heading east— in the wrong direction. The four other copters followed suit.

Shit-zu nearly wet himself right then and there. The high

officers around him knew something was wrong. He screamed at the video crew documenting the takeoff to stop taping immediately. The flag soldiers stopped waving their banners and the music was shut off. Frenetic radio calls were sent up to the chopper squadron. Finally, the pilot in the lead copter realized he was going the wrong way. He banked hard again, turned 180 degrees, and pointed the nose of his aircraft due west. The rest of the copters quickly followed.

Sighs of relief went through those on the ground, not the least of which came from Major Shit-zu. The flag men began waving their banners again; the awful music was turned back on. The video men resumed taping.

Reorganized now, the handful of Dauphins went into a ragged arrow formation and flew over the ceremonial troops at one thousand feet.

Then, as one, they climbed again, and soon disappeared over the mountains to the west, heading for a place the Chinese called Mou Ku for "evil holes," more commonly known as the Paswar.

Chillik Military Air Field
Eastern Kazakhstan

Several hundred miles west of Xianganga, at a smaller, darker air base, five more helicopters were waiting to take off.

They were, in total, the entire aircraft inventory of the eastern military district of the armed forces of Kazakhstan, the huge country that bordered Kyrgyzstan on the north and China on the east. The helicopter squadron consisted of two Hind gunships, two Hook troop carriers, and a Hip provisions aircraft. All of Russian manufacture, the copters were not in very good shape. Essentially left behind by Soviet military forces when the Soviet Union collapsed, the elderly choppers had been beset by maintenance woes and a dreadful lack of spare parts. Indeed, since becoming part of the Kazak military, they had spent much more time in their hangars than in the air. Hoping to keep their flying skills fresh, the choppers' pilots had spent their days training on ancient Sega helicopter video games.

Now they too were heading for the Paswar. The regional headquarters of the Kazak secret police, located in the district capital city of Karatau, had apparently intercepted some unusual radio traffic that indicated some kind of object had fallen out of the sky the night before, landing somewhere near the border of Kyrgyzstan and China, in the area of the Paswar. For whatever reason, the secret police believed this object was actually a top-secret American spy satellite, or at least the remains of one. They'd convinced the Kazak military it would be in their country's best interests to attempt a recovery of this object, and possibly sell it or parts of its wreckage to the highest bidder.

But this hastily conceived mission already had the makings of a disaster. Besides the poor shape of the copters, the Kazaks had little in the way of navigation equipment or communications sets. The ten pilots involved had less than five hundred hours of actual flying time combined. The ninety-three soldiers being stuffed into the Hooks were not Kazak special-operations troops, but draft-age conscripts with poor weapons, ill-fitting helmets and field suits, and zero combat experience. Few of them had even heard of the Paswar, never mind knowing where it was.

There was no formal ceremony to mark their departure. No flag-waving or music blaring through loudspeakers. Not even a formal intelligence briefing. The senior man for the force was a thirty-two-year-old lieutenant who, up until the day before, was the supply officer for the Kazak base at

Chillik. He was simply told to "reconnoiter the impact zone" and report back any unusual activity.

His only means of communication would be a cell phone.

After some delay in finding the correct maps of the target area, the five helicopters took off.

The Hinds went first, both gunships rolling down the bumpy runway, leaving behind twin storms of smoke and dust. The first Hook followed close behind, lifting into the air via a smoky, noisy takeoff.

The second Hook then began rolling down the runway, followed closely by the Hip provisions chopper. Too closely, as it turned out. Whether either helicopter ever actually made it off the ground would never really be determined. The only thing clear was that, probably due to a stuck throttle, the Hip copter went down the runway at twice the normal takeoff speed and crashed into the rear end of the Hook. Both copters went over in a kind of slow motion and slammed into the ground, exploding into a huge burning heap at the end of the runway.

The base's rudimentary crash-and-rescue teams rushed to the scene of accident, but it was no use. Both copters were totally involved in flame, and continued to explode for some time afterward. There was simply no way anyone could have lived through the crash.

Overhead, the three other copters began circling the base. With nearly fifty of their comrades suddenly dead and all their provisions gone in a flash, there was some question as to whether they would abort the mission.

But a radio call between the copters and the commanders on the ground put a quick end to the confusion.

"Proceed as ordered," was the gist of the stern message from the ground.

Having no other choice, the three aging copters slotted into a fragile triangle formation, then turned as one and headed east.

4

The USS *Bataan* was six hours out of the Persian Gulf when the message came in.

The ship had just completed a three-month cruise of the Mediterranean and the Middle East. It was now on its way to San Diego, where it would undergo a sorely needed year-long refit. If it wasn't for the poor weather in the Gulf the last few days delaying its departure, the ship would have been halfway home by now. But as it turned out, it found itself passing about a hundred miles off the coast of Pakistan this steamy April morning.

The message arrived at precisely 1100 hours. It was buried in so many encryption files, it looked like nothing more than two pages of alphabet soup at first. The *Bataan*'s communications officer thought for sure it was a mistake, a random burst of Comsat static that somehow made its way down to the ship. Such things had happened before.

But the comm officer followed the decoding procedures and, like peeling layers back from an onion, he eventually got to the heart of the communiqué. It was just one sentence: The captain of the *Bataan* was to phone the White House Situation Room—immediately.

The *Bataan* was an LHD, Navy-speak for Amphibious Assault Ship.

It looked like a miniature aircraft carrier. It had a flight deck about half that of a Navy supercarrier, and its center island looked like an outhouse compared to the virtual skyscrapers found aboard the *Nimitz* or the *Stennis*. The *Bataan* did not handle the F/A-18 attack jets or F-14 fighters as those ships did. Like a dozen or so other vessels in its class, the *Bataan*—or the "Batman" to its crew—was essentially a water taxi for the Marines. It was dedicated to putting men on a beach, quickly, efficiently, and with tons of fire support.

It was able to do this in many ways. By flooding a specially built lower compartment, landing craft could be put to sea via an opening in the stern. Up top, the ship carried squadrons of big CH-46 Sea Knights, each capable of lifting twenty-five troops plus all their equipment. Harrier jumpjets and UH-1 Sea Cobra attack choppers provided protection from the air. All this stuff was driven by the Marine Corps; the Navy guys just ran the ship. No surprise that on a normal cruise, if the ship's crew totaled a thousand men, the number of jarheads on board was usually twice that.

The *Bataan* was part of the Gator Navy, the sea-invasion arm of America's senior service. Though by their nature, amphibious operations guaranteed some excitement, even in training, being part of the Gator Navy was not considered glamorous duty for career sailors. In the highly political world of the U.S. Navy, being assigned Gator was, at the very least, a step sideways on the way to the top.

And rarely, if ever, did a message come in for the captain to phone the White House war room.

But there's a first time for everything.

Captain John "Bear" Currier was the commanding officer of the *Bataan*. He was in his office filling out his morning report when the communications officer delivered the coded message to him. The captain could not help but be surprised by the communiqué. Had the message been decoded properly? The communications officer assured him it had been. Even the phone number included in the message checked out.

Currier thanked him and asked that he close the door on the way out. Then Currier picked up his POTS—for Plain Old Telephone System—and started dialing the White House number.

His call was answered on the first ring.

When Currier emerged from his office ten minutes later, he was not excited exactly, nor enlightened. Rather, he was somewhat amused.

The reason for the conversation with the White House was to inform him that his orders had been changed. He was told to slow the *Bataan* down to five knots and switch to a circular course, this in order to maintain his present position. A number of "transitional personnel" were due to arrive on board his ship at any minute; they would be coming by two different modes of transport. To assure their arrival was as secure as possible, Currier was to clear his deck of all aircraft, save for a single SAR chopper. All personnel not essential to the operation of the ship were to be sent to their quarters until further notice.

Additionally, a secure cabin was to be made available to the ingressing personnel—with armed guards posted out-

side. The new arrivals were to be given access to any means
of transportation and equipment the *Bataan* could offer, including aircraft. All these arrangements had to be made as
quickly as possible. As Currier understood it, these personnel would be using his ship as a jumping-off point for a
hurry-up special operation that was so secret, only voice
communications could be used in discussing it. Only Currier, his ship's intelligence officer, its executive officer, and
the commander of the Marine contingent could be made
aware of the new situation.

But why the *Bataan*? Was it because Currier's operational record and crew reports were known to be among
the best in the Navy? No. The reason the ship was being
called on was simply a matter of right place, right time.
Whoever these transitional people were, they had to get
close to the Southwest Asian mainland as quickly and quietly as possible.

And the USS "Batman" just happened to be floating by.

Currier made all the necessary preparations. The majority
of the crew was sent to their quarters. The ship's speed was
reduced drastically and the 360-degree course laid in. The
deck was cleared except for one Sea Knight, which was
sent aloft and told to take up station about a thousand yards
off starboard. Two deck officers were also needed to stay
up top.

Currier informed his XO, his intelligence officer, and the
Marine CO. They were all out on the flight deck less than
ten minutes after Currier got off the phone. There they
waited as the late morning haze rolled in, promising another
hot afternoon in the making.

Right on time, an odd sound appeared on the wind. It
was an aircraft, but not a typical one. Ears accustomed to
hearing big Sea Knight choppers take off and land knew

well their distinctive sound. This was not it. Nor was it the
racket made by a CH-53 Sea Dragon, or a Kamen Sea
Sprite, or any of the other rotary aircraft that, at one time
or another, found their way to the deck of the *Bataan*.

This was different.

They saw it a few seconds later. It was coming out of
the northeast, tearing through the low humid clouds with
an urgency not seen with helicopters. That was because this
aircraft was not a helicopter. It was a V-22 Osprey.

The Osprey was a combination rotary craft and airplane.
About the size of a small commuter airliner, it had two
huge movable propellers located at each end of its wing.
The big props could be turned up to the horizontal, which
allowed the craft to take off and land like a chopper; when
moved vertically, they pushed the Osprey along in level
flight like a more conventional aircraft. While adding substantial versatility to usual helicopter missions, the V-22
could move at close to 325 mph, more than double most
choppers. It could also boast a range of more than two
thousand miles in some circumstances, a distance unheard
of in chopperland.

The officers on deck had seen these aircraft before, of
course. Though they were a relatively new design, and the
models were a long time getting out in the field, seeing an
Osprey was not as much of a rarity these days as, say, five
years before. Yet right away, something about this particular V-22 struck the officers as unusual.

Every Osprey any of them had ever seen before had been
painted in either assembly-line white or Marine gray-green
camo. This V-22 was painted dull black. It carried no country markings or aircraft ID numbers, and its fuselage was
studded with bumps and bulges, each one containing, they
supposed, some kind of high-tech radar or EW doodad. Its
nose was weirdly extended and thick with various antenna

extensions. Its underwings were heavy with pods and weapons' points. All this made for a very strange, almost sinister configuration. It gave this V-22 a mysterious air akin to that of a stealth plane.

"Who does *this* thing belong to?" Currier asked the Marine CO.

The Marine could only shrug. "It's not one of ours," he replied. "You can be sure of that."

The V-22 went around the carrier once; then its wings began their vertical translation. The aircraft slowed down so abruptly, it looked like an aerial hot rod suddenly slamming on its brakes. In seconds it moved into a perfect hover above the ass end of the ship, its engine wash—muted, yet powerful—spilling over the carrier deck like a small typhoon.

Five seconds of this and the aircraft finally came down. Its wheels hit the deck once and stayed there; there was no bounce. One of the deck officers directed it to a parking spot, its huge props already beginning to spin down. Looking out at the small greeting party on the deck, the men in the Osprey's cockpit saluted. Currier and the others saluted back.

The V-22 came to a halt and lowered a ramp from its back end. Two dozen black-camouflage soldiers clambered down the incline lugging heavy weapons and enormous field packs. They looked more like a SWAT team than a military unit.

They were directed to the nearest hatchway by the second deck officer, and quickly disappeared belowdecks. In all, it had taken them less than thirty seconds to come aboard.

No sooner had this happened than a second aircraft appeared in the sky.

"This *must* be serious," the XO said, pressing binoculars

to his eyes. "These guys are actually sticking to a schedule."

The second airplane was a huge C-5 Galaxy cargo jet, the largest airplane in the U.S. Air Force's inventory. It came out of the east, the opposite direction from the Osprey, and slowly began circling the *Bataan*.

Dropping down a bit lower with every orbit of the ship, it reached an altitude of about 750 feet. At this point, it leveled off, pointed its nose to a course parallel with the LHD, and slowed to a crawl. Engines screaming for power and height, the rear door of the big plane opened and something came tumbling out. It was about the size of a small compact car and shaped like a huge thimble. It was painted in very bright Day-Glo orange.

This thing was sometimes called a WIP, for Wet Insertion/Personal. This contraption with the filthy name was usually employed to assist stricken ships in emergency situations, a way to get people from an airplane to a seagoing vessel (or near one anyway) in quick order. It was not known for its comfort, however, and placing it in the correct spot of ocean was not yet an art form.

Most WIPs were equipped with parachutes, but this one had been dropped by the C-5 at such a low altitude, the silks had barely opened when the capsule hit the water. There was an enormous splash as it went under once, then twice, before finally coming to the surface and staying there, at least temporally.

The *Bataan*'s loitering Sea Knight moved in, and was soon hovering above the capsule. Divers went into the water, and in a scene not unlike the old NASA spacecraft recoveries, hooked a cable sent down from the Sea Knight onto the big orange blob. Once secured, the capsule was lifted out of the water, flown sideways, and gently placed onto the deck of the LHD.

No sooner had it touched down, however, than there was a bright flash, followed by a sharp explosion. The capsule's hatch cover blew off, went nearly straight up in the air, came down hard, bounced once on the deck, then went over the side of the ship.

Amid the smoke and steam from this, two men emerged.

"Quite an entrance," the Marine commander said dryly. "But are we sure these guys are in the right place?"

It was not an unreasonable question. The two men looked like they'd been swept up from a bar in Margaritaville and suddenly deposited here on a Navy ship a half a world away. Both were wearing flowered shirts, baseball caps, torn jeans, sneakers, and sunglasses. One was holding a beer can. They seemed slightly dazed and a tad crumpled by their unusual means of ingress.

They were Jazz Norton and Bobby Delaney. Both in their thirties, with Norton slightly taller, slightly younger. He had movie-star looks and a lean but rugged exterior. Delaney, who was known by various nicknames, including "Slick" and "Cowboy Bob," was wiry, slightly bowlegged, his face permanently tanned and weathered. He was the one holding the can.

Though they didn't look it, these two were part of a government special-operations group so obscure, so secret, it didn't even have a name. This tiny unit was built around helicopters—even though its personnel was not. Norton and Delaney were actually ex-fighter pilots. They'd spent much of their careers flying F-15's for the U.S. Air Force. Despite this, they and a few others like them had been tapped by the CIA's Special Foreign Projects Office for a secret helicopter mission about eighteen months before. This mission involved tracking down and destroying a rogue AC-130 gunship, left over from the Persian Gulf War, that had been wreaking havoc around the Middle East.

The mission, flown in badly disguised Russian helicopters, turned out to be perilous, bloody, and totally fucked up by the CIA from beginning to end. Yet somehow the unnamed chopper unit had succeeded when it was actually expected to fail. The gunship was recaptured, its war-criminal crew eliminated. Despite dozens of impediments put in its way, the ad hoc unit had fulfilled its mission.

It was probably the worst thing they could have done. For no sooner had they recovered from that escapade than they were called on again, this time to help a Russian special-ops unit win back a battered ex-Soviet aircraft carrier that had been taken over by elements of its crew after fierce internecine fighting. Again the chopper unit pulled the fat out of the fire. Again, they had been too successful.

Because not nine weeks later, here they were again—wherever "here" was.

Captain Currier introduced himself and the three other officers, then personally led the pilots below to the ship's intelligence room. Two heavily armed Marines were standing guard outside.

"I'll leave you here," Currier told them. "I hear you might be borrowing one of our aircraft?"

Delaney and Norton shrugged as if on cue. Currier was indeed a bear of a man—not too tall, but obviously very powerful. Yet his affable face gave him the look of a regular Joe. Norton told him: "Eight hours ago, we were fishing for blue marlin off Key West. Next thing we know, we're dunked here. Bottom line: I think you know more about what's going on than we do."

Currier smiled a bit.

"Well, not exactly," he said. "But I understand an officer in there will brief you fully." He nodded toward the intel room. "And you know, off the record, I'm due for a transfer once we get back to San Diego. I've been the CO of this ship for thirty-two months, and in all that time this might be the most exciting thing that's happened since I came aboard. In any case, good luck, with whatever you've been called on to do."

He shook their hands and started off down the passageway.

"Any time you want to join the party, Captain," Norton called after him unhappily, "just let us know."

They went through the door into the dimly lit intelligence room, and were relieved to see a gang of familiar faces looking back at them.

The two dozen or so black-camo soldiers who'd alighted from the Osprey were now crowded into this compartment, squeezed around a tiny metal table. Norton and Delaney knew them well. It was Team 66, the special-operations ground unit they'd worked with on the previous two missions.

Made up mostly of Marines, Team 66 was organized back in 1991 to take care of some postwar messes around the Persian Gulf. The highly classified unit went on to see action in Bosnia, Somalia, Central Africa, and Asia. Their specialty was putting out fires too small for the big units like Delta Force, or taking on ultra-dangerous assignments the SEALs simply weren't interested in, or were too busy to do.

Team 66 had been well named. They were like a collection of utility infielders. Most had just missed making the big leagues—that is, the SEALs, Recondos, Delta, or any number of other deep programs run by the U.S. military. Some had fallen short simply because of things like a five-percent hearing loss in one ear, or a rare allergy. One guy was missing the tip of his left hand's index finger; others were color-blind, or wore glasses, or contacts. Many had flat feet. This underdog environment had them taking on jobs no one else wanted—and doing so with gusto. Their mission record, though top secret, boasted a success rate of nearly one hundred percent. They could do wet operations or para-drops. They were as good in the jungle as in the snow. They were excellent at silent combat; they could work all the latest weapons. Rescuing hostages, tracking terrorists, handling nuclear or biological threats—Team 66 excelled at them all.

That was why their handlers never hesitated to loan them out to the CIA or the NSA or any other Spook outfit needing some firepower, quickly and quietly, somewhere around the world.

Norton and Delaney shook hands with a few of the more recognizable troopers. Each man seemed a bit distracted, though, and reluctant to speak. Sitting ramrod straight in a chair at one end of table was the team's CO, Captain Chou Koo. A tough-as-nails Asian-American officer who had led the unit since its inception, he was known to most simply as "Joe Cool."

They shook hands, and Chou eyed their ragged clothes. "Working undercover again guys?" he whispered.

"Well, with everyone so bent out of shape to get us out here so fucking quick, we didn't have time to dress up all fancy like you guys," Delaney told him in his Colorado twang. He was still clutching his beer can, as if he might never see another one again.

"Okay, so now we're here," Norton said to Chou. "And we're supposed to get briefed. So let's get on with it. What fucked-up situation do those assholes at the CIA want us to get into this time?"

Chou smiled, which was really an occasion. "I have no idea." he said.

Norton and Delaney stared back at him for a moment.

"But they said an officer in here would give us the low-down," Norton told him. "Ain't that officer you?"

Chou shook his head. "Nope, not on this one."

"Well, then who the fuck is?" Delaney asked.

Chou just pointed to the other end of the table. There was a person sitting there, dressed in night camos just as Chou's men were, almost lost in the dim lights and the sea of black. But this person was not like the other Team 66 troopers, for one simple reason: She was a female.

A very beautiful female . . .

"Welcome aboard, gentlemen," she said, standing up. "Nice of you to finally join us."

She was Commander Amanda Lawrence, USN, and to say that she was gorgeous was like saying the ocean was wet.

She was blonde, of course, about five-five, maybe 105 pounds, with a shape even the floppy black combat suit could not hide. But her appeal went way beyond all that. She was *unusually* beautiful. Her eyes, her lips, her nose, ears, cheeks, and chin—if each was found on six other women, they would not have worked as well as this. On her, the combination was stunning. She'd been mistaken for French, German, and Swedish in the past. But she was one-hundred-percent American, the sweet combination of all. Both pilots were simply dumbstruck at first sight of her, Norton especially. He had survived several serious relationships in his thirty-three years, and had dated a lot of models, actresses, and waitresses in between. Yet before this moment, he believed he'd seen only two truly beautiful women in his life. He would now have to add one more vision to that list.

She'd graduated Annapolis, Norton would learn later, seventh in her class. Her father was a retired admiral, her brother a Marine colonel. She had done time as a systems officer, first at the Pentagon, then on loan to NORAD and the U.S. Space Command. She was an expert in satellite photo analysis. She spoke seven languages. Somehow along the way, she'd managed to get both her pilot's wings and ratings for helicopters—and several bump-ups in her grade level, all in a brief six-year career.

Dear old Dad might have helped with the promotions, but with an IQ of 148, she was authentically as bright as she was beautiful. So when the CIA's Special Foreign Projects Office put out a request for military liaison officers, offering nothing but excitement and adventure, she applied, and—well, here she was, looking to Norton and Delaney like something from a dream.

She introduced herself. Norton swore he could see a faint halo hovering above her head. He and Delaney dropped into their seats.

"Commander Amanda? *Really?*" Delaney whispered to him. "When the hell did we get so lucky?"

All Norton could do was shake his head. "Beats me," he said.

She began the briefing by unfurling a map of Asia and hanging it on the wall. Though her hair was pulled back into a ponytail, it was slowly coming undone, as were the top two buttons of her combat suit. Upon seeing this, Norton began to lose all sensation in his chest. She opened a thick notebook to page one, checked her watch, then took a deep breath. All eyes were on her.

"I'm afraid we don't have much time here, gentlemen, so I'll be quick," she said. "Simply put, we've got a space shuttle down."

She let the words hang in the air for a moment, but not even the slightest murmur went through the room.

"At 2200 hours two days ago," she went on, "a shuttle was reported falling out of its designated orbit. All attempts to contact this spacecraft proved unsuccessful. Subsequent reports said it came back to earth, most likely somewhere in Southwest Asia. Its exact location is not known, but we have a real good guess. Our mission here is to find it. Quickly. And I mean within the next eight hours."

She tacked a recently printed-out satellite photo on the wall next to the map. It showed some frightening mountain topography in great detail.

"If this picture looks like a God's eye-view of the Himalayas to you, you're not too far off," she said. "Using tracking gear too secret to mention, our friends in Washington have identified a possible touchdown site somewhere in this particular area. But as you can see, we're talking about some of the most rugged terrain imaginable, all of it snow- or ice-covered. As a result, the satellite imagery has been inconclusive."

She looked up to find a sea of faces just staring back at her, wheels barely turning. Shuttle down. Snowy country somewhere. Okay, we got it. Just *please* don't fix your hair.

"Now, you're probably wondering," she pressed on. "Does anyone really think this thing came down in one piece? In that terrain? The answer is: No one knows. There *is* an emergency landing site for shuttles in Pakistan. It's possible this shuttle had some catastrophic problems, lost its radios, and was trying to make it down there—but overshot the safety zone. But we don't know because, as I said, communications were never reestablished."

She waited a beat. "Then, of course, there is the chance that it didn't come down entirely on its own."

Dead silence still enveloped the room. Blank stares were all she could see. Norton found himself wondering: How long was her hair exactly? And were her eyes greenish blue or bluish green?

She checked her watch again and started talking faster. Time was getting short.

"Now, what does that mean?" she asked with a quick shrug—even this made her look pretty. "I happen to have some familiarity with the orbiters. It probably comes as no surprise, though it is not generally known, that under certain circumstances, they can be operated entirely by ground stations. So what happened here? Certainly no one on the ground in the U.S. tried to bring them down. Could it have happened another way? We don't know."

Again, she looked up from her notes. These were really weighty things she was talking about here. Yet no one had moved an inch.

"Now, I'm not saying someone *forced* it down on purpose or by mistake," she emphasized. "And even if that *did* happen, my office wouldn't tell us anyway. That gives you some indication of how tight the lid is on this one. But I guess we have to say at this moment, anything is possible,"

She returned to the map. "This is known as the Paswar," she said, pointing to the nasty piece of real estate near the convergence of China, Kyrgyzstan, and Tajikstan, the same area depicted in the satellite photo. "It may be hard to believe, in a day when you would think every square inch of the Earth has been spoken for, but this is uncharted and unclaimed territory. No one wants it. It's that inhospitable. Yet this is the current best guess where the missing shuttle came down. Strange, isn't it?"

As one, everyone in the room nodded, slowly, silently, like participants in a Pavlov experiment.

She shook her head and looked down at her notes again. She'd worked for CIA Specials Projects for almost a year now; this was not the first time she'd given a top-secret briefing. Nor was it the first time she'd elicited this sort of dumbo reaction. Her father, the admiral, had told her she was too pretty for the job, and at moments like this, she almost believed he was right.

Still, she forged on.

"To underscore this theory, our intelligence people tell us that military units in surrounding countries may be gearing up for some activity in the target area. So, my office wants us to get to this Paswar place as quickly as possible and take a look around, especially in the valley right at its center, which is actually an ancient crater."

She let her eyes sweep the roomful of ogling troopers once again.

"I'll be blunt," she said. "It's going to be very difficult getting to this place from here—it's still almost a thousand miles away—and guaranteed, it will be no fun at all when we arrive. The weather conditions are almost always terrible—that's another reason why close-in satellite photos have been useless. But the security is so high for this predicament, and the clock ticking so fast, our leaders, including our Commander in Chief, feel this mission cannot be undertaken from a land base, even if one could be found in time. So this ship has been chosen and we've been selected to go."

She smiled sweetly. The walls around them began to melt.

"Personally, I'm hoping that all we'll have to do is get to this place and snap a few pictures, just enough to tell them that this thing *isn't* there. Then we can all go back home."

She returned to her notes.

"I have mission briefs prepared for all of you," she announced. "I urge you to read them quickly but thoroughly and then saddle up. We've got to launch from here in exactly one hour."

Finally she closed her notebook.

"For transportation, most of us will be using the Osprey. But I understand that two of you will be flying one of this ship's Sea Cobras as a kind of fighter escort for us. Majors Norton and Delaney? It says here that you are proficient in all types of rotary aircraft. Is that so?"

Dead silence still. It was getting weird now. No one in attendance had ever gone through a mission briefing quite like this. There had been no discussion, no questions, no bitching. Nothing. It was silly, but everyone seemed transfixed by the lovely Navy commander.

She looked right at Norton. "So, is that true? Are both of you able to strap on that chopper and fly it?"

Norton could barely move, never mind speak. He glanced at Delaney; he too was frozen in place. Chou was the same way.

A weird thought went through Norton's mind. Maybe this was all a ruse—something cooked up by those idiots at the CIA to study the reactions of special operations troops being briefed by someone who made the Playmate of the Month look like an old cow.

"Well, Major Norton?"

"I'm sorry, ma'am," he finally croaked. "But may I ask you something?"

She seemed delighted that there was actually going to be a question. "Certainly," she replied.

"Did you say that wherever it is we're going, you will be coming with us?"

She nodded happily. "I'm the field operations officer on this mission, so yes, I will be going along."

Suddenly one of the young Team 66 troopers blurted out, "Excellent!"

It was an embarrassing moment—but the trooper had spoken what was on everyone else's mind, especially Norton's.

"Yeah," Norton murmured. "That *is* excellent."

5

The island of Hawaii

The worst part of it was, Gene Smitz really believed he'd fallen in love.

Her name was Ginger. He met her in a bar called "Get Lei-ed," a nice place along the beach near downtown Kailua. She was a redhead, of course—his weakness—and was very cute in that third-shift sort of way.

He'd been sitting at the rail, watching a replay of the Dodgers game, when she appeared out of nowhere. Bikini top, cutoff shorts. Bare feet. She asked if he had a cell phone she could use. Hers had run out of juice and someone had vomited on the pay phone. He obliged, of course. She made her call, thanked him, then introduced herself. They began talking, and the rest was history.

Early on she said she thought he was a college student. Smitz grimaced when he heard this. *Everyone* thought he was a college student. It was his glasses. Tortoiseshell with round Lennon frames. Against his boyish face and under-nourished form, they apparently screamed "political science degree."

Truth was, Smitz had graduated college almost ten years before.

They'd met late, almost quarter to eleven. But it made no difference—the club stayed open all night. So they sat at the bar and talked for hours. She was a bit of a wiseass at first, which was okay with Smitz. But as the night progressed, she became warm and funny. She was a real small-town gal, transplanted from Ohio six years ago by a boyfriend who then went south on her. She'd been virtually alone every since. She loved baseball, the Stones, gambling, and sex.

By three A.M., after a dozen drinks, Smitz was ready to propose.

Somewhere around five in the morning, she mentioned she'd always wanted to take a helicopter ride up to see the famous Kilauea volcano. At that point, Smitz would have ridden a rocket to the moon with her. The sun was just coming up anyway, so catching his second wind, Smitz made some calls and secured some reservations. The next thing he knew, they were in a taxi, racing through downtown Kailua, heading for a place called Earlybirds, an outfit that specialized in sunrise flights up to Kilauea.

Though Ginger had professed some concern about flying in helicopters—a subject Smitz knew much about—she seemed not at all nervous as they walked out to the helipad, where a small helicopter was already warmed up and waiting.

Smitz climbed in first only because Ginger insisted that

she take the front seat. No sooner was he in, though, than she closed the door and locked it tight. She gave a thumbs-up to the pilot, who started lifting off right away.

Smitz began to protest—that was when he realized the pilot was holding an ID over his shoulder, just about eye level so Smitz could see it. It identified the pilot as an employee of the CIA.

Smitz needed no more than a glance at it. He recognized an authentic Company work badge when he saw one.

He looked out the window as they lifted off, and saw Ginger waving good-bye to him.

"Damn . . ." Smitz whispered.

She was holding up a CIA badge too.

It was times like these that Smitz really hated his job.

He'd been an operative for the CIA's Special Foreign Projects Office for nearly ten years now. In that time he'd become both world-wise and world-weary. He'd started out as an errand boy for the senior agents within his department, sanitizing their expense accounts and doing very low-level briefings. But all that had changed eighteen months before when he too had been tapped to join up with the unnamed chopper outfit and sent to the Gulf, where they tracked down and eliminated the crew of the rogue "ArcLight" AC-130 gunship. During that mission, Smitz had shot four turncoat CIA agents to death. In cold blood. From that moment on, he was an errand boy no more.

The mission to recover the Russian aircraft carrier had been his last big operation, but he'd done a bunch of smaller things in the Balkans and the Caucasus since. When working alone, his forte was deep penetration and close surveillance. Shoot-outs were not uncommon, but so far Smitz had escaped any real work-related bodily harm. Though his success rate was very high, he still maintained a love/hate relationship with his superiors, mostly the latter. To them he was a rogue, a loose cannon, valuable, but also problematic. In his mind, he felt it was better that they give him the job, then leave him alone. He was rarely shy about voicing that opinion.

The only thing they agreed on was that he was best when working, and there was no shortage of jobs to give him. In the past eighteen months, he'd worked so much, in fact, that the office had ordered him to take a vacation—or at least the accounting department had. Use your vacation time or lose it permanently. He'd caved in and set out for Hawaii, believing, foolishly as it turned out, that even at the CIA a man's two-week vacation was still considered sacred.

In the end, it had lasted less than twenty-four hours.

"Any chance that this might be, you know, a mistake of some kind?" he leaned forward and asked the pilot.

The pilot just shrugged. "I'm a lowly taxi driver, pal," he replied, yelling over the noise of the chopper.

Smitz switched tactics. "How much they paying you?"

"Enough not to take a bribe," the pilot replied. Then, after a pause, he added: "That's what you were referring to, I assume?"

"You have engine trouble. You set down on the nearest beach. You go to get help. I wander away."

"Well, stuff like that has been known to happen," the pilot yelled over his shoulder.

Smitz reached for his wallet.

"How much you want?"

"How much you got?"

Smitz counted out his wad of bills.

"Fifteen hundred bucks . . ."

The pilot looked around and then laughed at him.

"Yeah, right . . ." he said.

They flew along in silence for the next thirty minutes.

Smitz had little to do but admire the deep blue ocean, flashing by below. Except for a few fishing boats and the occasional Navy vessel, the water was wide-open and empty.

He had actually started to doze when a sharp turn to the left nudged him back awake. They were approaching a ship. It was a Naval vessel, but it carried no flags or hull markings and it was painted all white. Like an old hospital ship without the Red Cross. There were no other ships around it. There was no land in sight.

The pilot pushed the small copter over and glided in for a landing.

Smitz was taken off the chopper by two crewmen in nondescript combat fatigues and brought to a tiny cabin three decks below.

This compartment was empty except for a folding chair and sizable flat-screen TV hanging on the wall. The two men went back out the door and locked it behind them. Not a word was said.

Smitz examined the flat-screen TV. It was at least six feet high by eight feet long, and took up the entire wall. There was a tiny camera attached to a motorized swivel hanging off one corner; a microphone was taped to the other corner. An interactive beast, Smitz thought. Much too expensive for a typical Navy ship.

But, of course, this ship was hardly typical Navy.

Smitz had heard of vessels such as this. They were known by various names, one being a C2 ship, for command and control. Basically they were supposed to be like

floating administrative offices, called out whenever the
Navy was making war somewhere—or about to.

The strange thing about this one, it was painted white.

Smitz collapsed into the chair. He just assumed that he
was being sent on some new assignment, something time-
pressing and already fucked up. That was the only possible
reason that would necessitate the need for the Company to
track him down, ensnare him, and eventually snatch him
up as they did. He would never have gone willingly. But
using a redhead? He considered that hitting below the belt.

But instead of someone walking into the cabin and hand-
ing him the ubiquitous white envelope with red tape—these
things always carried secret instructions direct from the
president—Smitz would be getting his orders via a different
medium this time.

And, some would even say, from a higher source.

Exactly one minute after he'd entered the room, the giant
TV screen came to life. It happened so suddenly, Smitz
nearly fell off the chair.

The thing was so bright, and the sudden blast of static
so loud, Smitz felt it rip right through him. He was, of
course, working on his second twenty-four hours without
sleep, this after a rough night at the bar. The shock to his
system was a bit more than he would have normally expected.

Once his vision cleared, he found himself looking at a
picture of a large oval table set up in a very dimly lit room.
One wall of this place was actually a huge electronic map
of what looked to be the entire globe. Everything else
seemed to be made of glass and finely toned wood.

Seven men were sitting around the table. They were all
in their late sixties, if not older. They were dressed in comfortable cowboy duds—denim shirts and jeans. A few had
beards; several had long gray hair pulled back into pony-

tails. All seven were smoking something: pipes, cigars, cigarettes. Each man had a coffee cup in front of him.

None of them were smiling.

They were staring out of the screen at Smitz as if he was
the missing link. He could hear the whine of the tiny TV
camera zooming in on him. A few awkward moments
passed. Finally, one man spoke.

"Mr. Smitz, could you show us your ID, please?" this
man asked. "Hold it right up to the camera, if you could."

Smitz did as requested. The seven men took some time
studying the ID. They seemed to relax a bit, though. The
man at the far end of the table spoke again; his demeanor
was almost casual.

"Sorry for the inconvenience, Smitty," he said. "And we
do apologize for interrupting your vacation—truth is, we've
been looking for you for two days. We knew you were in
the islands, we just didn't know where. When one of our
bloodhounds spotted you, well, we just felt it was easier to
get you out here this way than by more typical procedures."

"What he means," the guy sitting next to the speaker
said, chiming in, "don't give your cell phone to every pretty
girl who asks for it. That's like setting off a homing bea-
con."

There were some smiles now from the others around the
table.

"I assume by all this it must be important," Smitz replied
with a twist of sarcasm. He had no idea who these people
were—but he had to proceed on the assumption that they
were high-ranking CIA types. Cloistered. Super-Spooks.
Even the Thunderball-type chamber they were sitting in fit
the bill. Everything—just like in the movies.

"It *is* important," the first man replied. "Extremely important."

"Well, I'm a captive audience," Smitz replied with a yawn. "So, shoot."

All seven men sat forward a bit.

"One of our space shuttles has come down unexpectedly," the lead guy told him bluntly. "We don't know where exactly. We are drawing together as many elements as possible to locate it. But at this moment, it's just . . . well, missing."

They let this rather fantastic news sink in a bit. Smitz's first reaction was one of quick and deep skepticism. A shuttle? Missing? Wasn't that the plot to at least one 007 movie? He stared back at the seven men for a moment. Might this be an elaborate prank, cooked up by his office mates just to fuck up his vacation? That too was pretty farfetched. But in his ten-year career with the Agency, he knew it was wise to consider all possibilities.

"A shuttle is a big thing," he said finally. "I mean, isn't that the equivalent of, let's say, a 747 going down somewhere? How could you miss it?"

"Well, we do know it came down in a remote area," the number-one guy replied, choosing his words carefully. "Very remote."

"Are we talking Siberia? Antarctica?" Smitz asked.

"Close," was the man's reply.

Smitz thought he could read the writing on the wall.

"And you want me to go find it?"

The lead guy shook his head no. "Others are taking care of that."

Smitz was stumped. "What's my role then?"

The speaker hesitated a bit. Finally he said: "We want you to find out *why* it came down."

The reply caught Smitz by surprise.

Interesting, he thought.

"The problem here is the time element," a third guy said. "We know you're used to working on a tight schedule, but this one will be one of the tightest. We cannot let time fly on this."

By now, Smitz only had about a million questions.

"But how do you want me to go about this?" he asked. "I mean, where do I start?"

The lead guy spoke again. "An up-to-the-minute briefing paper is being prepared for you as we speak. It should be in your hands within thirty minutes. You are to read it, absorb it, then destroy it. Then you will be flown back to Pearl Harbor, and a military flight will take you where you have to go. Support elements should be in place by that time to help you in your mission."

Smitz almost laughed. This *was* right out of a bad spy movie; but then again, so had his life been for the past two years. And it *was* his job, and he didn't know how to do anything else. He had no choice but to play along.

He looked up at the screen again. His best guess was that these guys were located somewhere in the American desert. And the fact that there were seven of them was intriguing— even if he didn't know exactly why.

"May I ask two questions?"

"Go ahead," the lead man replied. "But please hurry."

Smitz wet his lips. "Who are you guys?"

There were a few more smiles around the table. One guy lit his pipe again.

"That's classified," he said between puffs. "Next question?"

Smitz thought a moment. He'd been close to the TV and newspapers since arriving on Hawaii. He'd seen nothing about a shuttle going missing—or even one being up in orbit.

"I haven't heard anything about NASA losing one of its shuttles," he finally said. "How come?"

Again, there were a few smiles from the seven old men. The lead guy spoke again.

"Who said anything about NASA?" he asked.

6

Aboard the *Bataan*

It was on La Jolla Beach one summer afternoon that Jazz Norton saw the most beautiful girl in the world.

He had just finished Air Force flight school in Texas and was due to get his wings in two weeks. With several days off, he drove his Jeep to southern California, where he did nothing but drink and tan. She'd walked by him, carrying a surfboard, but looking way too gorgeous to actually want to use the thing. Their eyes never met. Norton probably saw her for ten seconds at the most before she disappeared into the crowd of bodies. Beyond the cutsie face, the long blond hair, and the killer shape, something about her, at that moment, on that day, struck a chord so deep inside him that it rang there for years. She was pure beauty. Nothing would ever let him forget her.

That is, until he saw the girl in Central Park.

It was seven years later, the early fall. He was in the city doing some high-level recruitment work for the Air Force when he decided to walk around the Big Apple's infamous common. She went by him on roller blades, actually said hello, nearly lost her balance, regained it—and was gone. Norton froze in his tracks that day, stunned by the vision that had just flashed by him. Big smile. A white blouse. Jeans. The sun on her hair. Red roller blades. He actually doubled back and tried to find her again, but never did. Since that day, on many occasions, even while in the presence of other women, he'd thought: Where was that girl? What was she doing at that very moment?

These were strange things to be thinking about now. Norton was well aware of that. Lying as he was on a borrowed bunk, in a borrowed billet, dressed in a complete combat suit, his high-tech rifle and oversized Fritz helmet lying across his chest, a thick mission briefing book unopened in his hands. Everything was going up and down in sync with his heart.

La Jolla. Central Park. The Arabian Sea. Were there three more unlike places in the world?

Commander Amanda was absolutely different from the first two—he was very clear on this. What famous person did she look like? What movie star? Norton couldn't get this particular question out of his mind. Cameron Diaz? No. Ashley Judd? Maybe. Michelle Pfieffer? Well, just a bit, with a little of his favorite B-movie actress, Kelly Maroney, thrown in. That was what was so fascinating about Commander Amanda. She *resembled* a lot of people, yet no one could possibly look like her.

Norton felt his chest begin to pound again. Yeah, this was strange. He was about to go on what could be a very hairy mission—the briefing book, or at least the few pages that he'd glanced at, read like a horror story. He knew he would be wise to study it all, yet he couldn't. All he could think about was this girl. This Amanda person, whose face just wouldn't leave him. This was not the Jazz Norton he knew. He was not thinking clearly—or rather, he was not thinking clearly about what he should have been thinking clearly about.

Had his brain been starved of oxygen anytime recently? Had he injured it while being hurled into the ocean at about 110 mph? Because this was not like him. After all the women and girls and babes and floozies he'd been with, to think of one he'd just met so intently, so obsessively . . . it was scary.

The banging at his cabin door finally broke him out of the spell.

It was Delaney. He could tell by the ferocity of fists banging on steel.

"It's open!" Norton yelled, finally rolling off the bunk.

Delaney barged in, looking like a spaceman from a sci-fi movie. Dressed exactly the same, so did Norton for that matter. Their attire was strictly Team 66. The secret unit usually had access to the latest in special-ops gear. The combat suits sent down from the Team's aircraft looked top-shelf.

Essentially the suit was a heavy-duty coverall with lots of utility pockets and places for belts and a pair of brand-new all-weather, heated-lining boots to match. The Fritz helmet was sized about ten percent larger than a standard battle hat. This because its insides were festooned with microphones, headphones, and internal mounts for things such as tiny video cameras, IR, or NightVision goggles. It could also double as a crash helmet. Supposedly the padding could take a three-hundred-mph hit without making a dent.

The suits came with the latest in flak-jacket fashion. They were battle vests made of Kevlar, of course, specifically

KM2. But these jackets were different because they had two long pockets running through them. Inside each pocket was a boron carbide plate. The standard KM2 could stop a bullet from a 9-mm handgun. With the boron plates in, the jackets could stop a machine-gun round. Or at least, that was what the collar tag said.

Delaney collapsed onto the bunk.

"Dorothy Mays, July issue, 1979," he said to Norton.

"What?"

"Dorothy Mays," Delaney repeated. "Playboy Playmate of the Month, July. 1979. That's who Commander Amanda looks like."

Norton was caught off guard. Had Delaney been thinking about her nonstop too?

"July, '79, you say?" he mumbled, trying to act nonchalant.

"Seven full-color pictures," Delaney went on. "Foldout was a pool scene. Full scooty. Two couch pictures, her home, interior. One black-and-white pic on the beach. Another of her feeding a parking meter in Aspen."

"How were the articles in that issue?" Norton asked, trying to get a word in edgewise.

"Turn-ons: skydiving, baking sugar cookies, and eating bananas . . ."

"That's a good sign."

"Turnoffs: taxis, rude people, and apples. And I quote: 'It scares me to bite into one. I'm always afraid there'll be a worm inside.'"

Delaney smiled broadly, as if he'd just recited a passage from the Bible. Norton just stared back at him.

"What color is the sky in your world?" he asked him.

Delaney didn't miss a beat.

"Yellow, of course . . ."

•　•　•

They spent the next few minutes checking their weapons. Both had been issued a high-tech M-16, one which had every conceivable gizmo attached to the barrel and stock, plus six clips of high-velocity ammo. They synchronized their watches—it was exactly 1245 hours local time. They shook hands, a custom of theirs before embarking on a mission, and then set off for the flight deck.

Typically, Delaney never stopped talking.

"I'll tell you this, Jazzman, the scenery on this mission will be a whole lot better than it was when we were hiding in bat shit in Iraq or freezing our asses off on that Russian garbage scow. Too bad she's not riding up with us. Chou and his guys will have all the fun. I hear you can really spread out on some of those Osprey things."

Delaney's comments immediately pinged Norton the wrong way.

"You know, there's a reason why they don't send women into combat," he said.

Delaney was confused. "What do you mean?"

"What the hell do you think I mean? Seeing one blown full of holes might affect your morale a bit, don't you think?"

"Blown full of holes? What are you talking about, Jazz?"

Norton stopped in his tracks. "If you're in combat with a beautiful female, you'll probably take greater risks trying to save her than you would normally—and things like that can fuck up a mission, as well as your own personal well-being. You know how ugly it can get when you hit the ground on one of these things."

Delaney was shaking his head. "No, what I don't understand from you is why you think this is a combat situation. All we're doing, Jazz, is taking a little trip inland. A hoot and scoot. Snap a few pictures, shit, we'll be back here before midnight chow. And I hear the food on this tub is excellent."

"A little trip inland?" Norton fired back at him. "Are you nuts? We're practically flying to the top of the Himalayas, for Christ's sake. Over a bunch of airspace that ain't our own. Going to a place no one wants. And if anything goes wrong, it ain't like anyone's going to come after us anytime soon."

Delaney just shook his head. "Jeez, Jazz, why don't you just suck *all* of the energy out of this thing? Compared to what we've been asked to do in the past, this one will be a breeze. And you know, *she'll* be on the ground with us once we get up there. And we'll see her at the refueling stops. And when we get back, you just *know* she'll be doing the post-mission briefing, and we can stretch that freaking thing to at least a couple hours, even more."

Delaney got a faraway look in his eyes.

"Then, who knows," he went on. "Maybe some asshole will want to steal a Russian ICBM or something and we'll get to work with her again, like real soon."

Norton just shook his head. It was obvious. Delaney had it almost as bad as he did.

"I thought you had a girlfriend," Norton said.

Delaney froze for a second. There was a girl back in the Keys he saw a lot. Her name was Mo.

"Well, yeah, but, this is . . . *work*-related," he finally stammered.

"So's the hole in your head," Norton told him.

They reached the deck to find the Osprey making all kinds of noise.

Its gigantic propellers were creating a sonic disturbance bordering on bone-rattling. Norton could feel it go right to the pit of his stomach. Even as the last of the Team 66

troopers climbed aboard, the strange aircraft seemed too
anxious to go, as if it would leap off the deck at any second,
leaving a string of black camo soldiers falling in its wake.

The *Bataan*'s crew had already started one of the ship's
Sea Cobra helicopters. It was warming up about fifty feet
in front of the V-22. Long, slender, looking like some gigantic pissed-off bug, the Sea Cobra was almost as futuristic in appearance as the Osprey, even though the chopper
design had been in service for almost thirty years.

Simply put, the Navy copter was the oceangoing version
of the Army's well-liked AH-1 Huey Cobra. A legitimate
hot rod, the Huey Cobra was a Vietnam-era machine famous for being the first rotary aircraft developed specifically as a gun platform.

Cobras were also known for hauling ass. Some models
could hit more than two hundred miles per hour. They
could maneuver like a small jet, and had a reputation for
being tough to shoot down. Norton had never flown one
before; neither had Delaney. But they knew the basics, plus
they had detailed flight manuals with them. Besides, after
the pigs they'd been asked to fly in the previous two missions, how difficult could flying a good old American chopper be?

Sea Cobras could go out loaded for bear too. An M-28
turret gun was standard equipment. Hard points on its
small, side-mounted winglets held places for a half dozen
TOW missiles, or rockets, or even gun pods. But then, there
was the question of fuel. Like everything that flew fast, the
Sea Cobra burned fuel quickly. And there was one big difference between this bird and the Army's land-flying ani-
mal: The Navy chopper had two engines, as all aircraft
designed to fly over water should. This was considered life
insurance. But as a result, where a landlubbing Cobra could
eke out 350 miles before needing more gas, the Sea Cobra

could go only about three hundred miles on a good day
before needing a fill-up.

The problem was, the Paswar was nearly a one-thousand-
mile flight from their present position—and that was just
one-way. So the *Bataan*'s crew had done a quick custom-
izing job on the Sea Cobra. Gone were the TOW-missile
racks. In their place were long silver fuel tanks, two per
side. They looked not unlike bombs themselves. The extra
gas would extend the copter's range by about two hundred
miles. However, sometime before that bingo point, the two
American aircraft would have to set down and pump gas
from the Osprey's reserves into the smaller gunship. Depending on what went on once they reached the Paswar,
between them they should have just enough gas to make it
back to the *Bataan,* again with a quick pit stop somewhere
on the way home.

Norton and Delaney began a walk-around of the Sea Cobra, but after a few seconds, Delaney deliberately wandered
away. To Norton's eyes, the Navy chopper appeared to be
in excellent shape. Well maintained, with very few patches
and scratches, and even a new paint job. Instead of its usual
gray coat, this particular bird was now covered in dull black
camo, making it look like the Osprey's little brother.

Just below the pilot's step, someone had painted in red
scroll: "Do anything, go anywhere." This was the unofficial
motto of Cobra pilots. Norton took a closer look at the
bulbous oversized fuel tanks. The "do anything" part he
had no trouble with. It was the "go anywhere" that had him
thinking now.

He climbed into the pilot's position, which was the second seat in the tandem two-seat layout. He'd won a previous coin flip with Delaney, meaning he'd be flying the
bird on the way up. Norton was a bit surprised to find the
Sea Cobra's cockpit so cluttered, this even though such

things as the ALQ-144 radar jammer, the backup systems for the communications rig, and anything having to do with the firing of the TOW missiles had all been yanked out to make the chopper lighter and thus more fuel-efficient. Still, he seemed surrounded by dials, buttons, TV screens, and switches. There was one good reason for this, though. Because this particular copter was actually a Navalized version of the Army's brand-new AH-1SX, it carried, among other things, a C-Nite sight, the same thermal-imaging technology used by the M-1 Abrams battle tank. As its name implied, this device would allow the Sea Cobra some measure of NightVision, which could only help in a bad situation.

But as far as firepower went, as configured now, this Sea Cobra was a flying gun that could see in the dark, nothing more.

Norton thanked the flight mechanics for their prompt changeover. He climbed out of the chopper and walked back toward the ship's island. There he found Delaney reemerging from belowdecks. Commander Amanda was with him. So the snake had slithered off to intercept her, Norton thought. They didn't call Delaney "Slick" for nothing.

Norton stopped about fifteen feet away from them and pretended to adjust his flak jack. He could see Delaney and the beautiful officer were deep in conversation, but Norton detected a puzzled look on Commander Amanda's very lovely face. This was good. Whatever they were talking about, Delaney was confusing her.

"We're good to go, Slick," Norton called over to him nonchalantly. Preempted, Delaney began blurting out his farewell. Commander Amanda straightened a bit and saluted him.

"Good luck, Major Delaney," she said. "Have a good flight."

Delaney gave her a thumbs-up and walked a bit dramatically out to the Sea Cobra.

Norton saw his chance. He walked over to her.

"Don't worry about him, ma'am," he said as coolly as possible. "I'll keep an eye on him for you."

She gazed up at him, surprised by his words. Hair mussed slightly by the hot afternoon breeze, she looked into his eyes. Norton looked right back. A lump began to form in his throat. She was wearing practically the same outfit as he. Yet even dressed up for war, she looked more beautiful than he'd thought possible.

What the hell is she doing way out here?

"Did you review the mission paper, Major Norton?" she asked him.

"Yes, I did," Norton lied. "Looks like a very executable plan."

"Well, that's nice to hear," she replied sweetly. "I was up all night writing it."

She took a breath. "Well, you take care of yourself too, Major. We'll see you at the first refueling stop."

They were almost the same words, but when she said them to him, she did not salute. Instead, she reached out and touched his arm lightly. Norton felt a spark go right through his flak jacket, down to his boots and back again.

Apparently Kevlar didn't stop everything.

"I'll try to do that, ma'am," he heard himself say.

She smiled.

Then she hurried over to the waiting Osprey, climbed aboard, and was gone.

7

For the first three hours, the dash for the Paswar went by without a hitch.

By the time they had lifted off, the *Bataan* had closed to within twelve miles of the Pakistani coastline. The American two-ship formation—the V-22 "Ozzie" in the lead, the smaller sleeker Sea Cobra following close behind—had made landfall about twenty miles north of Karachi, and maintained a belly-scraping altitude of three hundred feet ever since.

The plan to go in low and fast was an attempt to sneak under the Pakistani radar net. According to the mission paper, the country's detection net was porous, with the majority of its screens pointing toward India. Most importantly, it had a bottom floor of five hundred feet. If the Americans could stay below that magic number, the chances of their detection would be reduced dramatically.

The V-22 had the better navigation systems on board, so naturally it lead the way. Once Norton got into the rhythm of the unusual aircraft's flight idiosyncrasies, he had no problem staying in position on its tail and holding steady at the breakneck two hundred mph airspeed. Rising only for the occasional hill, or going around the rare jungle mountain, the V-22's follow-the-leader flight plan had been flawless. Radio technicians inside the Osprey were monitoring all Pakistani military frequencies. So far, there had been no indication anyone knew the two aircraft were traversing their airspace.

This was not to say that all the territory they'd flown over was uninhabited. Pakistan was a very crowded place, especially in the south. It was almost impossible not to be flying close to some kind of population center at any given moment, be it a city or a small village. But the occasionally twisting flight path took this into account, and any pockets of civilization they passed over were comparably small and isolated. Plus, they were going so fast and flying so low, by the time anyone on the ground saw them, they were already overhead and gone.

"This is sort of like the Ploesti Raid," Delaney concluded about thirty minutes into the flight. "Those guys went in real low too."

He was referring to the famous World War II bombing raid made by B-24 Liberators flying out of North Africa against the German-controlled oil-processing complex at Ploesti, Rumania. For the crucial part of that historic flight, the B-24's had gone in extremely low, this after scaling some sizable mountains earlier in the journey. But Norton recalled that the Ploesti raiders arrived over the target in utter confusion, and had been flying so close to the ground that some were damaged by small-arms fire and slow-moving flak trains. One even suffered a pitchfork in its engine, the pitchfork being thrown by a farmer as the big bomber flew over at an altitude of just fifteen feet.

Norton really hoped they wouldn't see any pitchforks this day.

They *had* seen some unusual sights, though.

At one point they spotted a train moving briskly through the jungle right below them. It paralleled their course for a short time, long enough for them to get a good look at it. Several of the railcars had been lashed together with huge chains and were carrying a load so long and so wide, it seemed impossible that it could stay balanced on the relatively thin flatbed cars. Whatever they were hauling was covered with a bright blue tarpaulin and bundled in such a way that Delaney remarked: "What are those guys moving . . . a whale?"

At another point, they flew over a small jungle lake, in the middle of which was floating a huge barge, something more likely seen out on the ocean. Covered by a massive plywood roof, the barge was anchored to strong points all along the shoreline, and indeed its size took up nearly three quarters of the lake's area.

"Floating casino?" Delaney wondered.

It was as good an explanation as any.

Then there was the wedding they almost crashed.

Or at least, they thought it was a wedding. They came upon it just as they reached the first refueling stop. This place was code-named Exxon One, for obvious reasons. It was located on a two-hundred-foot rise next to a long flat plain about 450 miles inland, roughly halfway to their goal.

The site was selected by Commander Amanda after she had reviewed the most up-to-date satellite photos available of the area. And, according to these pictures, Exxon One *was* the perfect landing place . . . twenty hours or so before, when the satellite pictures had been taken. But now, the situation had changed.

The area surrounding Exxon One was high desert, an abrupt change in the topography they'd been seeing since making landfall. But now, in the middle of this rocky plain, and close by the hill where they were to set down, a huge tent had been erected with a makeshift parking lot surrounding it. The tent was big enough to fit a circus inside, and was painted red, white, and green, the traditional colors of Pakistani marriage ceremonies. So many Mercedes-Benz cars and trucks were parked around it, it looked like a prestigious car dealership had sprung up out in the middle of nowhere.

The lay of the land around Exxon One was such that the tent and the cars were not visible until the Osprey and the Sea Cobra were practically on the ground. By the time they saw the hubbub out on the plain, it was too late to abort the landing. A quick flash of navigation lights from the Ozzie confirmed they had to set down, which was good, because the Sea Cobra was running on fumes by this time.

The two aircraft landed atop the designated hill with no problem. Even before Norton killed his engines, troopers from the Osprey were running fuel lines from the back of their plane to the tanks fitted to the side of the Sea Cobra. Norton and Delaney did not argue with their haste. No one wanted to stay on the ground any longer than they had to.

They climbed out of the small chopper and met Chou at the bottom of the Osprey's back ramp. Together, they made their way to the crest of the hill, and after lying down flat, looked out on the suddenly bustling plain through their binoculars. They could hear very loud scratchy music blaring from the tent site.

"Another party I wasn't invited to," Delaney said. "I wonder if anyone would notice if I cut in the food line."

"Not exactly a chapel in Vegas, is it?" Chou observed. "I wonder who's getting married."

"Judging from the wheels parked around that thing," Norton replied, "I'm guessing the daughter of the richest guy in Pakistan is getting hitched—if there is such a thing as being rich in this country."

Suddenly they were joined at the crest by the very beautiful Commander Amanda. Crawling up beside them like a pro, she was clearly agonizing over this sudden development.

"Oh, my God," she said, getting her first good look at the huge tent and the commotion about a half mile away. "I put us down right next to a Barnum and Bailey circus!"

"It's okay," Norton told her, trying his best to sound comforting. "If they had heard us come in, half of them would be crawling up this hill by now. And look—the tent flaps are all pulled tight. And you can hear that awful music way up here. It must be destroying their eardrums inside. Don't worry, they'll never know we were here."

His words did little good, though. She felt terrible about the situation. "Wait till my boss hears this," she groaned. "I'll be back to making coffee for him."

She took off her crash helmet. The ponytail was long gone, and her long blond hair fell about her shoulders. All three men were stunned. Norton had to thump himself on the chest to get his heart going again. She was even more gorgeous than before.

But she was also all business.

"I have to check my map book," she said, quickly scribbling notes on the back of her hand, again like a pro. "But when we lift off again, I think if we go south about a mile and a half and then swing around, we can get right back on course again."

She pulled her hair back up, slammed her helmet back

on, and began scrambling back to the Osprey, all before any of them could say another word to her.

"Damn . . ." Norton whispered.

"Well, that was . . . *brief,*" Delaney said, clearly disappointed. Even the stoic Chou seemed bummed out that she had left so quickly.

A Team 66 trooper ran up and told them the refueling was already fifty percent complete. Chou checked his watch again.

"We're still running ahead of schedule," he announced. "That's good news—I hope."

With that, Chou got up and accompanied his trooper back to the refueling operation. Delaney announced: "I gotta take a squirt. Don't go anywhere without me."

He toddled off, and now it was just Norton looking out from the bluff. He began studying the mountains that lined the northern horizon. They looked like an enormous set of jagged white teeth.

"Not quite the Himalayas," he thought. "But close."

Some of the peaks seemed to tower over him already, even though they were still fifty miles away. They would have to get around them somehow. But how high were they? And just how high could the Sea Cobra fly?

How could you possibly go on a mission like this and not read the mission plan? he imagined Commander Amanda asking him.

"Guess I just can't help it," he would have told her.

Norton's daydream was broken by Delaney, standing in a clump of bushes about fifty feet away from the crest, gesturing frantically. He wanted Norton to come over to him.

"What the hell could he possibly want?" Norton mumbled to himself.

He climbed down from the bluff and into the bushes

where Delaney had disappeared. He found his colleague standing next to a path near a small clearing about twenty feet down the hill. He had mercifully finished his bodily function and was pointing to something on the ground.

Norton walked up beside him. "This better be good," he growled.

Delaney indicated the bed of moist sandy clay near his feet. Someone had drawn something into it.

"Check it out, Jazzman," he said to him. "What's that look like to you?"

Norton studied the sketching for a moment. It was crude, probably made with a stick or finger, and done quickly at that.

But there was no mistaking what it was supposed to be. High tail. Thick wings. Stubby nose.

It was a space shuttle.

"I'd accuse you of peeing this thing into the ground," Norton told Delaney. "But it's too damn good for that."

They were genuinely puzzled. They were out in the middle of nowhere. They were looking for a shuttle. Yet they were still at least five hundred miles away from where they were supposed to begin the search.

So why was this thing drawn here?

"You think any mook who lives way out here has enough smarts to draw this thing?" Delaney asked.

Norton looked around. As far as lack of civilization went, it wasn't like they were in the middle of deepest, darkest Africa. But they were damn close.

"Does Pakistan have cable TV yet? Can they get on the Internet?" he wondered aloud.

"Beats the shit out of me," Delaney replied.

At that moment, they heard the Osprey's engines starting up again. The refueling was complete.

It was time to go.

"What should we do?" Delaney asked. "Scratch it out?"

Norton thought a moment, then said: "No, let's leave it. Maybe it will bring us good luck."

8

Twenty minutes after leaving Exxon One and diverting south for a mile or so, they were back on course and about ten miles away from the foot of the massive mountain range.

The snowcapped peaks looked absolutely huge now.

"What mountain range is this?" Delaney called back to Norton.

" 'How the hell should I know, Connie?' " Norton replied without missing a beat. "They ain't the Himalayas, but they must be close cousins. Look at the size of these fuckers."

Since leaving Exxon One, Delaney had actually spent some time reading the Sea Cobra's flight manual and reporting key information back to Norton. Under these conditions, the copter's maximum altitude was about twelve thousand feet, a bit less than two miles. Some of the mountains facing them were at least that high. Norton had wondered if the elevation and cold would affect his aircraft's

turbofans or not. Either way, the flight path ahead looked
rather challenging.

The good news was they didn't have to fly over the
mountains. As confirmed by Delaney, who had finally read
the fine print in Commander Amanda's mission document
as well, the Ozzie was carrying a very accurate virtual-
terrain-guidance system known as J/O-LANTIRN, or according to her extensive acronym list, the JOL. Supposedly
it could fly an aircraft through some of the tightest turns in
the Grand Canyon, at top speed, at low altitude—while on
automatic pilot.

So, no—they weren't going to fly over the mountains.
The plan said they were going to fly between them.

About two miles away from the foot of the first peak, Norton's ears perked up. Commander Amanda's voice was suddenly in his headphones.

"JO/LANTIRN is engaged," was all she said. Still, her
words sounded like those in a song. Norton wondered if
she still had her helmet off and her hair down. Was she
riding up front in the Ozzie or in the back?

Norton forced his mind back to business. The Ozzie's
super terrain-guidance system was now running the show.
From the Sea Cobra's point of view, the change was apparent right away. Smooth and graceful while under a pilot's control, the Ozzie was now flying in a slightly
herky-jerky motion, moving a bit this way, and a bit that
way, the result of the aircraft's four redundant computers
constantly adjusting its flight path as dictated by the JOL.
It looked great—but the Sea Cobra didn't have the luxury
of a high-tech computer brain to do the flying for it. It still
relied on wires and cables and Norton's hands and feet to
stay on the Ozzie's tail, all while maintaining top speed.

They went down to less than one hundred feet. The

opening between the bottom of the first two peaks lay dead
ahead. If something went wrong now, Norton thought, there
wouldn't be much to pick up in the way of debris. At this
altitude and speed, one wrong move and they'd be little
more than a black smudge on the side of some huge snow-
covered mountain.

As they came up very fast now, the space separating the
first two peaks seemed very slim indeed. But as advertised,
the Osprey found the right path between them and went
twisting through the very narrow space. Norton mimicked
the airplane's movements exactly—and just like that, they
were through too. The next narrow space came up very
quickly as well. They did the same thing. The Ozzie twisted
a bit and went around the bend, while Norton kept the Sea
Cobra no more than one hundred feet off its rear end.
Boom, just like that, they were through once again.

What they were doing was following the path of a raging
river that had cut its way through these high snowy peaks
eons before. The Ozzie followed the twisting, turning river
like a bird finding its way home. Before turning controls
over to the terrain-guidance system, the pilots had articu-
lated the V-22's big propellers to a point halfway between
vertical and horizontal. This gave the Ozzie unequaled ma-
neuverability without much drain-off in speed. It went
twisting and turning through the canyon passes with the
greatest of ease.

Meanwhile, the Sea Cobra had to plow along through the
thick canyon air the old-fashioned way: by disturbing it,
briefly. Norton's fingers were already going numb, his grip
was so tight on the controls. Delaney was quiet for the most
part, though Norton could see his colleague shifting in his
seat, trying to apply some body English to Norton's race-
car steering.

"How long do we have to do this?" Norton yelled up to him. "Just two or three minutes, right?"

This made Delaney laugh. "Try more than ninety minutes," he said. "Maybe I'll take my nap now . . . the exciting part is over."

No sooner were those words out of Delaney's mouth than a shrill ringing began blaring in Norton's headphones. Suddenly the cockpit was vibrating with warning buzzers. Norton's control panel lit up like a Christmas tree. Delaney's did too.

"Talk to me, Slick!" Norton yelled ahead. "What's this all about?"

Delaney began pushing buttons and slapping flat panels. It took him about three seconds to figure out what was going on.

"I'm reading these things right," he reported. "Someone is hot-painting us. . . ."

Norton couldn't believe what Delaney was telling him: They were being tracked on radar, probably one hooked up to some kind of antiaircraft system, probably one that was very close by and pointing down at them.

"Who the fuck has a look-down radar set out here?" Norton shot back.

They were still twisting and turning through the canyon, following the contours of the river, sometimes coming as close as twenty feet to the top of the raging icy water. This was already inhospitable terrain. The cliffs seemed to become taller and more jagged the faster they went.

So it was a good question. Who *would* have a radar set way out here?

"Picking up a lot of radio chatter now," Delaney reported. "What should we do?"

"Tell the Ozzie," was all Norton could advise at the moment. He was too busy flying the chopper to suggest anything else.

Delaney was quickly talking to someone up in the Ozzie. Whether it was Amanda or not, Norton couldn't tell. But the conversation lacked any radio protocol and went like this: "What? *What?* Who? *Where?* Are you shitting me?"

A moment later, they went around the next curve—and found themselves suddenly facing a small aerial army.

Helicopters. At least a dozen of them. Many were on the ground, straddling the river. But at least six were in the air or in the process of taking off. One more was perched on an outcrop of rock, with a radar set standing next to it. All of these helicopters were painted dark gray.

Norton saw all this in the span of one second. In the next two seconds he ascertained that the airborne helicopters were gunships, not unlike the one he was flying. And the fact that they were in a hover, lined abreast, indicated they'd been waiting for the Americans to come around the bend.

These gunships all had air-to-air missiles slung under their stubby wings. In one last mad moment, Norton imagined he could see the warheads of these missiles illuminated in a reddish glow.

No doubt about it—this was an ambush.

"That's now a *very hot* paint job!" Delaney yelled back to him. "Jessuz . . . they're going to fire at us!"

A burst of static punctured Norton's eardrums. When it cleared, he could hear Delaney yelling: "Jazz! Who the fuck are these guys?"

Norton didn't know and didn't intend to stay around long enough to find out. With no hesitation, he yanked back on the chopper's controls; an instant later they were traveling straight up.

"Holy sheeet!" Delaney yelled as he found his toes suddenly pointing skyward.

Two air-to-air missiles went by them a heartbeat later. It was pure luck they didn't vaporize the chopper right then and there. It was only that they'd been fired at such close range that their guts didn't have enough time to acquire the Sea Cobra properly. Still, the sight of the two missiles whooshing by them was enough to call in the cleaning lady.

But at that moment Norton was more concerned with pushing the Sea Cobra straight up at top speed. Can you do this to this rig? he wondered. The aircraft was shaking violently and the rotor began to buck. Then the twin engines let out a simultaneous cough. This was not good. They were going into a stall. Norton felt a shudder go through his body. If he lost his flight envelope now, they'd be picking them up with tweezers.

He stayed with it, though. Pulling the Sea Cobra right over on its back, he went for the whole ball of wax and tried to complete the loop. This maneuver mandated that he look hard over his left shoulder; all he could see was the snowy peaks rushing by him—upside down. When he turned his head forward again, he found himself staring into the Ozzie's right-side propeller. The V-22 had enacted almost the exact same escape maneuver—straight up—but just a second or two after Norton. The result was nearly disastrous. The Ozzie was twisting skyward just as Norton was coming down, all in a very tiny piece of airspace.

"Jink it, Jazz!" Delaney cried. "Jink this fucker!"

Jink it he did. Norton pushed the aircraft left just as he was at the bottom of his loop. He pulled back power—and prayed. A second later, they cleared the Osprey's tail wing by no more than a dozen feet.

"Jesus, I could see Chou looking out at me!" Delaney yelled.

The maneuver saved their lives—at least for the moment. Because at the end of all this jinking and jerking, they found themselves almost in the same position as when they had first spotted the gray-camo gunships. And the mysterious choppers were still hanging there, air-to-air missiles warming up again. There was no way Norton was going to pull another gut-wrenching loop. This time he decided to take the direct approach.

"Does that popgun work up there?" he yelled to Delaney.

Delaney didn't reply. Instead he just engaged the gun switch, and suddenly the chopper was vibrating wildly again. Smoke obscured their vision for a moment. Delaney had fired off a dozen or so rounds, sending them off in all directions.

Norton simultaneously yanked back on the power controls, slamming them forward in their seats as the Sea Cobra slowed to a bone-crunching crawl. Norton adjusted slightly to the right. One of the gunships was now floating no more than twenty-five feet off their nose.

"Do it!" Norton yelled—but Delaney needed no prompting. He pulled the trigger again, and another long stream of cannon shells burst from the chopper's chin turret and slammed into the gray gunship. One of its rotors went flying off immediately; its engine exploded an instant later. Norton went right as just the fiery debris went left. He increased power, and finally they were moving forward again.

The V-22 went right over their heads. Tracer rounds were pouring out of several of its gun portals, perforating another gray gunship hovering nearby. Back under manual control, the Ozzie pilots hit the gas. They were clearing the area; the unspoken implication was that the Sea Cobra should too.

Norton jammed the controls down. He wanted to gather

some energy for a steep climb out. But just by the physics of the maneuver, he and Delaney found themselves looking down on a big troop-carrying chopper that was parked alongside the raging river.

"Take it, Slick!" Norton yelled forward—but Delaney had already flipped the gun back on. Norton could see the cannon shells impacting all over the huge copter, tearing up its fuselage from the flight compartment on back. A two-second burst was more than enough. Energy gained, Norton yanked on the controls again and they climbed up and out, twisting around the next bend in the river canyon.

The Ozzie was in front of them now, sprinting along at top speed. In all, the small battle had lasted less than thirty seconds. Still, they did not know who their opponents had been—only that they probably were not Pakistanis.

Norton was absolutely drenched in sweat now. That might have been the most intense, in-close aerial combat he'd ever been involved in. His heart was literally beating out of his chest.

That was when he looked behind him, and saw three of the gunships were in fast pursuit.

"Jessuz!" he yelled now. *"Who are these guys?"*

The Kamov Ka-50 was a helicopter with many names.

It was a gunship, built in Russia, a middle-shelf knockoff of the U.S. Army's better and bolder AH-1 Apache.

The Ka-50 was long and slender like the Apache, and its job description was similar: busting tanks and anything else that moved in a combat environment. In its way, the Russian gunship was revolutionary in its design—but some revolutions are better left undone. The Ka-50 differed from its contemporaries in several unusual ways. First of all, it had no tail rotor. The Kamov featured a coaxial main rotor, meaning two rotors were essentially stacked on top of each other, a design element—or some would say flaw—made famous by the Kamov helicopter people. Thus, there was no need for a tail rotor—but at the very least, this could make for tricky flying.

The Ka-50 was also peculiar because it carried just one man aboard, the pilot. Instead of having a second set of eyes, ears, hands, and feet on board, the Ka-50 was loaded down with a number of automation devices, mostly heads-up stuff and controls for bulky helmet-mounted displays. Many more pounds were devoted to computer navigation devices, all of them automated. It was innovative, but it would have been much easier just to put another guy on board.

Even stranger, though not unique, the pilot had an ejection seat, one that went straight up when activated. Who wants an ejection seat that shoots the pilot up into not one, but two spinning rotors? Kamov's solution: Install explosive devices on the rotors designed to blow the spinning blades off the aircraft—and *then* fire the pilot out of the cockpit.

In a word: *who-fa* . . .

The Ka-50 could pack some heat, though, at least on paper. It carried one 30-mm cannon, an array of Vikhr-M laser-beam-guided antitank missiles, Shturm AT-6 radio-guided anti-anything missiles, or Kegler air-to-surface missiles. Free-flight rocket pods, 23-mm gun pods, and AA-11 Archer air-to-air guided missiles—it was all impressive stuff. Trouble was, the Ka-50 was so new to the landscape, and untested in combat, that no one was really sure if any of it actually worked.

Then came the name thing. Because the Russian military was broke, they couldn't afford to buy many of the new gunships for themselves. But the model was offered for sale overseas and as such, it was called Werewolf by some, Black

Shark by others, and Helicopter Soldier by still others. And
when some customers wanted a two-seat version, Kamov
complied by designing something called the Alligator.

The rap on the Ka-50 was simple: Flying a gunship in
the heat of battle is a demanding thing to do, especially for
just one man. That was why sometimes not everything
worked as advertised on the Russian-built chopper—and
sometimes nothing worked at all. Even more mysterious, it
was said, just when it seemed like everything was going
along fine for the Ka-50, the helicopter had a strange habit
of simply falling out of the sky.

That might be why the NATO reporting name for the
Ka-50 was the one that most people used when referring
to it.

The name that stuck was the Hokum.

And three of them were now in hot pursuit of the American aircraft.

The three Russian-built gunships were flying in a staggered
single-file formation, the first two aircraft out front, the
third chopper bringing up the rear. Twisting and turning
through the low river canyons, they were anticipating catching up to the fleeing Americans around the next big turn.

And that was exactly what happened—but not how the
Hokum pilots had planned it.

The three gunships approached the particularly wide turn
in the river known as Shamilili Gorge. The distance between the mountains blew out to 1200 feet down low, and
almost twice that up high. The Hokum pilots took the corner into the gorge at around five hundred feet.

The Americans were waiting for them.

The Ozzie and the Sea Cobra had reached the northern
side of the gorge thirty seconds ahead of the Hokums. In
that time, the Ozzie was able to pull up short and elevate

its big props to full horizontal. Again, the effect was like slamming on the brakes. In the same fluid motion, the V-22 spun around on its axis, turning its nose back to where its rear end had been seconds before.

This done, it activated its virtual air-defense suites and picked up the approaching Hokums. The Ozzie went down to five hundred feet, the exact altitude of the approaching gunships, and turned slightly to the right, allowing its three gun portals a clear field of fire. Once all this maneuvering was done, Norton took up a position about one hundred feet to the left of the Ozzie. Delaney had the chin gun primed and ready.

The first two Hokums came tooling around the corner as expected. A combined barrage of cannon fire greeted them; they could not avoid flying right into it. Hit squarely on its fuel tanks, the lead Hokum went up fast. The second Hokum, having about a two-second heads-up as to the presence of the American aircraft, veered hard left to avoid his partner's fate—and slammed right into the gorge's overhanging cliff. It too went up in a ball of fire and smoke.

The American aircraft held their positions and waited. Thirty seconds. Forty. One minute. The third Hokum never showed up.

One of the tenets of successful combat was knowing when to break off an attack. Two Hokums had gone down, one from weapons fire, the other trying to avoid it. That was twice lucky. Simply put, it was easier for the Americans to leave the area rather than wait to engage the third Hokum in some kind of spinning slow-motion dogfight in very close quarters, or linger long enough for the rest of the gray-camo helicopters to catch up.

So off they went, the Ozzie first, the Sea Cobra right on its tail. Falling back into the same twisting, turning flight pattern, they began to follow the contours of the immense river valley again. Norton opened his throttles wide. He was just about to tell a dazed Delaney just how kick-ass the Ozzie could be when a storm of yellow flashes went streaking by his cockpit.

Norton spun his head around to see that the third Hokum was now bearing down on them, its gun pods flashing nonstop.

"Jessuz Freaking Christ!" he yelled as he immediately dumped altitude and got out of the line of fire. "This guy sure doesn't know when he's not wanted!"

Norton's headphones were suddenly screeching with radio calls from the Ozzie. They were no longer in the wide gorge. Their airspace now was very tight, with a trio of jagged, soaring snowy peaks overhead. The lack of maneuvering space trumped any chance the Ozzie could pull its about-face trick play again.

It would be up to the Sea Cobra to deal with the third Hokum.

Norton kept diving. For a moment it looked like they were going straight into the raging waters of the icy river. Delaney let out a yelp just an instant before Norton gave the controls a mighty pull. The Sea Cobra responded with surprising agility, and in a snap they were going up again. Though awash in gut-wrenching g-forces, Norton managed to crane his neck and see that the Hokum had followed them down, and was now following them back up again.

Norton was a fighter pilot. Driving choppers was not his chosen profession. And being behind the controls of the Sea Cobra did not relieve him of instincts honed while flying F-15's. So he did what he would have done in a jet fighter. He went straight up—again. He looked below and saw the Hokum was mimicking his maneuver perfectly, but in mirror image.

Norton went to full power; this time the two engines barked in response. The Sea Cobra was suddenly tearing a hole in the sky. Delaney was screaming at the top of his lungs. After about ten seconds of this nonsense, Norton dared to look below them again. He saw what he wanted to see. The Hokum was faltering—it just couldn't take the strain of the rivet-rattling brutally vertical flight. When the Russian-built copter fell away, Norton simply peeled over and rode his tail down. Still bellowing, Delaney opened up with the chin gun and let Norton maneuver the chopper in order to adjust the fire. The big cannon shells began sparking off the rotorless tail of the Hokum. Its pilot tried just one evasive stunt. He yanked left. Norton stayed with him, and the fire stream intensified. Finally, inevitably, the rounds found the Hokum's fuel tanks. It went up, very quickly, just like its predecessors.

Now just a ball of flame, it slammed into the icy river seconds later. Norton overflew the burning wreckage just once. Seeing no life on the ground, he pulled up and grabbed some altitude.

In seconds, he was back on the Ozzie's tail and they were flying north again.

9

The Paswar
Three hours later

Norton was feeling dizzy.

It was to be expected, he supposed. He was exhausted. Flying through a black sky, surrounded by nothing but snow and ice. And he was cold. Very cold.

Their sprint through the winding river canyon had lasted all of two hours, but ended without further incident. They'd spent the last sixty minutes flying up the sides of ascending peaks. It was a slow process, climbing in increments of a hundred feet or so, trying to avoid ever-present snow squalls. But gradually, they were nearing their goal at the top of the world.

They had very little conversation during this leg of the flight. They had passed on to Chou what they'd seen drawn in the sand back at Exxon One. They had spoken briefly about their shared suspicion that the shuttle they were supposedly looking for was probably not one operated by NASA, or at least not one that was being flown in the public eye. This was not a big surprise for the two pilots. They'd heard the rumors of other shuttles being flown secretly by the military. If true, no wonder there was so much hush-hush surrounding this latest incident. Losing a shuttle that the public knew about was one thing; losing one that they did not know about—well, that was something else again.

It was close to 1900 hours now; the night had come on very quickly. It was hard for Norton to fathom that just a short while ago he'd been standing on the deck of the *Bataan*, sweating in the very humid breeze. At the moment he felt like he'd never be warm again.

The Sea Cobra had been slowly losing power over the past hour. All the panel lights were fading; the controls were getting sluggish. Shortly after climbing out of the river canyon they'd been forced to shut off all nonessential electrical devices in an effort to conserve power. The heater was the first thing they had to kill. The condensation from their breath was now frosting up the cockpit's windows.

The juice was draining off the copter's main power lines; Norton thought simple fatigue might be the cause. Choppers like the Sea Cobra weren't used to flying so many hours in a row. It was almost like the aircraft needed a nap. But it also had something to do with the altitude that they now found themselves at. They'd just passed eleven thousand feet and were still ascending. Just as a mountain climber would find it difficult to breathe at such cold and lofty heights, so too did the Sea Cobra. Making the bad situation even worse, their fuel was also back down to very critical levels. It was so low, Norton had avoided looking at his fuel gauges. Some things he didn't want to know.

Despite all this, Norton was close to awestruck by the

forbidding, almost terrifying beauty of the eerie, frozen surroundings.

"If the Moon had snow," Delaney said as they topped yet another mountain peak, "I think it would look like this."

Indeed, it was otherworldly. Even though there was no moonlight, the snow on the towering peaks was so glaring, it was almost blinding them through their C-Nite extension goggles. Yet it was impossible to fly without the thermal-image devices.

One thing was obvious, though: For grunts and jet jockeys alike, there was a big difference between what a satellite photo showed and the reality of topography. No photograph could ever do this place justice. Nothing could adequately capture its frightening beauty.

It had taken both of them a while to come down from the adrenaline rush following the knife fight with the Hokums back down in the valley. Who were they? Why had they been lying in wait for the Americans? Certainly this mission, with all its tighter-than-tight security measures, couldn't have been compromised. Or could it?

They didn't know, and the fact of the matter was, they didn't have time to think about it. Not now. What was most important was to get to their LZ in the good shape and do what had to be done.

If any mooks were waiting for them on the return trip, they would deal with it then.

Finally, they saw the signal they'd been waiting for—the Ozzie was flashing its navigation lights.

"What's that supposed to mean again?" Delaney called back to Norton.

"We're within five miles of our LZ," he replied. "And not a minute too soon."

"Does that mean I can turn my heater back on now?"

"Better not," Norton cautioned. "It might be a good thing that we're used to the cold now. I don't think there's going to be a whole lot of the warm and fuzzy where we'll be landing."

They cleared one last peak, and that was when they finally saw it. The Paswar.

"Well, isn't this freaky-deaky," Delaney exclaimed. "What planet are we supposed to be on again?"

"I'm not sure anymore," Norton replied.

Now *this* was a strange place.

Commander Amanda had been right: The Paswar was indeed a big hole, or more accurately, an ancient crater. It was about a half mile across, nearly perfectly round, and surrounded by a continuous ring of peaks. It was probably two miles around, and its crown was flat and festooned with small clumps of scraggly summit pines. The interior of the crater was, for the most part, sheer ice. Only a few outcrops and small cliffs broke this pattern, and most of these were more than halfway down. The floor of the crater itself was almost entirely obscured by blowing snow.

Strangest of all, unlike the summits they'd passed by the dozens since climbing up here, the predominate color of the ice pack up here was not white, but blue. Translucent blue—that was the only way to describe it. But this didn't make sense. Both Norton and Delaney had been to the Arctic. They had seen blue ice before. But it was always near ocean water, or packed in icebergs. At the moment, they were higher than some airliners flew. Why would there be blue ice up here?

But then, as they turned right, following the slow-moving Ozzie's lead, something weird began to happen. The color of the ice turned green. It was true. At first it seemed almost pale blue. But now it all looked green, or more accurately, emerald.

But then, after another jink to the right, the ice pack began to shimmer yellow. A bank back to the left again, everything was blue again. It was a massive optical illusion, caused by who knows what. But it was very bizarre.

"Did I say this place looks like the Moon?" Delaney said, witnessing the change in hues. "I think I meant Jupiter."

They flew along for another two minutes, the Sea Cobra following close behind the Ozzie as the lead ship, its lights still blinking madly, searching for an adequate flat surface where both of them could set down.

They finally found a place up near the crown of the crater wall. It was a piece of snow and ice that was flattened out in roughly the same size as a football field, bordered by summit pine on three sides.

"LZ in sight," Norton heard Chou announce over his headphones from the Ozzie.

Norton gave a word of silent thanks. His hands were so cold, his fingers felt frozen to the control column.

The Ozzie went in first. With the darkness and the blowing snow, visibility was almost down to zero. The V-22's landing approach only added to this problem. Its powerful props kicked up more spray than two big choppers landing at once. It started descending gingerly, as if its pilots weren't certain what they were landing on was real. Was it solid ice or simply frozen-over snow? Would they slide off the other side of the crater or sink from their own weight?

Finally, the Ozzie touched down—and stayed there. The icy spray went more than two hundred feet up in the air, but the stiff winds soon dissipated it. A cloud of exhaust followed it up as the engines wound down. It was almost as if the aircraft itself let out a sigh of relief. They'd made it. And in one piece. At least for the moment.

Now it was the Sea Cobra's turn.

Norton slowed to a crawl and went into a hover about a hundred feet up. He positioned the Sea Cobra over the midfield point of the landing zone. The Ozzie was parked about fifty yards away.

"What can you see down there, Slick? Anything?"

"Yeah, a lot of snow . . ."

Norton finally looked at his fuel gauge. It was way below the red line. Its warning lights were blinking dimly. Norton could just see the last of his gas making its way through his engines.

"I think we're clear now," Delaney yelled back to him. "Go straight down, partner. . . ."

At that moment there was a loud *pop!* Then came an almost deafening backfire from the twin engines. Suddenly the Sea Cobra was going straight down—*very* fast—its engines DOA.

"Yeah, good!" Delaney was yelling, not yet aware of the situation. "Dead on, Jazz . . . ah, maybe you can ease the throttle a bit. . . ."

They hit a second later. The rotor had continued spinning—that was the only thing that saved their lives. But they came down so hard, they bounced back up, came down, and bounced again. They came down a third time; this time harder than the first two. But at least it was for good.

"The freaking Eagle has freaking landed!" Delaney announced in mock triumph.

Norton didn't have anything to do once the chopper finally came to rest. Nothing to shut down. Nothing to secure. Everything had died the moment they hit the ground.

They opened the canopy and climbed out. Delaney met Norton at the bottom of the access step.

"Great landing, Jazzman. Makes me glad you were doing the driving."

Norton stamped his feet on the ground. He needed to convince himself that he was on terra firma again.

"I'm glad you enjoyed the ride," he said. "Because you're driving on the way back."

They took a look around. The sky was so clear, the wash of stars above them was absolutely spectacular. The stars looked like handfuls of diamonds spread across the inky blackness. The wind was blowing—it was almost a constant hum, and oddly musical in a way.

"I've been to a lot of places," Delaney said. "But nowhere ever looked like this place."

They made their way over to the Ozzie. Its rear ramp was lowered and the Team 66 troopers were hustling their equipment out into the cold. Four squads were hastily setting up NightVision scopes along the crater's edge. Others were assembling long-range IF cameras.

Norton and Delaney walked past these soldiers and scanned the inside of the Ozzie. They both had the same priority. They were frozen, tired, and disoriented, true. But they were also very interested in the whereabouts of Commander Amanda.

Chou climbed down from the flight compartment and read their minds right away. "She's still up front," he told them. "Trying to find a secure uplink."

Chou pulled the collar of his combat suit closer to his chin. "Well, we're here. And just like she said, let's snap some pics and then get the hell out."

A trooper came slipping and sliding up to them.

"I need a word, sir?" the young soldier asked.

"What is it?" Chou replied.

But the trooper just shook his head.

"Begging your pardon, Captain," he said. "But this you have to see for yourself."

Chou, Norton, and Delaney followed the trooper to his position. The man had set up a NightVision station close to the edge of the crater. He indicated that Chou should look through the NightVision scope.

Chou did so . . . and began swearing under his breath.

"Son of a bitch, I don't believe this," he said.

The scope was not pointed down into the crater, but directly across it. Norton and Delaney tried to see with their naked eyes what Chou was looking at, but it was so dark, and there was so much blowing snow, it was hard to pick out anything beyond the great precipice in front of them.

Finally, Chou abandoned the scope and Norton took his place. It took a few moments, but finally he realized he was looking at the other edge of the crater, maybe a distance of two thousand feet away. What he saw in the scope's telescopic lens was someone on the other side, looking back at him.

"You're kidding me," he mumbled. "We've got company?"

Delaney went to take a look. "Really? Way the fuck up here?"

At that point, another of Chou's men came scrambling up. He was holding a portable NightVision scope.

"Captain, take a look over there," the man said, pointing to a spot a bit further north of them.

Chou did as requested, while Norton turned the other NightScope too. Again, he was startled to see someone staring back at him.

Then another trooper ran up. He'd been manning a NightScope on the team's western perimeter. He pointed out a target; again Norton turned his scope in that direction.

Again he saw a pair of NightVision goggles looking back at him.

"Damn it!" he cursed through gritted teeth. "Were we so dumb to think we'd be the only ones with this stupid idea?"

They scanned the entire top rim of the crater. To their amazement just about every inch of habitable space on the top had been occupied. By helicopters. There were at least a dozen parked along the rim. And they had not come empty or unprepared. Not only were hundreds of cold eyes looking back at the new American position, so were the barrels of many large weapons including machine guns, cannons, rocket launchers, heavy-duty mortars, even a couple of small howitzers.

In a place that no one wanted, at the top of a strange mountain few people knew existed, there were now enough soldiers and weaponry to equip a small army.

Or start a small war.

10

Paris

The hastily disguised SR-71 Blackbird spy plane entered
the landing pattern above Orly Airport just behind a Swissair 747 and in front of an Egyptair DC-10.

It was late afternoon and raining. The airport was
extremely busy as usual. The long sleek hypersonic spy
plane was given final clearance to land, and touched down
thirty seconds later, wheels skidding on the slick runway,
a long-drag chute deploying to help slow it down. On the
plane's tail, its fuselage, and the parachute itself were letters
identifying the jet as belonging to NOAA, the National
Oceanographic and Atmospheric Administration. The airplane was here as part of a worldwide study on global
warming in the upper atmosphere—or at least that was the
cover story. In reality, this could not have been further from
the truth.

As the Swissair jumbo jet turned off and headed for its

assigned terminal, the SR-71—acknowledged as the fastest airplane known to man—continued all the way to the end of the runway, where it rolled onto an auxiliary taxi lane and finally came to a stop.

The pilot killed the engines and raised his duo-canopy. Airport support vehicles were passing by the plane, which was still sizzling after a hypersonic one-hour-and-ten-minute dash across the Atlantic. There were even busloads of passengers being ferried by. Yet the pilot could see no one on board those large vans giving him or his jet a second look.

"Only in France," he said to himself.

He peeled off his helmet, then twisted around and looked into the plane's rear compartment. The man strapped in the backseat appeared quite dead.

"We have arrived, sir," the pilot said, hoping to see some signs of life from his passenger. "Are you okay?"

Gene Smitz finally began to stir. He managed to pull his helmet off, only to find his hair was literally standing on end. He looked as if he'd driven across the Atlantic on the back of a motorcycle rather than in the jump seat of the fastest plane in the world. His eyes were watery, his mouth still frozen in a sickly death grin. He had everything but bugs between his teeth.

He sat up a bit, sucked in some of the wet, fume-clogged air, and then dropped his full-to-the-top sickness bag to the tarmac. They'd left Hawaii no more than a few hours ago, and except for several aerial refuelings, had flown at top speed literally halfway around the globe. Exciting stuff—even for an authentic CIA type.

Smitz, however, did not enjoy the ride.

"I've never been more sick in my life," he gasped to the pilot.

The pilot laughed. "I get that a lot," he said.

• • •

Smitz somehow managed to unstrap himself and climb down from the long black jet.

It was a ten-minute trudge over to the airport's main terminal. He had no coat, no hat. He was dressed in the same clothes he'd been wearing so long ago when he'd walked into the "Get Lei-ed" on Kailua Beach. He needed a shower very badly. His teeth needed serious brushing as well. He looked up at the huge Air France terminal.

"No one will notice," he mumbled to himself.

The mission paper promised to him by the seven mysterious old men turned out to be exactly two pages long, most of which was taken up by alphanumeric encryption codes. The kernel of the information was so sketchy, Smitz was convinced that the seven men were either lying to him, or had forgotten to give him the other eighteen or so pages that were supposed to be part of the document. Or, never letting go of his original thought, that this was still part of some elaborate gag orchestrated by his CIA office mates to fuck up his first real vacation in years. If that was the case, they had succeeded beyond their wildest dreams.

The first legible item on the brief instructed him to meet a contact here at Orly, in the coffee shop at the main passenger terminal. This contact would give him some "information relevant to the current situation." Thanks to his Adam's-apple-busting flight in the SR-71, Smitz was actually five minutes early for this appointment.

He reached the terminal, fished around in his pants, and came up with just enough change to buy a cup of bad coffee. He took a seat at the table closest to the window, as instructed by the brief. He sipped the bad café au lait and grimaced. If his stomach could keep this stuff down, he thought, then he just might be on the road to recovery.

He happened to glance at his reflection in the window,

and was horrified by what he saw. He frantically pushed his hair back and tried to rub the exhausted look from his eyes. Using a napkin moist with spit, he wiped the last traces of vomit from around his lips. Another napkin cleaned his glasses. By the time he returned to his coffee, a man had taken the seat across the table from him.

This man was wearing a trench coat and fedora. His face was thin, effete, his eyebrows neatly trimmed. A pencil-thin mustache barely graced his upper lip. In sum, he looked like someone from a Pink Panther movie.

He took out an ID card and flashed it so quickly, Smitz wasn't able to see anything more than a scramble of French words and a bad picture. But the CIA man didn't need to check the veracity of the man's credentials. All Spooks looked the same, especially to other Spooks. This guy was authentic. Smitz could just tell.

"I would ask you how your flight was," the man from French Intelligence told him. "But I think that's a bit obvious at this point."

Smitz just sank further into his seat.

"Do you know where I can get a decent cup of coffee?" he asked the man in reply.

The French agent smiled. "Yes, at the Four Seasons—in New York."

Smitz finally gave up and pushed the coffee cup away from him.

"Okay, so here I am," he said. "What have you got for me?"

The French agent lit a cigarette and blew the smoke around the small coffee shop.

"I'm here to offer you assistance, of course," he replied, his voice dripping with sarcasm. "The entire resources of the DGSE are at your disposal."

"Sorry, I usually work alone," Smitz said derisively.

The French agent just scoffed at him. "Pardon me, Mr. Smitz, but you seem to have me at a disadvantage. This is not the movies. We don't have martinis, either shaken or stirred. What we *do* have is some information that will help you on your quest."

"You're so sure I'm on a quest?"

The agent smiled again. "Monsieur, just about everyone in the world knows you are on a quest."

He pulled an envelope from his briefcase.

"Here is your first piece of evidence," the agent said sourly. "It will appear in tomorrow's editions. Try to use it wisely. That would be my suggestion."

Smitz ripped open the envelope. Inside was a story from a French English-language newspaper. The gist of the article was that police in Rome had no clues in the theft of a blimp owned by the Italian soda-pop company Chinnotto. The dirigible, which was built in the shape of a huge soda can, was used to fly advertisements over soccer games. It had disappeared en route to a match in Athens two weeks before.

"We have no new clues," an Italian national police spokesman was quoted as saying. "It's as if the airship vanished into thin air."

Smitz just hung his head in his hands. He was too tired to laugh, too tired to cry. He'd been up for forty-eight straight hours now, and was sitting a half a world away from where he'd taken his first drink, so long ago. How he wished he had that scotch and water in front of him right now.

"I get my ass shot out of a cannon to come over here— and all for a news story about a fucking coke-can blimp being stolen?" he asked the French agent bitterly.

But when he looked up for his reply, the man in the trench coat was long gone.

• • •

Thirty minutes later, Smitz was flopped on a bed on the seventh floor of the La Maison hotel, one mile down the road from Orly Airport.

He was now too exhausted to sleep; he'd barely had the strength to splash water on his face. An airliner took off nearby and shook the hotel to its foundations. Rain continued to splatter on the windows. Smitz felt a shiver go through him. He wondered what Ginger, the CIA flytrap, was doing at that moment. Ensnaring some other overworked agent probably . . .

Weird mission or not, he needed some shut-eye, a bath, some food, and some decent coffee—in that order. He'd told this to the SR-71 pilot—despite rocketing around the globe with him, Smitz still didn't know the man's name. The pilot had simply given him an international pager number. When Smitz was ready to move again, all he had to do was give the pilot a beep. His hypersonic taxi would be ready on a half hour's notice to take him wherever he wanted to go—except back to Hawaii.

Smitz wearily reached for the remote control now and switched on the TV set. At the moment he couldn't think of a better sleep aid than ten minutes of bad French TV. He began flipping through the channels, past the financial reports and the Continent's weather, and landed on an amateur variety show.

Perfect.

Smitz already felt his eyes start to droop.

That was when the phone rang.

It startled him so much, he lunged for the phone and answered it on the first ring.

The voice on the other end was twangy, American, and sounded like it was coming from Mars.

"Hello, Smitty . . . turn to Channel 32, please . . ."

"Hello? Excuse me?"

"Turn to Channel 32 . . ."

. Smitz switched to Channel 32 as instructed. It was all static. But just as he was about to hang up, the picture cleared, and suddenly Smitz was looking at the same dark chamber and the same seven elderly ponytailed men he'd first seen on the C2 ship off Hawaii.

"Whoa . . ." he exclaimed.

The seven men looked like they hadn't moved an inch since the last time he saw them. They were still smoking, still drinking coffee, still dressed like fat and happy cowboys.

"How was your flight?" the top guy asked him over the phone.

Smitz couldn't reply right away. He was still trying to sort out the implications of what was happening here. Just how connected *were* these guys? They'd not only tapped into the hotel's phone system. They'd been able to splice into its cable TV system as well. And how did they know what hotel he'd checked into in the first place?

"My flight was terrible," he replied defiantly, but still a bit spooked. "Next question?"

"You received the information from our friends at French Intelligence?"

Smitz almost laughed—but then he wondered if these guys could somehow see him through the TV set.

"I received a newspaper story about a blimp being stolen," he answered. "I fail to see the connection."

"So do we," the lead guy admitted. "That's why it was put in your hands. If you track down the people who stole that blimp, we have reason to believe it will point you in the direction of those responsible for bringing the shuttle back to Earth."

Smitz just stared back at the TV set. "Do you realize this blimp is shaped like a giant soda can?" he protested.

There was no reply, no reaction at all from the seven men.

"Just find out who stole it and why," the lead guy said. "And hurry. We're talking about a matter of hours here. Minutes even."

Smitz was stumped. "But how do *I* chase this thing down? The cops in Italy don't know who stole it."

Some of the seven men laughed. "Of course they do," the lead guy said. "A police spokesman was quoted in that newspaper article. Since you've arrived on the Continent, it has been determined that this person knows more than he let on. So, track him down. Get what he knows, by any means possible. If what he tells you is valuable and you need some backup, it can be arranged for you. But the important thing now is for you to get moving."

"Moving where?" Smitz half-whined into the phone.

"To Rome, of course. Now beep your beeper and get going."

Smitz bit his lip. He'd been in the spy biz in some capacity for nearly ten years. Nothing in all that time even came close to the wackiness of this.

"Can I ask you guys a question?" he spoke into the phone.

The seven men shifted uneasily in their seats.

"This shouldn't become a habit," one man warned him. "But go ahead."

Smitz wanted to word this carefully.

"Let's say you boys find out where the shuttle is, *and* who brought it down," he began. "What happens next? I mean, a shuttle is a big thing. I'm assuming you want to recover it—or what's left of it. But to do so, you'll need a lot of muscle. A lot of people doing a lot of heavy lifting.

A lot of people means a lot of mouths, a lot of loose lips you have to make sure stay shut."

"What is your question exactly?" the lead guy asked him impatiently.

"If this spacecraft is such a big secret," Smitz said, "how are you going to pick it up, and move it—without half the world knowing about it?"

The seven men just stared out of the TV at him.

Finally the lead guy spoke again.

"Let's just say we're working on that."

11

The all-black, unmarked C-17 Globemaster cargo jet had just passed over the border of Utah and Nevada when its radio set came to life.

"Please identify yourself and give status," a strange disembodied voice requested.

The pilot answered the call himself. Unlike the other members of his crew, he'd flown this part of Nevada airspace before.

"We are U.S. Air Force special flight, en route from Pease, New Hampshire," he said. "Crew of four, two passengers in transit for delivery. Need final heading and landing clearance."

"Roger, Air Force special," the voice replied. "Change course to three-seven-emerald, special grid C. You are cleared to land. Suggest you initiate tactical defense procedures."

The rest of the flight crew looked at each other. Did they hear that right? Initiating tactical defense procedures was usually a prelude to entering a combat situation. Yet at the moment, they were flying about seventy-five miles north of Las Vegas.

"Relax, everyone," the pilot told them. "Let's just do it by the numbers."

They turned north as instructed by the three-seven-emerald command, killing all but essential lights and communications, and activating their tactical-defense-procedure suite. They were flying at fifteen thousand feet, just above a thick cloud layer. It was late afternoon and the sun was already dropping below the horizon.

They began descending through the clouds, lining up for their final approach. On breaking through at eleven thousand feet, however, the crew was astonished to see the ground below them lit up with fires and explosions.

Or at least that was what they thought they were seeing.

"What the hell is . . ." the copilot blurted out before stopping himself.

The pilot reached over and pushed the airplane's threat-warning systems to full power. The panel lit up like a Christmas tree.

Now, as they passed through ten thousand feet, it appeared that a huge battle was raging in the hills and desert below them. Tracer streaks were crisscrossing the landscape. Bright red and yellow explosions, characteristic of TOW missiles and cannon fire, illuminated surrounding mountains.

There were also other aircraft in the area. The C-17's defensive radar system was picking up at least a half-dozen fighter-size aircraft, all within a ten-mile radius of its ever-descending position.

"We are getting indications that we are being painted," the copilot reported, not quite believing what he was saying.

"Painted? By what?" the pilot asked calmly.

"SAMs, air-to-airs, Triple-A—you name it . . ."

An instant later, a huge explosion went off a hundred feet from the C-17's nose. The big airplane shuddered from one end to the other. Then another explosion went off, this one just above the right wing. Then a third, just below the tail.

The airplane's flight-control systems shot into the red. Buzzers and warning signals began going off inside the cockpit. According to the cargo jet's flight computer, the C-17 had just taken three near-hits from high-velocity surface-to-air missiles. They should have added up to a fatal shot. Yet, the plane was still flying.

Up ahead, being revealed through the last wisps of clouds, the stunned crew members could see an airfield. It had two long runways, both north to south, both lit up with long lines of green landing lights.

But something seemed very wrong here as well. The base appeared to be under heavy attack. Explosions were going off all over the place, including on the runways.

Still, the C-17 dropped in altitude. The control tower at the base transmitted a very routine message to the cargo jet, clearing it to come in on the left-side runway, and stating there would be no further communications until it was down.

Three miles out now and descending through four thousand feet, the C-17's crew could see tanks, APCs, and soldiers moving in the murk below them, lit up by the nonstop explosions.

Two miles out and at 2,500 feet, the airplane was rocked again by a series of explosions going off all around it. Yet it passed through them unscathed.

One mile out, down to less than one thousand feet, the crew could see vicious gun battles going on near the end of the runway. Their was no other way to explain it: The air base itself was under heavy attack. Troops in the hills were trying to get in, while troops in a defensive perimeter around the air base were trying to keep them out.

"Must be someone's birthday," the pilot murmured. "Okay, let's lower the gear."

The C-17 crossed the runway threshold less than thirty seconds later. The closer they got to the ground, the more apparent it was that they were landing in the middle of a titanic battle—deep inside the Nevada desert.

Five seconds later, the C-17 was down.

It rolled through a series of explosions that seemed to be caused by heavy-duty mortars—or not—and steered toward a single HumVee waiting at the end of the runway. Possibly the strangest sight of all was that of a ground crew member, standing at the edge of the runway, waving two bright orange wands as a way of directing the taxiing C-17—all while explosions were going off all around him.

"It's freaking weird here today," the C-17's pilot murmured.

The C-17 rolled up to its parking spot, its engines still screaming even as they were winding down. The forward access door was opened and a ladder was hastily lowered to a small group of men waiting below. At that moment, all of the firing and explosions suddenly stopped.

Two of the men scrambled aboard the C-17 and made their way up to the flight deck. Both men were wearing desert-warfare combat suits. Fritz helmets, coveralls, belts, and boots—everything was standard issue. Except for the color.

Their uniforms were gray.

Confederate gray.

"We are here to take charge of your passengers," one man told the flight crew. "And we're in a hurry."

The pilot nodded back toward the rear compartment.

"Hey, man, they're all yours," he said. "They haven't stopped whining since we picked them up."

"What are they wise to so far?" the other man asked.

The pilot just shrugged. "From what I can tell," he said, "absolutely nothing."

The two men scrambled back out of the C-17, and on their signal, the waiting HumVee roared up to the rear of the airplane. This HumVee was painted in broad black and white stripes, not unlike those on a referee's shirt. Its driver was dressed in an all-white uniform with a red armband.

The C-17's rear access door opened and two men in suit coats and ties stepped out. They were Jimmy Gillis and Marty Ricco. Both were in their mid-forties. Both were sporting buzz cuts. Both had the same dazed look on their faces. They were part-time pilots. Weekend warriors for the New Hampshire Air National Guard. They flew KC-135 aerial tankers, the so-called flying gas stations in the sky. As a team they'd been doing air-to-air work for nearly twenty years.

Less than five hours before, both men had been sitting in the auditorium of their children's school in Portsmouth, New Hampshire, watching an Easter play. Then some men from the CIA had appeared, and now, suddenly, they were here—plunked down in this very strange place in the middle of the Nevada desert.

They didn't seem all that surprised, though—that was the odd thing. Angry, tired, depressed—yes. But surprised, no. They too had been part of the top-secret unnamed chopper unit that had tracked down the rogue AC-130 gunship and recovered the nuke-filled Russian aircraft carrier. Like the other members of that ad hoc team, they too had been somewhat unwilling participants in those missions.

And the look on their faces now said it all: *Here we go again . . .*

The men in the gray uniforms hustled Gillis and Ricco into the back of the HumVee. One man took out a small white card and read the paragraph on it to them: "You are now inside a top-secret government facility. During your stay here you will not take any photographs, make any recordings, make any radio transmissions, or keep any personal notes. Do you understand what I've just read to you?"

"Sure, like a criminal understands his Miranda rights," Ricco replied harshly.

"Good enough," the man in gray said.

He signaled the HumVee's driver and the striped vehicle took off in a cloud of dust.

As soon as it left the small airport, the strange battle began again.

The HumVee roared along a winding, barely paved road-way, hitting speeds in excess of eighty miles an hour. They were going so fast, and the road was so bumpy, both the six-four Gillis and the five-six Ricco were hitting their heads on the HumVee's roof, even though they tightly strapped in.

They sped past many strange places. It was difficult to see, they were traveling so fast, but one place looked like a village more likely found in the Caribbean, specifically Cuba. It was on fire—or at least it seemed that way. Another place resembled a Southeast Asian hamlet, something right out of Vietnam. Still another bore a remarkable like-ness to a typical Balkan town, complete with tiny white-washed houses and red clay roofs. There was evidence that fierce battles were going on around these places. Explo-sions, smoke, and endless streams of tracer rounds could be seen lighting the sky over their heads. M-1 tanks, mobile guns, Bradley Fighting vehicles filled the road at some points; the high-speed HumVee roared right around them. Dozens of soldiers, some wearing regular Army uniforms, others dressed in the enigmatic gray, were also seen moving about.

This was obviously a training facility of some kind— Gillis and Ricco had heard of similar places before. The National Training Center, a huge tract of land where tank forces learned how to fight desert wars, was in the high desert of California not far from here. Fort Hood, in Texas, boasted a life-size version of a typical "Central European City," complete with thin, cobblestone streets and crowded thoroughfares, all the better for troops to learn how to maneuver themselves around in tight spaces.

Down in Florida, in what used to be Homestead Air Force Base, there was said to be a hangar in which a full-scale jungle environment had been created, complete with live creepy-crawling things and B-52-sized mosquitoes; this was a place to train pilots in realistic conditions should they ever find themselves shot down in the jungle. A similar artificial environment was rumored to be built into a mountain in Alaska, a training area for polar operations.

But this place—this seemed to be an amalgamation of all those places and more. One apparently devoted to training America's special-operations units. And just like the NTC, this place had its opposition army, the Grays.

But never in their wildest dreams did Gillis and Ricco think any training facility could be this elaborate. This big.

This real . . .

After twenty miles or so, the striped HumVee reached a steep desert road that wound its way up to the top of a huge mesa. There, Gillis and Ricco were instructed to climb out.

They did so, after which the driver wished them luck . . . and drove away.

No sooner had the HumVee left than they heard a helicopter approaching. A moment later it came out of the sky, heading right at them. It was flying so low and so fast, both pilots instinctively ducked.

They recognized the chopper type right away. It was an MD-530 Night Fox, a small, fast, observation copter used mostly by special-operations units. It was painted in the same black-and-white stripes as the HumVee.

The chopper slowed down, turned, and came into a hover right above their heads. They were instantly covered with sand and dust, kicked up by the copter's powerful downblast. It finally landed and its only passenger stepped out. He was a slight, almost scrawny man, mid-thirties, with a dark complexion and a thin mustache. He seemed to be swimming in his uniform, which was standard desert issue, except it was all black. He was wearing no identifying patches or nameplates.

"Welcome to the Nevada Special Weapons Testing Range, gentlemen," he said. "I'm Lieutenant Moon. I hope your trip wasn't too uncomfortable."

Neither Gillis or Ricco replied.

Moon checked his watch. "Well, we're in a bit of a hurry here," he said. "So, if you'll just climb aboard, we can . . ."

Gillis took two steps toward him. Moon's nose came up to Gillis's chest.

"What the fuck are we doing here . . . *Lieutenant*?" Gillis half-shouted at him, the last word coming off his tongue like a bit of spit. Both he and Ricco were majors in the Air Guard; theoretically, they outranked this guy.

Moon looked up at Gillis like a man contemplating a redwood tree.

"This place is filled with sites built to simulate potential

combat situations," he said, almost as if he were reading a
script. "The weapons are all laser-generated, some are even
holographically projected. I think you'll agree, they are
very real-looking—and they sound and feel real too. What
we say around here is: 'They can do everything but kill
you.' "

"You're not answering the question," Gillis barked down
at him.

Moon was nonplussed. "You've been sent here to train
for a highly secret special operation," he said with a shrug.
"One that has a very short fuse."

"What *kind* of special operation?" Gillis demanded of
him.

Moon shrugged. "I'm sorry," he said. "Officially, my orders state there can be no briefing until we go over your
equipment."

Gillis glowered at him.

"And *unofficially*?"

Moon just shrugged again. "You've got chopper experience and you've got big-plane experience, true?"

"True . . ."

"Then that's what the people in charge are looking for."

"And who might they be?" Ricco asked.

Moon ignored the question. He checked his watch again
and indicated they should climb into his chopper.

"Sorry, we really have to go," he said. "So, if you don't
mind?"

They squeezed into the MD-530 and took off.

Turning north, they rose above the mountains and mesas.
They spotted formations of tanks and troops moving along
desert roads below. Other helicopters could be seen scoot-
ing along the horizon. Dusk was approaching quickly, and
at some points it seemed like the whole desert beneath them

was lit up with the strange holographic lights.

After about a fifteen-minute flight, they reached their destination. It was a large isolated hangar, built close to the side of a mountain. A long north-to-south runway disguised as a four-lane highway stretched out in front of it. Moon set the small chopper down right next to the hangar. A sign above the main entrance read: "Welcome to Area 51-1/2."

They climbed out and Moon led them inside the hangar. At first glance it appeared the big barn held just one airplane. It was a Boeing 747 jumbo jet. It looked brand-new. Its wings and fuselage were still bare steel, with no paint, no ID numbers, and no other aircraft markings.

The airplane was not a typical airliner. It was actually a cargo-carrier version of the famous 747 design. There were no passenger seats inside. Rather its interior was a cavernous cargo hold. Its nose was hinged, and could be pulled open like a huge mouth. Ramps located inside raised and lowered automatically, making the airplane similar to the huge C-5 Galaxy cargo jet.

They followed Moon into the plane's huge cargo bay. It was dark inside, but there was enough light to see that strapped down on its main pallet was another aircraft.

A helicopter . . .

Gillis and Ricco moaned audibly.

"We should have seen this coming," Gillis said.

Moon hit a light switch. The cargo hold slowly became illuminated.

"Oh, damn," Ricco wailed. "They want us to fly this thing too? What the hell is it?"

It was a Sikorsky CH-54 Tarhe, more commonly known as the "Sky Crane." It was one of the most unusual choppers ever built. It looked like a huge insect. Four long legs with a bug-eye cockpit up front, and a long rotor and heavy engine providing the thorax in the back.

The Sky Crane had muscles. It could lift more than twenty thousand pounds by using a series of cables slung from beneath its empty midsection. Under the right conditions, the chopper could pick up and tuck in a load the size of a small railroad car.

The Sky Crane had been around for more than forty years. It had seen service in Vietnam, but few were left in military service. Oddly enough this one was painted all white.

"How did you guys get this thing to fit in here?" Ricco asked. Indeed, even though its rotors had been folded back, the copter seemed perilously squeezed into the hold of the aircraft.

"Magic, I guess," Moon replied.

They climbed up into the copter's flight compartment. It was more spacious than it looked from the outside. There were five seats inside; one of them faced to the rear of the copter. A set of duplicate flight controls was located next to this seat. These allowed the pilot to fly the chopper while looking toward the rear, extremely helpful when picking up huge loads, but clearly a technique that would take some getting used to.

Two thick flight manuals were sitting on the cockpit floor.

"Required reading?" Ricco asked Moon, kicking the two books.

The young officer just shrugged. "Maybe you won't need them," he said. "I was told you two can fly anything with a rotor."

"Don't believe everything you hear," Ricco said.

They climbed down out of the copter and left the 747 altogether. Gillis and Ricco finally took off their suit coats and loosened their ties. It had been a long day for both.

"Okay, so now we've seen the gear," Ricco said to

Moon. "What do they want us to do with it and how soon?"

Moon lowered his voice to conspiratorial levels. It was time to deliver the bad news.

"You are going to be asked to fly that 747 to a pre-designated site overseas with the Sky Crane in back," he began. "You'll land, unload the Crane, fly it to another site. Once there, you will retrieve an extremely sensitive cargo, transport it back to the 747, load it on, then take off and return back here—all in a matter of hours."

Ricco and Gillis stared back at him as if he was crazy.

"You're joking, of course," Gillis said.

Moon shook his head. "There's more. It looks like you'll be flying this mission in bad weather. Most likely at night. Most likely under hostile fire."

"Jesus H. Christ," Ricco swore. "Us and what fucking army?"

Moon continued to be direct. "No army. Just you two. Alone. No radio contacts, no support personnel. No back-ups."

Gillis glared at him.

"And just who is requesting we do this?" he asked.

Moon reached into his pocket and came out with two white envelopes. They were sealed in red tape. He handed one to each pilot, but Gillis and Ricco didn't even open them. They had seen them before. They were PALs—Presidential Action Letters. In effect, they were being ordered on this mission by the president himself, just like the last two times.

"You're here to train as quickly as possible for this mission," Moon went on. "But again, the clock is ticking. Other elements are already in place. To a certain extent, they are waiting on you—and the mission can't be completed until you deploy. And you can't deploy until you squeeze some training in."

Ricco and Gillis turned the letters over in their hands.

"Or, we could just kill you now, hide your body, and get out of this freak-show Disneyland," Ricco said. "While we're still in one piece."

Moon just shrugged. He didn't miss a beat.

"Well, that's certainly another option," he said.

An hour later, Gillis and Ricco were aloft in the 747.

The jumbo jet was not much different from the aerial tankers they'd been driving for almost twenty years. Still, they did not find the big Boeing very pilot-friendly.

Takeoff had been very tense. The runway/highway was long enough, but the winds ran crosswise over it. It took all their combined strength to get the beast off the ground and into a level climb. Between them Ricco and Gillis had many thousands of hours flying big jets. But not a minute of it would have been possible without support from ground personnel or their in-flight crew. But now, it was just them, doing the work of at least a dozen people. Could two people handle everything necessary to get such a huge airplane into the air, and keep it flying?

One way or another, they were going to find out.

In reality, though, it was the aircraft in the cargo hold that worried them the most. They had many fewer hours flying helicopters, not one minute of which they'd enjoyed. In the two previous missions with the unnamed chopper unit, they had been made to fly both the monstrous Russian-built Hook and the smaller, clunkier Ka-27 Naval helicopter, a real shitbox.

The gangly Sky Crane looked like a real mess to drive as well. Add to this, they were being asked to fly it at night, in bad weather, while people were shooting at them . . . well, there were many other things they'd rather do.

• • •

If the top-secret weapons range was strange during the day, it was absolutely bizarre at night. Both Gillis and Ricco had seen combat during the Gulf War. What was going on below them now mimicked it almost exactly. Troops moving about, high-speed mobile equipment kicking up dust across the desert floor. Very realistic tracer streaks crisscrossing the sky. Some of the "explosions" were incredibly bright, and even at twelve thousand feet it seemed that they could feel the concussions disturbing the air around them. Even more remarkable, all this was taking place very close to civilization. They could see the glow of Los Angeles on the far western horizon, and the lights of Las Vegas dead to their south.

They were not alone in the air either. They'd seen many jet fighters transiting through the same airspace as they were. F-18's, F-16's, F-15's, even a few F-117 Stealth Nighthawks—Gillis and Ricco had to initiate evasive action twice in five minutes to avoid colliding with one of these birds.

It seemed the sky was very crowded above this very strange place.

They were airborne about ten minutes, flying in circles, and fighting the high winds, when their radio suddenly burst to life.

A very distant voice—maybe Moon's, maybe not—began giving them a heading and direction, their instructions on where to land. But the radio transmission was weak and full of static. When Ricco punched the coordinates into their flight computer, the screen began flashing a gobble-dygook of numbers back at them, and then froze up completely. It took four times of inputting the information before the flight computer caught on. Only then did they find themselves turning east, going even deeper into the mysterious weapons-testing range.

They were over the landing site inside fifteen minutes. It was a relatively flat stretch of desert, ringed by high mountains on all sides. Another fake highway/runway ran through the middle of it, but this one was much shorter than the one back at Area 51-1/2. There were luminescent stripes painted on the highway, but they presented a less than perfect landing strip. Even with NightVision goggles on, the stripes could barely be seen. This was due in part to the fact that the night illuminators were not working as well as they should.

Both Gillis and Ricco were beginning to feel the pressure now. They were dressed in standard blue flight suits, and it suddenly seemed very warm and stuffy inside the 747's cockpit. They had to set down on a narrow piece of road in a valley the size of a postage stamp, at night, with cranky NightVision goggles. No wonder both of them were beginning to sweat.

"We should have killed Moon when we had the chance," Gillis said.

They prepared to land, doing a standard approach and going 180 in order to line up nose-south on the empty roadway.

The jumbo came down just as rough as it went up, and they needed all their strength again just to hold the huge plane steady. The winds were even worse than at 51-1/2, and the NightVision goggles just refused to operate at full power. They fought the controls all the way down, finally slamming onto the bumpy roadway and bouncing for a full quarter mile before all the gear agreed to stick. They continued to roll out for another mile, though, every nut and bolt in the jumbo jet sounding like it was coming loose as the thrust reversers took their own sweet time to fully engage. On top of it all, the Sky Crane was rocking mightily in the back. As they stood on the brakes, both men knew if the big copter somehow escaped from its tethering, the shift in weight would be enough to flip them over and end this bad dream once and for all.

Finally, they somehow rolled to a stop. Both pilots just sat in their seats for a full minute, not talking, barely breathing, bathed in sweat.

"I just want to see my wife and kids again," the normally unflappable Gillis finally whispered. "Just one more time. That's all I want. . . ."

"Me too," Ricco replied.

It took them fifteen minutes to secure the big plane; the shutdown procedure was complicated and repetitive. Then, opening the giant door in the front became a nightmare when the fuses kept blowing every time they tried to get the hinge to swing loose automatically. Finally, they wound up pushing the big door open by hand, a long and tiring struggle as the thing fought them every inch of the way.

They had been assured by the so-called procedure list that unloading the CH-54 Sky Crane would require little more than the push of a button. The copter's pallet was on a computer-driven skid. The pallet's cables were set in winches located on the lip of the loading platform. The pallet itself was sitting on a long set of rollers.

Reading their instructions from a bad Xerox copy, Ricco took up station at the bottom of the ramp, while Gillis stayed up in the cargo hold itself. He located the magic button and gave it a push. Nothing happened. He tried again. Still no result. Gillis checked the fuses again, making sure the plane still had enough power flow, and punched the button again. Still nothing.

Gillis just shook his head in frustration. Then he wound up and punched the button so hard, he would later learn that he cracked the knuckle on his ring finger. Suddenly motors started whirring and cables moving. The next thing Gillis saw was Ricco running away from the loading ramp at top speed. They had both expected that when the big copter came down, it would slowly ease its way down the ramp. In reality, it came down with the speed of a locomotive, necessitating Ricco's hasty retreat.

The Sky Crane hit the desert floor hard, rolling out in a storm cloud of sand and dust. Gillis ran down the ramp, and eventually found Ricco wandering around in the swirl.

"Son of a bitch! I thought that thing was going to flatten me," Ricco exclaimed.

"You're not that lucky," Gillis told him.

Now they had to get the big copter ready for flight, again a task usually attended to by a score of ground personnel. There were long guide wires hanging from each of the folded-back rotor blades. Theoretically, if they pulled on those wires, the rotor blades would snap into place. But while Gillis jerked the blades into position, they would not lock in. Ricco was forced to scramble to the top of the copter and lock each blade in place individually. This took another twenty minutes, and resulted in Ricco becoming soaked in lubricating oil and grease.

"Can anything get more fucked up?" Ricco cried, climbing down from the top of the copter.

"Don't ask," Gillis warned him in reply.

They finally climbed inside the Crane and prepared to start the engines.

Gillis and Ricco had taken a cursory look at the chopper's controls upon first seeing them; at that time they had recognized all the vitals they would need to actually fly the thing. But now, illuminated by the eerie green light of the control panel, everything looked as if it had somehow tripled in number and complexity. Both men started hitting buttons and throwing switches, following the start-up procedure as written in the flight manual, but nothing seemed to be happening.

After much checking and rechecking, Ricco discovered that only half their auxiliary batteries had been engaged, a detail left out of the flight-procedure list. Starting at the beginning again, they finally got the chopper's power plants to spark to life, but right away, the aircraft's engines sounded awful and sluggish. When Gillis added power, the engines coughed twice and quit.

That was when a long line of explosions began lighting up the hills to their west.

"Oh, great," Ricco said, eyeing the very realistic-looking flashes. "Just what we needed."

They continued struggling with the copter's engines; like a balky car on a cold winter's morning, the damn things just did not want to start. Meanwhile, the faux explosions were getting closer to them.

"Now tell me again," Ricco said. "Those things are harmless, right?"

The bright flashes were now about a half mile away.

"That's what they say," Gillis replied, barely looking up from what he was doing.

Ricco's eyes stayed glued on the explosions to the west. They were getting closer. The ground below the chopper was actually shaking from their concussions.

"How do you think all this works, Jimmy?" Ricco asked him, whistling in the dark a bit. "You think each side gets points? Then you trade them in for microwaves and things?"

Gillis was barely paying attention.

"I already got a microwave," he said, still grappling with the engines' controls. "I don't need another one."

Finally Gillis got the engines to turn on, and stay on. For a moment anyway. They quit after three or four seconds. Gillis tried again. They started again, then stalled again. He tried a third time. The salvos were now just a quarter mile away. The reflections from the explosions were throwing weird shadows around the chopper's cockpit. Gillis tried the engines yet again—and this time, they stayed on. The rotors began spinning slowly at first, but gaining speed with every second. The fake explosions were now just a thousand feet away.

"What say we just fly this thing down to Vegas and play some craps?" Ricco asked him.

"Don't tempt me," Gillis replied. "In my mind, I'm already halfway there."

It took another two minutes, but they finally lifted off in a cloud of dust, just as the fake explosions began impacting all around the dormant 747.

The Sky Crane barely clawed its way into the air, and another five minutes passed before it reached a paltry 1200 feet in altitude. The copter was powered by two Pratt & Whitney turboshaft engines; each could kick out about 4800 horsepower on takeoff, but once in forward flight, they could barely push the ship to a one-hundred-mph cruising speed. The fastest chopper in the world the Sky Crane was not. In fact, it was one of the slowest.

Once they had settled down, Ricco looked over at Gillis. Both of them were drenched in sweat.

"Now what?" Ricco asked.

No sooner were the words out of his mouth than their radio set came alive. Both men jumped in their seats, it had happened so quickly.

"You will stand by for further orders," the same disembodied voice told them again.

"Gee, was that creepy enough?" Ricco asked.

Gillis looked over at him and put his finger to his lips. The message was clear: no chitchat. They were obviously being bugged here. The less they said, the better.

Their flight computer came alive a few seconds later as well. A long stream of numerical codes began flooding the screen. Ricco began pushing the buttons and throwing switches, and when the numbers became properly shaken, stirred, and descrambled, they provided them with their flight plan.

They were to proceed to an area about twenty miles north of their current position. Using their crappy NightVision goggles, they had to locate a place described as "a very deep sink." Somewhere at the bottom of this depression they would find their "retrieval target." They had to figure a way to get down low enough to actually hook whatever the hell it was and bring it back to the 747.

"Sounds like a lot of fun," Ricco said.

"Yeah, I can't wait," Gillis replied wearily.

Again they flew over the strange war-gaming reservation, barely paying attention to the simulated battles going on below them.

After a very sluggish ten-minute flight, they reached their designated area. Ricco began searching the terrain below, constantly adjusting his NightVision goggles, usually to no effect.

They were orbiting two towering mesas, but he was

having a problem picking out the "deep sink" that supposedly sliced between them.

"This *must* be the place," Ricco said. "But it's so fucking dark down there, I can't see a thing."

Gillis yanked back the throttles and went into an even slower orbit around the gorge. Turning the Sky Crane at this altitude was like trying to drive a truck with three flat tires. It was low, loud, and slow. Once again, Ricco scanned the ground below them through the near-useless Night-Vision goggles. Finally, after five frustrating minutes, he spotted an object way, *way* down at the bottom of the chasm.

"Okay, there *is* something down there. It looks to be about the size of a car. . . . Wait a minute. It *is* a car. . . ."

"A car?" Gillis asked.

"I'm serious," Ricco was saying, banging his Night-Vision goggles again. He was looking almost straight down. "Christ, it looks like an old Lincoln Continental."

"Marty, really?" Gillis was saying.

"I'm not shitting you, Jimmy," Ricco insisted. "That's a Lincoln down there. It's white, got the big fins, the big grille. I'm guessing it's about a '69 or '70."

Gillis was instantly furious.

"What the *fuck* is going on?" he asked. "They drag us all the way out here. To this freaking bad dream . . . to pick up . . . *a car?*"

But Ricco wasn't listening to him. A very bright red light had suddenly emerged from deep inside the gouge. It was heading right at them.

"Jessuzz, Jimmy!" were the only words Ricco could spit out. A second later the chopper was rocked by a tremendous explosion.

Or at least it seemed like an explosion. There was a

bright flash. An earsplitting noise. And the copter nearly went over from the concussion.

But then, a moment later, all was calm again. No smoke, no fire. No warning lights indicating they'd just lost half the aircraft. All they had were spots in their eyes, big ones, the equivalent of having a hundred or so lightbulbs go off in their faces at once.

Still, Gillis fought the controls for a few harrowing seconds—it took his psyche that long to realize they weren't really in danger.

"Jesus . . . Jesus! . . . *Jesus!*" Gillis said three times with three different inflections. "What the fuck was that?"

Before Ricco could respond, another explosion went off, this one about ten feet from their nose. It was even brighter than the first, and twice as loud.

Then came another. And another.

"Christ, Jimmy drop this thing!" Ricco cried. "These assholes are shooting at us!"

Gillis needed no further prompting. He put the chopper into a dive that had them lose more than five hundred feet in just a few seconds. By the time Gillis yanked it back to level flight, they were nearly even with the top of the twin mesas.

That was when the tracer fire began.

No sooner had Gillis turned the chopper around than they were enveloped by a swarm of orange tracers. They could hear popping going off all the way down the fuselage in back of their cockpit. Not quite the sound of bullets tearing through the metal, but damn close. Every which way Gillis jinked the big copter, the tracers followed. It was like they were caught in an out-of-control amusement park ride.

"God damn, they don't pay me enough to do this crap!" Ricco bellowed.

They were somehow able to steady the chopper and put

it into another, less hectic dive. The tracer fire stopped. But now they had other problems. The gorge was only two hundred feet across; the Sky Crane's rotors cleared seventy-two feet. Gillis's hands were frozen to the controls, keeping the chopper's long blades equidistant from both sides of the rocky depression.

Down they went, into the dark abyss, until they could finally see the bottom of the gorge with the naked eye. And sure enough, sitting out on a small outcrop of rock shaped not unlike a huge sandy pedestal was a 1969 Lincoln Continental.

"That's our target?" Gillis exclaimed.

"It's got to be," Ricco replied, craning his neck to see out the chopper's side window.

Gillis just shook his head. "This has got to be the most fucked-up enterprise I've ever been involved in."

"I'll second that," Ricco replied, unstrapping from his seat. "But something tells me the party hasn't even started yet."

Gillis brought the Sky Crane down almost level with the old car's position, hovering long enough for Ricco to jump out. He landed hard, toppling over in the downwash and managing to knock the wind out of himself. Gillis maintained his hover, wondering if Ricco was still conscious—or even alive. When he started waving back up to him, Gillis slowly turned around, came back at about fifty-five feet, and went into another hover.

The Sky Crane had a dozen cables hanging down from its skeletal belly. It was with these cables that they would lift the "retrieval target." Gillis hit the cable-release lever in order to drop them—but of course, nothing happened. He hit it again. Still nothing.

"Jessuz, does *anything* fucking work around here!" he

screamed in frustration. He yanked the lever again. The cables finally dropped.

As Gillis held the hover, Ricco ran the cables through the Lincoln's interior and then under its front and rear axles. It was hard work, in the dark, in his greasy, smeared uniform, with the downwash blowing all sorts of things around. At times he could barely see his hands in front of him.

Throughout all this Gillis had held the Sky Crane steady—he was flying like a pro. Back when he was first sucked into the secret chopper unit, he and Ricco had gone through a rigorous training period that changed them almost overnight from tanker pilots to chopper jockeys. Lots of this training took place in very realistic helicopter simulators. Gillis flew many more hours in the missions that followed. The result was he had become a fairly good helicopter pilot, better than he would ever admit to himself. But he was still light-years away from actually liking it.

Finally, after ten minutes, Ricco had the car all but wrapped up.

That was when the tracer fire started again.

Ricco had hooked off the last cable when the gorge was suddenly deluged with tracers, ricocheting down from the tops of the twin mesas. Gillis looked down and saw Ricco doing a weird kind of dance trying to avoid getting hit with the flashes of laser light. *Damn, how real they looked!*

Finally he saw his partner give him a very shaky thumbs-up. Gillis immediately pulled the cable lever back—and thank God this time it worked on the first try. The car rose slowly into the Sky Crane's open-air belly, not exactly even, but close enough for what they had to do with it. Once it was secure, Gillis went down to get Ricco, all the while flying through the storm of bright phantom bullets.

His partner jumped on board with much enthusiasm, and immediately began screaming for Gillis to climb out. Gillis pushed the pedal to the metal, and slowly but surely the big copter began to rise.

The tracers followed them all the way up, past the tips of the mesas and beyond. Only after the Sky Crane began moving forward again, fading slowly into the night, did the laser-generated gunfire finally stop.

They returned the way they came, flying at 1200 feet, passing over dozens of pyrotechnic battles taking place below.

Finding the big 747 was no problem. They set down by the empty highway, with Gillis maneuvering the big Sky Crane right up to the mouth of the huge cargo jet. Ricco jumped out and guided him in the last few feet. They lined it up just right on the first try.

As Gillis proceeded to shut down the big copter, Ricco climbed up into the 747 and started its quartet of huge engines. All this took about ten minutes. Then they winched the Sky Crane back to the cargo plane's cables, pushed the magic button, and watched as the big copter was gobbled up again by the jumbo jet. Both men were amazed that this time, everything worked—first try. Even more astounding was that they could do this all by themselves. Just the two of them.

"Why have we been fucking around with ground monkeys all these years?" Ricco joked as they reengaged the 747's doors and watched them close automatically.

Takeoff was hairy, but relatively problem-free. They flew directly back to Area 51-1/2 and set down, rolling up right next to the hidden hangar. Moon was waiting for them as they climbed out.

"Well, we got your car back," Ricco told him. "Next

time, don't leave the keys in the ignition. You never know where it will wind up."

"I drive a Jag," Moon told them without batting an eye.

"And I drive a minivan," Gillis shot back. "And my guess is, the Lincoln was just a substitute for what they really want us to pick up, right? Same size? Same weight?"

"Correct, more or less," Moon replied.

"Are you saying we're flying offshore to steal a Mercedes or something?" Ricco asked.

"Not quite," Moon answered. "But, all things being equal, do you think you've got the hang of it?"

Both pilots laughed wearily. "If you mean did we live through it the first time, the answer is yes, I think," Gillis told him. "But as far as getting the hang of it, that's another story."

Ricco nodded, stretching his aching back. "I hate to say this." He yawned. "But if you want us to actually do this right, we *will* need at least a dozen more sessions."

Moon just shook his head.

"That won't be possible," he told them. "My suggestion is that you use the facilities in the airplane barn, get cleaned up, get some coffee. You're due to ship out at any moment."

Gillis and Ricco couldn't believe what they were hearing.

"Listen, Moonpie," Ricco said. "It will take us at least a week of jerking this thing around before we are ready to fly someplace and actually do it."

Moon just kept shaking his head, though.

"The way this thing is coming down," he told them, "you'll be lucky if you get that cup of coffee in."

12

The Paswar

No one was sure who fired first.

All Norton saw was a long line of red streaks arcing over the crater, almost like the trail of a meteorite burning its way to Earth.

The noise that followed was unmistakable, though. It was not the tinny *rat-a-tat* of an infantry rifle. No, this was big, brassy, serious stuff—the tune of a heavy-caliber machine gun. Like the opening notes of a grand Wagnerian opera, that single refrain set off an explosion of weapons fire all around the crater's top. Cannons, mortars, artillery rounds— in seconds the sky above the Paswar was lit up like the Fourth of July in winter.

Not two seconds after these first shots were fired, Chou yelled the two words that no one in the American contingent wanted to hear: *"Dig in!"* The Team 66 troopers snapped to instantly, though, as if they did this sort of thing every day. With pickaxes and hammers, they began chopping into the hard ice surrounding the American position. It was like hitting solid rock—still, they pounded away. In just minutes they'd created a string of icy foxholes, igloo-like firing stations, and a twenty-foot trench running along the lip of the crater. It was crystal-clear now—the Americans would be staying awhile.

This was not the way it was supposed to be. In the most basic terms, this was really just a reconnaissance mission. Their orders were to ascertain if the missing shuttle was lying at the bottom of the crater. Facing hostilities was not included in the game plan. Maybe it was haste, or maybe it was arrogance. But the idea that someone else would fly up to the Paswar so quickly apparently never crossed the minds of the geniuses who had put the mission together. The battle back in the canyons against the Hokums should have been ample warning, but even Norton had to admit he'd never dreamed that another special-ops group would be waiting for them once they arrived here, never mind this many.

But, since they were under strict orders not to break radio silence until they knew the shuttle's fate, calling for help or even to report their predicament was out of the question. They had little choice then: With the darkness and the wind and weather, seeing anything inside the crater would be impossible before daylight—the NightVision stuff wasn't even registering on the crater floor, that was how cold it was. So, they would have to hang on here until at least first light, to see if anything was really down there.

That is, if they survived the night . . .

Just who was shooting at who was almost impossible to determine. The first chain reaction of gunfire seemed panicky, desperate. Hunkered down in the newly carved trench, Norton and Delaney had followed the gunplay, using the

NightVision scopes on their M-16's. Team 66 troopers were all around them, their weapons at the ready. Chou himself was never too far away, teeth chattering as he reeled off the names of the various weapons being fired, knowing them simply by the noise they made.

A loud *whomp!*

"That's a 120-millimeter heavy mortar," he reported. "Russian-built. Soltam. Old stuff."

A sizzle, then a crack . . .

"AGS-17 Plamya grenade launcher . . . that thing's an antique!"

An earthshaking series of *Blam! Blam! Blam!*

"Wow . . . that sounds like a 12.7 Russian-built AA machine gun."

No surprise, much of this ordnance was actually hitting ice—*ancient* ice, undisturbed for eons until now. Each impact would release a cascade of illuminated ice crystals that lasted but a second before disappearing forever. In that instant, though, they looked like nothing less than an explosion of diamonds, hot glittering facets too quickly melted away.

It was strange, beautiful . . .

". . . and fucking weird," Delaney kept saying over and over. "This is one fucking weird place. . . ."

No one disagreed with him.

Early on Chou had told his men to hold their fire—that is, until someone fired on *them.* But when the gunplay erupted from just about every point along the crater's rim, it didn't take too long before one of those long sprays of red tracers found its way to the American encampment and lit it up like a dozen Roman candles. No sooner had the first barrage gone over their heads than Chou's fire teams opened up with their heavy 50-caliber machine guns. The big American weapons proved to be the brightest and the loudest of all. And while their intensive return volley did not stop the incoming fire completely, it reduced it substantially.

Still, no one felt entirely safe in their current location. Far from it. Every time a big round exploded anywhere near the American position, the ice beneath them would shake, rumble, and groan. Since they were up so high, with such a perilous drop below them, this was not a reassuring feeling.

With all the exploding ordnance and the resulting smoke and confusion, it took a while for the Americans to realize that the heaviest fighting was actually going on up around the northeast part of the crater, some distance away from them. Indeed the tracer streams and elliptical mortar trails became nonstop in that area. Using their NightVision scopes, Norton and Delaney watched the vicious hand-to-hand combat at the far end of the crater for nearly three hours. Faceless soldiers dressed in heavy parkas, fighting each other endlessly over the most inconsequential outcrops of rock. Norton had never seen blood spilled through a NightVision set before. He now knew it oozed hot and yellow. And at times, the weapons fire was so intense, it actually hurt to look at it through the NightVision lens.

Through all this, the wind increased and the temperature plummeted. The snow squalls were so sudden and brutal, it was sometimes impossible to see a hand in front of your face. Everyone was extremely cold, especially the two pilots. Even though they were now wearing lightweight, battery-heated snow-ops camos courtesy of Team 66, Norton was certain he'd never be warm again.

There were other problems as well.

"Take a look around you," Delaney said to Norton during a brief lull in the fighting. "Tell me what you see."

"Snow, ice, snow, and more ice," was Norton's frigid reply.

"Right," Delaney said. "And what is the color of all this snow and ice?"

"Mostly white," Norton replied.

Delaney nodded grimly. "So, what's wrong with this picture?" he asked.

Norton studied the American position, and finally discovered what Delaney was getting at.

It was the two aircraft, the Osprey and the SeaCobra, parked about fifty yards behind the trench. They might have looked sinister and mysterious in their dull black paint jobs when they left the *Bataan*. But up here, at the top of the world, with all the snow and ice, once the sun came up, their opaque finish would make them stick out like two very sooty thumbs.

"Yeah, let's make a note of that," Norton said, shivering. "When flying missions to the Himalayas, try not to paint the fucking airplanes black."

As if on cue, another long stream of tracer fire went over their heads.

"And while we're on the topic of fucked-up things, here's another question for you," Delaney said, leaning in a little closer to be heard over the huge firing guns. "Isn't it about time for our guardian angel to appear?"

This time Norton knew what his colleague meant right away. In the last two missions, they'd come in contact with a very strange Spook who went by the code name "Angel." Neither Norton or Delaney knew who this guy was exactly, only that he was a pilot and flew an aircraft that was so secret, if they had laid eyes on it, Angel said he'd have to kill them. And he was absolutely serious. His mysterious aircraft had, at the very least, VTOL capability and could go very, very fast. They knew this because this Angel character—he was a tall, blond Nordic-looking individual who wore a pure-white flight suit, a futuristic crash helmet, and plain black Keds sneakers—always seemed to appear via an aircraft, without the need of a runway, whenever they were facing their most desperate moments. Like now.

So, where was he?

"Maybe he's on vacation," Norton observed wryly. "Just like we should be."

It was now 0330 hours.

The fighting on the north end of the crater was raging again. The sky was filled with bright fiery ordnance flying back and forth.

Suddenly, someone jumped into the trench with Norton and Delaney. They were surprised to see it was the very beautiful Commander Amanda. They assumed she'd been inside the Osprey since landing, trying to secure a line of communications in order to contact the higher-ups when the time was right. But whether it was the altitude, the weather conditions, or even interference from all the gunfire going on, she'd not yet been able to open a line out, thus adding to their predicament.

This glitch did not stop her from doing other things, though.

She was carrying her laptop and a notebook with her now, a huge helmet bobbing on her head. Norton's heart froze when he saw her. He didn't want her up here, where one stray bullet could end her beautiful life. His first instinct was to hustle her back to the relative safety of the Ozzie. But at the same time, he knew she would never stand for that. She was not only gorgeous and smart, she was also not a wuss. Not by a long shot.

Besides, she had something very important to tell them. Something that would eventually save all their lives.

Or at least some of them anyway.

"I took one of the NightVision scopes and did a quick survey of the people who are up here with us," she told Norton, Delaney, and Chou as they gathered around her. "Luckily, none of these mooks are shy about displaying their national colors and insignia on their aircraft or uniforms. I mean, we're the only ones up here who aren't waving a thirty-foot flag."

She checked her notes. Norton inched a bit closer to her. So did Delaney. So did Chou.

"My survey confirmed that we are sharing the immediate area with armed forces from seven different nations," she went on. "They brought lots of weapons, lots of soldiers—and lots of helicopters. Yet there's not a Hokum in the bunch. That's interesting, isn't it?"

She pointed toward the far eastern edge of the crater. "There's a large contingent of troops at about the two o'clock position—over there, where most of the fighting is taking place. No doubt about it, those people are Chinese special ops.

"Over there, right next to them, at about one o'clock, we have the Pakistanis. Over there, at twelve o'clock, those are Afghans, authentic Taliban fighters, I suspect. Then, see that green-and-white-camo chopper at about eleven o'clock? Those people are Kazakhstanis. Beside them, those bluish-camo choppers—they are Tajikistanis. Beside *them,* those people are from Kyrgyzstan. Then way over there, on the other side of the Chinese, are the Indians."

Another barrage of gunfire went over their heads. All three men made an effort to protect Commander Amanda. The Team 66 gunners promptly returned the volley, letting loose a barrage of machine gun fire so loud, it echoed like thunder around the crater.

"All this got me thinking," Amanda went on, once the

noise had quieted down and she had disentangled herself from her protectors. "*We're* the strangers in this neighborhood. The Chinese, the Pakistanis, the Kazaks, the Tajiks—they've all been here for centuries. Hoping that I have at least a passing knowledge of geopolitics, that can really only mean one thing. . . ."

"That they want to eat us?" Delaney asked her, deadpan.

She gave him a slap.

"That they think *we* want to eat *them*?" Delaney tried again. This time, no slap.

Norton took the high road. "That they are all related?" he asked, giving it a shot.

"No," Amanda said with a shake of her head. Her hair was falling out of her helmet. Suddenly Norton felt warm again. "It means they all despise each other. Isn't that great news?"

The three men went into their Sure-I-Knew-That routine. Of course they'd all hate each other in this part of the world. It just made sense.

"Now," she began again with some qualification, "that doesn't mean that they all hate each other exclusively, or that the Chinese dislike the Tajiks more than the Tajiks hate the Kazaks. Though I'm certain that's what all this gunplay is about."

"Yes, of course," Delaney said, as if he understood it all perfectly. "Please, go on."

She slouched down a little and rested her laptop on her knees. How was she able to do that? Norton wondered. He couldn't move an inch in this icy hole without some slipping or sliding. Yet she was able to remain so, well . . . elegant.

"This is what I came up with," she began again. "It might sound slightly stupid. But do you want to hear it anyway?"

Was she kidding? Norton thought. It was below zero, the

snow was flying, they were within range of many, many
big guns—and still, he would have given an arm and a leg
to hear her recite the alphabet.

"Yes, please . . ." he heard himself say.

She bit her tongue in the most precocious way and then
began reading from her notes.

"Well, interestingly enough, just about everyone up here
hates the Chinese—and the U.S. too, of course. But the
Indians are especially very belligerent toward the Chinese,
as are the Tajiks, the Kazaks, and the Kyrgyzstanis. Now,
the Indians hate the Pakistanis too, of course. And the Pakistanis hate the Indians—but they are also on very bad
terms with the Afghans, who I still can't figure out why
they decided to come."

She turned the page of her notebook.

"Now there are also regional animosities between the Kazaks and the Tajiks, but we can't forget that the Kyrgyzstanis were once part of . . ."

She went on like this for the next ten minutes, the three
men in the trench absorbing her every word, fascinated by
the amount of work she had done, and the information she
had at her fingertips. But to say they understood it all would
not be correct. And when a particularly intense barrage
started up, Norton touched her lightly on the arm and said:
"Better cut to the chase, Commander. This might not be
the safest place in a little while."

She flipped through ten more pages of handwritten
single-spaced text in her notebook before reaching the last
page.

"Okay, bottom line?" she said. "If we have any friends
up here, it's those people over there."

She pointed across the crater to the ten o'clock position,
the place where Captain Azzur and Company X of the Kyr-

gyzstani Armed Forces had landed in their antique Flying Bananas.

Finally the sky began to brighten.

The fighting at the northern end of the crater died down, as if the new day itself had caused the guns to stop. Relative calm returned to the Paswar. The wind blew. The snow squalls went away. The eight camps quieted down—some with wreckage still smoking, others with blood tainting the snow around them. The survivors had other things to do, now that the daylight was coming. They all wanted to know the answer to the same question: What, if anything, was lying at the bottom of the Paswar crater?

Chou and his men had been preparing for this moment for most of the night. They had set up two electronically powered telescopic cameras. These all-weather devices were able to take thermal images as well as regular tele-photo shots even at great distances.

"You know what the punch line to this joke will be?" Norton asked as the sun finally began to peek over the eastern mountaintops. "That there's nothing down there."

"You really think that?" Delaney asked him.

Norton nodded. "Nothing but snow and ice."

"Want to make it interesting?"

"Name it."

"A hundred bucks says you're wrong," Delaney told him.

Norton wearily slapped him five. "You're on, partner," he said. "And I want cash this time. Not one of your crummy checks."

Chou powered up one of the camera-scopes and took the first look into the valley. Even without the aid of a powerful camera lens, the place looked particularly forbidding in the cold light of dawn. The interior walls of the crater were much steeper than anyone had thought; some went almost straight down. A few outcrops of rocks, or in several places, piles of rubble stretching down the sides, were the only things that broke this pattern.

From this first glance, it seemed impossible to reach the bottom of the crater by hand and foot.

"That's why everyone brought helicopters," Norton thought, along with everyone else.

But even a chopper would have a hard time setting down on the crater floor. The sheer walls culminated in a sort of huge V shape with very rugged terrain below. The very bottom of the crevice was too narrow in many places for even a small chopper to negotiate.

Norton, Delaney, Amanda, and most of the Team 66 crew were now leaning over the lip, staring into the maw through binoculars, looking for anything that might be made of something more than snow and ice.

But they could see nothing.

"Man, I *knew* this was a wild-goose chase," Delaney said, flip-flopping after he scanned the valley floor with his spyglasses. "I mean, how dumb can we be? Of all the places on this planet to come down on, what are the chances that this thing came down *here*—the worst place on Earth?"

"Heads will roll back in my office," Amanda fretted, scanning the bottom as well. "And knowing those cowboys, mine will be the first one to go."

Norton, however, smiled wearily. He was glad they'd come up empty. Now they could just all go home and be warm and Amanda would be safe.

Plus he'd won a hundred bucks.

In fact, Delaney was actually reaching for his wallet when . . .

"Jessuz Christ!" Chou swore very uncharacteristically. "I think I see something."

"You've got to be kidding," Norton exclaimed. "Where?"

Chou had the camera-scope pointed toward the eastern end of the crevice, where it was its narrowest. That part of the crater floor had not yet been reached by the new sunlight. But in the brightening murk, an object began to come into focus.

Chou pulled Norton in front of the scope.

"Take a look," he told the pilot.

Norton pressed his eyes to the lens—and sure enough, at the far end of the crater, he could see a large gray object half buried under tons of snow.

It looked like the rear end of an aircraft. A large tail fin was most evident. What appeared to be rocket nozzles, big and black, and the trailing edge of one wing were also visible. Even though it was easily a half mile away from their position, the object looked enormous.

"Son of a bitch," Norton whispered. "Is it real?"

"It looks real enough to me," Chou declared.

Amanda took a quick look, then began to quiver with excitement.

"I've *got* to get this news back to base!" she cried.

But no sooner were the words out of her mouth than Delaney spotted some activity up near the Indian encampment.

"Hold on, what's this?" he asked.

Fog was still covering most of the crater top. But through the mist, they could see a line of Indian soldiers making their way down the sheer ice face toward the bottom of the crevice.

They were wearing snow-white camo uniforms, and carrying rifles, light machine guns, and an enormous Indian flag. One man was lugging a radio set. They were descending into the crater with considerable aplomb, in some cases using repelling gear.

Norton, Delaney, and Chou turned to Amanda. Her helmet was off. Her hair was down.

"Could this be the end of our ball game right here?" Norton asked her. "I mean, if they reach that thing first, they can make a case that it belongs to them—correct?"

"At the very least," she replied, biting her lip.

Once more, she started to climb out of the trench, intent on getting through to her superiors with the bad news—but Delaney started yelling again: "Look at that!"

He was pointing to a section of the crater wall about two hundred yards north of the Indian troops. Another line of soldiers was making the climb down.

They too were equipped with mountain gear; they too were heavily armed. They were trying to reach the bottom not by climbing straight down the icy walls, but by attempting to negotiate the handful of small, craggy peaks that punctuated the crater's sides.

"It's the Chinese," Amanda said, binoculars back up to her eyes. "And that means this whole soap opera just got five times worse. The Indians, we might be able to deal with. But the Chinese—they'll never give that thing up."

But then something else happened.

Puffs of smoke could be seen coming from the Chinese troops. Then some of the Indian soldiers began to falter. One man lost his balance and fell all the way down to the craggy floor of ice below. Not only did the Americans hear his screams, they heard his bones crack when he hit. His blood stained the heretofore-virgin white ice.

Now came more gunfire. The Chinese troops at the top of the rim began firing at the Indian encampment and vice versa.

"Jessuz, here we go again," Delaney said.

Surprised by the sudden attack, the descending Indian troops began fighting back. But the Chinese were better armed and were in a better position to fire on the Indians. The small craggy cliffs afforded them more protection. The Indians were without any cover. Soon, more bloody stains were dripping down the side of the crater wall as, one by one, the Indian soldiers were picked off by Chinese sharpshooters.

"This isn't fair!" Amanda cried out. "We've got to do something."

"I don't think we can," Chou told her. "Our primary directive is to recon this place, not to get involved in a shoot-out."

"What do you think this is?" Norton fired back at Chou. "*Star Trek*? We're already involved."

With that, Norton picked up his rifle and began firing at the Chinese soldiers. His stream of bullets came nowhere near them, but it distracted them long enough for the surviving Indian soldiers to scramble for what little cover they could find. Three went back up the rope to the top of the crater; three others made a quick, sliding descent to the crater floor.

Those three were the unlucky ones. The Chinese soldiers at the top of the crater began firing at them—and they simply had nowhere to hide. Two were perforated almost instantly. Once again, Norton began firing on the Chinese sharpshooters; Delaney did too. Even Amanda raised her gun and began shooting. But they were just too far away from the Chinese position to do any good.

But then suddenly, the Chinese position was rocked by a huge explosion. Somebody had hit an ammunition supply, and caused a blast so violent, it sent a shock wave right through the crater. Again, the ice beneath their feet began to moan.

Now a stream of red tracers went directly across the crater and slammed into the Chinese position. This gunfire was
coming from the Tajikistani camp. More Chinese troops
took up firing positions along the crater rim. Two small
howitzers were brought up; heavy mortars too. The Chinese
began firing directly into the Indian camp even as the Tajiks
were shooting at *them*. Then the Kazaks began firing at the
Tajiks. And the Pakistanis at the Kazaks. Inside of one
minute, the battle along the crater lip was raging once
again.

"Jesus, this thing is really getting out of hand!" Delaney
yelled over the renewed cacophony of weapons fire.

"Whatever happened to just white hats and black hats
shooting at each other?" Norton yelled back.

"That went out with the millennium!" Chou shouted to
them. "Welcome to the twenty-first century."

"Greed, territory. It doesn't matter anymore," Amanda
moaned loudly. "If someone gets in your way these days,
just shoot him."

He wasn't sure why, but at that moment a strange
thought went through Norton's head. He looked down into
the valley, where the large tail fin and the rocket nozzles
were located.

Then he pulled Delaney aside.

"Put your thinking cap on," he told his fellow pilot.

"I believe I left it at home," Delaney replied.

Norton pointed to the object at the far end of the crater.
"Let's say that's the Real McCoy down there," he began.
"It sure doesn't look like there are any survivors, right?"

"Right," Delaney agreed.

"Well, then, any recovery process would take weeks,
maybe even months," Norton went on. "They'll probably
have to bring it up piece by piece—and that's after they

dig it out. They'd need a lot of muscle, a lot of manpower, even under the best of circumstances."

"Yeah, so?"

"So if they had a good idea where it came down, why did they want us to hustle up here so damn fast? The *real* reason? I mean, let's face it, everything was *so* chop-chop, they forgot to put about a million things into the mission spec."

"Again, that's true. But what's your point?"

"Well, this is just a hunch—but I think what's happening here ain't so much about the shuttle—or the crew. I think it's about something else."

"What else could it possibly be?" Delaney asked, authentically curious now. "One of our shuttles crashed. A *top-secret* shuttle. People find out about it—and now everyone wants to claim it, just for the bragging rights alone. If they do, a big classified program is revealed—and the U.S. looks dumb. It just makes sense that our guys would want it back first."

"Yes, but look at it this way—our guys probably knew the crew didn't make it. After all, this wasn't a rescue mission they sent us on. It was a *recon* mission—to see what was left of it."

Delaney shrugged. "Get to the point, will you? You're giving me a headache."

Norton looked into the big hole again. "Maybe I'm way off," he said. "But maybe what everyone at CIA is having kittens about isn't so much the shuttle—or the fact that if someone else finds it first, a whole top-secret program will be revealed. Maybe it's something even bigger. . . ."

"But what could be bigger than that?"

Norton thought a moment. He really didn't know where these strange notions were coming from.

"I don't know," he said. "Like maybe something the

shuttle was carrying. Something inside its cargo bay. Maybe *that's* what they don't want people to find."

"Like a spy satellite or something?" Delaney asked.

"Maybe," Norton replied. "Though I can't imagine them going through all this just for one lousy satellite—but you never know, I suppose."

Delaney thought a moment. "Interesting theory. But if it ain't a satellite, what else could it be?"

Norton just shrugged. "What else is floating around up there besides satellites? Something worth all this?"

Delaney looked at the sky, as if the answer would be whizzing right over his head.

Finally he just said: "You've heard me sing this song before, but some things I don't want to know."

The sound of heavy mortars brought their attention back to the battle. In amongst the sequence of *whomp!* sizzle, and resulting explosions, another sound could now be heard: the unmistakable racket of a helicopter's rotors beginning to turn.

"Oh, brother . . ." Amanda exclaimed. "Look!"

The two pilots were back up to the lip in seconds. Across the crater from them, one of the big Pakistani MI-8 Hip choppers was ascending above the line of summit pines.

"Where the hell are they going?" Delaney yelled.

"If they're smart, they're going home," Norton yelled back.

But this was not the case. The Pakistani chopper banked left, leveled off, and then to the surprise of all, began descending into the crater.

"Oh, God, this is not a good idea," Amanda said.

She was right. The copter pointed its nose almost straight down, the pilots gave it the gas, and it began plunging into the huge ravine. A stream of gunfire followed it all the way down, the heaviest coming from the Chinese gun positions.

Those looking down on the Pakistani copter could see bullets ricocheting off the revolving rotor blades, that was how intense the fire was.

About two thirds of the way to the bottom, the chopper pulled up—a fatal mistake, probably brought on by indecision in its pilots. Being shot at in any aircraft was never any fun. Being in a chopper while under attack could be especially unpleasant. The Pakistanis found this out a few seconds later. A fusillade of Chinese rocket fire rained down on the hapless helicopter. Some of it found the fuel tanks—and that was all she wrote. First came a flash of flame, then a huge explosion. The helicopter dropped another hundred feet, colliding with a ledge and flipping over on its side. Its rotor blades disintegrated instantly, sending a blizzard of razor-sharp shrapnel flying around the crater.

The fatally stricken chopper now toppled the last three hundred feet into the crevice, bouncing a few times before finally slamming onto the crater floor. There was one last explosion. When the smoke cleared, nothing was left but mangled, blazing wreckage. Somewhere in the maul were the bodies of fourteen Pakistani soldiers.

What had been their plan? Why had they attempted what amounted to a suicide mission? Practically the only thing that survived the crash was a large Pakistani flag. It furled up into the air, and then came to rest not far from the blazing wreckage. It too was soon consumed by the flames.

It was the final note in a sad, almost pathetic display of misplaced bravery, one that hit the Americans right in the gut.

"God damn," Delaney mumbled. "Is that what's going to happen to us?"

The next ones to try were the Kazaks.

Taking advantage of the commotion surrounding the

shooting down of the Pakistani helicopter, they had warmed up one of their Hinds. Now the Kazak aircraft, one of just three remaining, rose up and over the scrub line, made a threatening pass near the Chinese camp, then plunged down into the crevice.

All this time, the squad of Chinese soldiers was still making its way down the crater floor. The Kazak chopper flew right by them. The Chinese soldiers sought cover and no gunfire was exchanged, but it was a brilliant maneuver nevertheless. It allowed the Kazaks to proceed to the bottom as the Chinese on the crater lip were reluctant to fire down at the copter for fear of hitting their own troops.

The Kazak Hind managed to touch down on the crater floor, finding one of the few spaces big enough to land on without encountering the closed-in walls. But at that exact moment, the squad of Chinese soldiers about 250 feet above them had found suitable cover. Now machine-gun and mortar fire rained down on the Kazak aircraft from the top lip with a cruel vengeance. The first three Chinese mortar rounds landed right on top of the Kazak copter, blowing the aircraft apart. More than a dozen men were trapped inside. Some stumbled out of the burning wreckage, their uniforms on fire, to die a grisly death at the bottom of the crater. Six men, however, somehow made it out of the chopper unscathed.

Stunned that they were still alive, this valiant band of Kazak fighters began scrambling over the rugged crater floor, heading toward the massive heap of snow that held the tail fin and engine nozzles. It was a distance of about 150 yards, all of it over some very rough and icy ground.

The action of the Kazaks, flag unfurled and flying behind them, naturally attracted the attention of the people at the top of the crater. Once again a cascade of bullets and mortar shells came down on the intrepid troopers. Two were killed immediately; two more were wounded, and then their bodies riddled with bullets—some Chinese, some Indian—as the men desperately tried to drag themselves to cover.

As soon as these unfortunate souls were dispatched, the fusillades concentrated on the last two remaining Kazaks. The soldier in the lead was carrying the colorful Kazak national flag. The man behind him was carrying a radio and a camera.

The man with the flag was shot down by the Chinese in brutally short order. But in a case of true gallantry, if not insanity, the last Kazak picked up his country's banner without missing a step and started running toward the snow mound.

He made it, just long enough to put down his weapon and start erecting the flag. But that was as far as he got. A Chinese barrage blew his chest away in a cloud of bloody mist. He fell over on his back, eyes looking straight up.

What he saw in his last dying moment was both the Osprey and the Sea Cobra making their own hellish descent into the crater.

Now it was the Americans' turn.

The original plan had called for the Ozzie to either land or get as close as possible to the crater floor, and deposit a squad of men near what they hoped was the secret space shuttle. But now, with the presence of hostile forces and the unexpectedly rough terrain, that plan had to be changed.

So the Ozzie would become the gunship and the Sea Cobra the hands and eyes of the mission.

They had taken off in the confusion following the slaughter of the Kazak fighters. No sooner had Chinese gunners killed the last of the Kazaks than the Ozzie swept down on the Chinese encampment. The three hatches on the Ozzie's left side were open and four Team 66 troopers were deployed in each, their M-16's sticking out of the openings, blazing away. The Chinese all dove for cover, stunned that the weird flying machine had been able to sneak up on them so completely.

While all this was going on, Norton and Delaney roared the Sea Cobra down through the crevice, dodging the still-burning wreckage of both helicopters and threading their way along the crater floor. They had additional supporting fire from the American position up on the crater lip, where six Team 66 troopers were handling the unit's heavy weapons. Whenever the Ozzie had to turn away from firing on the Chinese position, the Team 66 troopers would unleash a stream of rockets and machine-gun fire all around the top of the crater, keeping everyone's head down.

Working under this blanket of ordnance, Norton put the Sea Cobra down right next to the first pile of dead Kazaks.

He popped the canopy and both he and Delaney scrambled out. Flaming pieces of white-hot metal and sparks were flying all around them. The smoke was thick, as was the stench of burnt flesh. The crater floor now resembled a little piece of hell.

Norton and Delaney dashed over the rocky terrain and around the last of the fallen Kazaks. Delaney was first to reach the snow mound. He stopped dead in his tracks. Norton nearly collided with him. Standing still was not a wise thing to do at the moment.

"Jessuz, Slick!" Norton yelled. "What are you doing?"

"Look at that goddamn thing!" Delaney shouted back, pointing to the huge snow mound. Norton dove for cover near a craggy rock, yanking Delaney down with him.

From there they studied the tail fin and rocket nozzles, now no more than a hundred feet away. The nozzles seemed huge. The tail fin towered over them as well. But there *was* something strange about them.

Delaney broke away and started climbing the gigantic snow mound; Norton had no choice but to follow him. The Ozzie was right above them, suppressing all hostile fire—at least for the moment. Finally, they got to within twenty-five feet of the first nozzle. It looked real; there was no doubt about that. But now Norton sensed something was very wrong here—just as Delaney had a few moments before.

They started digging in the snow, madly, with their hands and rifle butts. It took what seemed like forever, but finally they reached the underside of the first nozzle. That was when it came loose from the snow and nearly fell on top of them. They got out of the way just in time. The nozzle toppled down the snow mound, hit the crater floor below—and broke apart into a million pieces.

"God damn it!" Norton swore.

It was made of wood.

So were the other two nozzles, the tail fin and the back edge of the wing. They were made of plywood and painted black and gray, and had been stuck into the snow to make it look like the shuttle had crashed here.

But there was nothing behind them.

It was all a fake.

13

Rome

They were known simply as Squadra Verde, or the Green
Team.

An offshoot of the famous Groupe Interventional Spe-
ciale, Italy's antiterrorist unit, they had a good reputation
around the special-ops biz. Over the last half decade, they'd
seen action not just in Italy, but all throughout the Med,
including the Balkans, Greece, and Lebanon. They were
known to be thorough, innovative, and when necessary,
ruthless.

Gene Smitz was sitting in the back of a tomato delivery
truck with sixteen of these special-ops soldiers at the moment. It was 11:45 P.M. local Rome time. They had been
double-parked in the same spot on the Corso Vittorio in
downtown Rome since ten that morning. No one had ques-
tioned them. No one had asked them to move. In a very

congested part of the very congested city, they'd blended in perfectly.

Sitting in the back of the truck with them was Lieutenant Victor Buonovilla, a press spokesman for the Carabinieri, the Italian National Police. He was wearing leg irons and handcuffs. His brother, Pio, ran the small airfield where the Chinnotto soda-can blimp had been stored. The lieutenant and his brother had been observed buying matching Ferraris just days after the big blimp went missing. This suspicious behavior was compounded when the policeman gave an extremely detailed account of the case to the news media— including information that would have been impossible for him to know without having access to the official files, which he didn't. After some less-than-gentle persuasion by the Green Team, the policeman admitted he and his brother had helped a little-known terrorist cell steal the dirigible. After further interrogation, he'd led them here to the Corso Vittorio.

While Smitz had spent most of the day either dozing or reading an ancient copy of *Sports Illustrated*, the commander of the Green Team, a guy known as Il Lupo, had been glued to a pair of headphones, monitoring a bug planted on the seventh floor of a *pallazzo* directly across the street. Two of Il Lupo's men were watching the front door of this building via a hidden camera. Lieutenant Buonovilla was told to ID anyone he recognized entering or leaving the place. So far, he'd seen no familiar faces.

This changed, finally, around ten minutes to midnight. Buonovilla identified two people entering the building as the local heads of the terrorist cell.

"One is the little brain," he said. "The other, the big brain. One knows nothing. One knows all."

Il Lupo gave Smitz a nudge.

"Our pigeons have landed," he said.

Ten minutes later, just as church bells nearby were peeling twelve, ten men from the Green Team, along with Il Lupo and Smitz, were working their way up the apartment house's staircase, heading for the top floor. The Italians were armed with machine guns and pistols. Smitz was carrying his trusty .357 Magnum.

They reached the seventh landing, and with admirable stealth, the special troops took up positions around the apartment door. Smitz moved closest to it—that is, until Il Lupo pulled him back. "You are our guest, Smitty," he said. "We will go in first."

Smitz just waved him off. There was no way he was going to let an Italian soldier take a bullet meant for him.

"This is my party," he told the Green Team commander. "I'm the first one through the door."

Il Lupo just shrugged. He signaled his men to get ready, then nodded to Smitz.

The CIA man checked his weapon's load. It was full. He took a moment to compose himself. It was now almost seventy-two hours since he'd been to sleep. He wanted to make sure that he knew what he was doing.

Finally, he nodded back to the Italians. "Okay, let's go."

The next thing Smitz knew, he was kicking in the flimsy wooden door. It exploded in a crash of splinters. He went through first, gun up in a two-hand stance, just like on TV. The room was alive with people scrambling this way and that.

Smitz started yelling: *"Scendi! Giu! Polizia!"* The only three Italians words he knew. Gunshots rang out. Flash grenades exploded. Somewhere a baby started crying.

Smitz made his way to the kitchen. Two men were sitting

at a table there; the individuals fingered by Lieutenant
Buonovilla. One was wearing a red ball cap, turned backward. The other was completely bald. They were too
shocked to move. Smitz put his gun between the eyes of
the man with the red cap. When the bald man attempted to
raise a small revolver, Smitz turned, shot him dead on the
spot, and had his gun back upside the first man's head inside a second.

"Scendi!" Smitz kept yelling. There was so much gunfire
going off in the rooms around him now, it was hard to hear
anything else. *"Polizia! Polizia!"*

But the guy in the hat seemed totally confused—and absolutely horrified that his colleague was now lying across
the table, half his head blown away. That was when Smitz
realized the guy probably didn't speak Italian.

So he started yelling at him in English—the universal
language of terrorist ops. "Don't move! *Don't move!*"

Suddenly the guy didn't seem so confused anymore.

The gunfire died down in the other rooms. Il Lupo appeared in the kitchen doorway and gave Smitz a big
thumbs-up.

"Sanitized . . ." he told Smitz.

Smitz pushed his gun deeper into the man's temple. He
pulled out a picture of a hot-air balloon.

"You seen this?" Smitz yelled in the man's ear. Was he
the big brain or not?

The man began shaking his head violently. His whole
body was trembling.

"No! No!" he began screaming, just as another round of
gunfire erupted from the next room over.

Il Lupo stuck his head back into the kitchen. "Sorry . . .
now we are sanitized."

Smitz pulled another picture from his jacket pocket. It
showed a drawing of the Beatles' Yellow Submarine.

"This? You seen this!?" he screamed in the man's ear.

No! No! The man was shaking his head.

Smitz pulled a third picture from his jacket. It showed the missing Chinnotto soda-pop blimp.

"This? You seen *this*?" Smitz yelled.

The man froze. He stared at the picture for three very long seconds—then began shaking his head again. *No! No! No!*

Smitz hit him in the temple with the butt of his pistol. The hat went flying one way, the man went the other.

Then he lowered his gun and breathed a sigh of relief.

At least he hadn't shot the wrong guy.

14

Nevada Special Weapons Testing Range

They came out of nowhere.

One minute Jimmy Gillis and Marty Ricco were pouring out yet another cup of coffee, seemingly alone inside the big hidden hangar. The next, the place was taken over by a small army of airplane mechanics.

There were probably forty of them in all. Like Lieutenant Moon, they were wearing nondescript black uniforms, ball caps, and sneakers. Keds seemed to be the predominant brand.

They began hustling around the big aircraft barn, coming up with ladders, movable scaffolding, electrical cables, face masks—and paint. Lots and lots of paint.

As the two National Guard pilots watched from an adjoining break room while slugging down their coffee, the mechanics began loading up more than two dozen high-powered paint guns. Then dispersing into teams of twos

and threes, they climbed the hastily erected scaffolding and
began spray-painting the big 747 jumbo jet.

A storm of paint fumes quickly filled the hangar—they
were so strong, Gillis leaned over and shut the door to the
break room. It seemed to seal tightly enough to keep out
the distinctive stink of the paint.

"I hear you can get really high sniffing that stuff," Ricco
said, making another pot of coffee for them. "So high,
you'll never know what killed you."

"Don't tell me that," Gillis replied. "I might just stick
my head out that door and start breathing deep."

They'd been inside the hangar for about three hours now,
still recovering from the hair-raising training mission earlier. They'd been able to shower, shave, and climb into new
sets of flying fatigues. Moon had provided them with steak
sandwiches and coffee creamer. They'd wolfed down their
meal, and had drained two pots of coffee in that relatively
short time. At any minute they expected the diminutive
lieutenant to return with word that they were shipping out.

The appearance of the ghostly maintenance crews only
added to the mystery of what the CIA had in mind for them.

They had stopped asking each other what they thought all
of this cost—the question was almost comical now. Certainly billions had been poured into this very strange, very
high-tech, very secret place. But there was no telling
whether all of it, or any of it, had been well spent. In some
ways, the weapons range looked less like a military training
facility and more like an elaborate movie set.

"But what's a few billion to the Pentagon?" Ricco had
said. "Even a hundred billion can be pocket change to
them."

It was true. A single B-2 Stealth bomber cost at least a
billion dollars. Dozens were already built. The new F-22

Raptor fighter would cost almost half that—and the Air Force wanted to buy hundreds of them. What was a few billion dollars for the Pentagon to build this place? A drop in the bucket . . .

But it sure made for one hell of a playground.

Even above the noise inside the big hangar, they heard the distinct whizzing of the MD-530 chopper approaching. Lieutenant Moon was coming in for a landing right outside the hangar door.

Gillis asked again: "And how does one guy manage to get his own helicopter? And a lieutenant yet?"

Ricco just shook his head. "Let's make that question four hundred and ten on our list of things to ask."

Moon walked through the door a minute later, trailed by a cloud of paint fumes. He was carrying a grocery bag with him.

"How were the sandwiches?" was the first thing he asked them.

"Primo," Ricco replied.

"And the coffee? Was it okay?"

"Yeah, it's great," Gillis assured him.

Moon reached into the bag and came out with a bottle of champagne.

"I thought you guys deserved a toast," he said. "It's a bit of a tradition around here."

He popped the cork, produced three plastic cups, and poured. Gillis caught wind of the label.

"Nineteen sixty-nine?" he said, noting the champagne's vintage. "Was that a good year?"

Moon just shrugged. "Beats me," he said.

They raised their drinks. Then Ricco asked: "What are we toasting again?"

Moon clicked his plastic cup into theirs.

"We are toasting your graduation from this place," he replied. "And for what was probably the shortest deployment here ever."

"You mean we really gotta leave?" Gillis asked, instead of tasting his champagne. "So soon?"

"Yeah, we just got here," Ricco chimed in.

Moon could only shrug. "Those are the orders," he said almost wistfully. "They just came through."

"But . . . we don't want to go," Ricco said in a perfect whine. He was only half-kidding. "This place is too much fun."

Moon noisily sipped his champagne. "I've actually heard that before," he said. "No matter how many people transit through this place, you'd be surprised how many of them get homesick for it real quick."

"That's because when someone shoots at you out here, it ain't real," Gillis told him.

Moon nodded slowly. "You can't beat that, I guess."

At that moment, they heard the familiar sound of an aircraft tow vehicle starting its engine. The big 747 was being pulled out of the hangar.

"I'm afraid that's your cue," Moon said.

They drained their cups, then walked out of the break room. The doors to the big hangar had been pulled back, and most of the paint fumes had been ventilated out. Sitting outside was the 747. The big plane had been given a super-rush paint job. It no longer boasted a stainless-steel finish. It was now painted bright white with garish yellow trim, with letters along its fuselage identifying it as belonging to Southwest Asia Airlines.

"Southwest Asia Air?" Ricco said. "Never heard of them."

"Neither have I," Moon said. "But you've got to admit, the guys did a real nice job on it."

"Yeah, fucking lovely," Ricco groaned.

"Should we assume that flying tow truck is still stuffed in the back of this thing?" Gillis asked.

"You assume correctly," Moon replied.

"Okay, then what's next?" Ricco asked.

Moon flipped open up his IBM NoteBook and flashed ahead to the appropriate screen.

"You'll find a complete flight plan already downloaded onto the onboard computer," he said. "But here's the short version. You're flying this monster to Hawaii, where you'll gas up and then, I assume, proceed to your primary. A contact will meet you when you set down on the big island. The plan is for you to look and act like just another commercial flight."

"With no passengers on board?" Ricco asked. "No seats?"

Moon just shrugged. "No one will notice," he replied matter-of-factly. "Our people there will make sure of that."

"How will we know our contact?" Gillis asked.

"You'll land normally," Moon said, reading from his screen. "An airport control vehicle will meet you out on the runway. Your contact is a very lovely redhead—her name is Ginger. She's a good friend of mine. She'll have your go-orders with her."

There was a long silence. The wind whipping through the desert had turned warm again. If there was a time for any last words, this was it.

"I know you don't know about our mission specifics," Gillis began, looking up at the huge airplane, its paint still wet in some places. "But why do I get the feeling we're going on a kamikaze mission here? Flying this big plane halfway around the world. Just the two of us. Carrying a screwy chopper in the backseat. Picking up cars? In very tight quarters? All in such a big hurry? I mean, can you read the tea leaves for us just a little bit? What do you think they have in mind for us?"

Moon pondered this for a long time.

"To quote someone I think you guys know fairly well," he finally replied, " 'I don't know—and I don't *want* to know.' "

15

In the Paswar

Suckers . . .

That was what they were.

Actually, *two*-time suckers. They'd been played like violins twice now. From overture to encore. Suckers times two.

Norton and Delaney had gone through this before. In their first mission, the one to retrieve the stolen AC-130 gunship that was running wild in the Persian Gulf, the unnamed chopper unit had attacked a secret air base where they'd been led to believe the rogue airplane had been hidden. But after a lightning-quick air assault, they'd arrived on the ground only to discover the base was abandoned and the aircraft they thought was the gunship was actually a mock-up.

Now it had happened again. Obviously the "shuttle" at the bottom of the Paswar crater had been put there to divert

their attention, and that of other countries in the area as
well. The ruse had worked perfectly—and Norton and Delaney had been made to look like chumps for the second
time in as many years. Even worse, they had no idea who
had gone to such great lengths to fool them.

And at the moment, neither of them cared.

"This is it for me," Delaney declared shortly after the
heartbreaking discovery. "I'm out of this freaking Spook
business for good. They can put me in jail if they want.
But I'm resigning from this James Bond crap. Let them get
some other sap."

Norton could only agree with him. This was not the line
of work he wanted to be in. What they had found on the
crater floor were more like props in a huge practical joke.
The problem was, dozens of soldiers had died before the
grim punch line was delivered.

Someone, somewhere, must be laughing very loudly, he
thought.

It was amazing how quickly the carnage stopped when
it became apparent there was no space shuttle—or any
other kind of spacecraft or secret U.S. warplane—at the
bottom of the Paswar crater. Even before Norton and Delaney had stumbled off the snow mound and back into their
Sea Cobra, many of the troops camped up around the lip
were packing their gear, starting their engines, and getting
ready to leave for home.

No gunfire. No parting shots.

Just weariness. And frustration.

And anger.

By the time the Sea Cobra had flown out of the crater,
the Ozzie had set back down at the American encampment.
Its huge propellers still turning, it was picking up the troopers who had manned the heavy guns during the failed operation. The Team 66 guys were hustling big-time now,

dismantling the last of their equipment and destroying any evidence that the special-ops group had ever been there. Seeing how the mission had gone, embarrassment was as much a concern as national security. The sooner they all got out of there, the better.

"C'mon, let's get this fucking show on the road!" Delaney was yelling as Norton put the Sea Cobra into a hover above the American camp. They had taken on their extra fuel from the Ozzie even before descending into the crater. Now, if the winds were right, they might make it back to the *Bataan* with the gas they had left internally and in the wing tanks. But that would mean they'd have to find a streak of good luck very soon—and that would be a first for this mission.

Finally, the Ozzie's engines began revving up to full power, a sign that it was getting ready to lift off. The last of the Team 66 troopers were climbing aboard, and Norton could see Commander Amanda was among them, pitching in by carrying a machine gun mount. He breathed a sigh of relief.

We'll fly back to the ship and she'll be safe . . . he thought.

It was almost absurd to admit it—he was certain he was just one face in many to her—but at that moment, Commander Amanda's well-being was probably the most important thing in his life. Although he would probably never see her again once they returned to the *Bataan,* he knew until the day he died, he would always think about her. Always wonder where she was. And what she was doing at that very moment. And of course, wonder if she ever thought about him . . .

His schoolboy daydream was interrupted by a crackle in his headset. It was Chou.

"We're about a minute from departure," he reported. "Do

you two see any positive aspects at this time in trying to recover any of what you found down in the crater?"

The two pilots replied quickly and without qualification.

"No," Norton said.

"Double no," Delaney replied.

Chou went on: "So what you're saying is that due to our fuel situation and the gas we would burn up in any recovery effort, that it would be counterproductive at this time to—"

"Yes," Norton interrupted him.

"Double yes," Delaney added.

"So noted," Chou replied, his ass duly covered. "See you up top."

The first explosion came about two seconds later.

It blew out the side of the crater wall about ten feet below the lip, right where the now-abandoned ice trench was located. The blast was so powerful, the concussion tossed the Sea Cobra more than a hundred feet into the air before Norton was able to regain control again.

The second explosion came a few seconds later further down the lip, where the Indian encampment lay. It made a direct hit on something combustible, because both of the Indian troop-carrying helicopters were obliterated, and anyone within a two-hundred-yard radius was killed instantly. In seconds, more explosions began going off all around the crater rim.

The Sea Cobra's radio came alive an instant later.

It was Chou. He was screaming at the tops of his lungs: "Gentlemen, we have a problem!"

Then they heard one of Chou's men shout: *"Bogies in the backcourt, driving for the net!"*

Delaney yelled back to Norton: "What the hell does that mean?"

Norton responded: "I think it's their air-threat guy. He's picked up aircraft heading our way."

Norton hastily scanned the skies. That was when he spotted one, two, three Hokum attack choppers. Then four. Then five. Then six. They were painted in the same mysterious gray as the ones they'd tangled with back in the river valley. This group was coming over the mountains to the west, gun pods blazing, heavy rockets firing off their rails.

"*Oh, Christ . . .*" Norton yelled. "Have we got our asses hanging out here!"

Now came more explosions. Rockets and tracers were flying everywhere. Suddenly the American camp was enveloped by mushrooming fireballs. One barrage of rockets impacted on the nearby tree line, blowing hundreds of burning branches and tree trunks in every direction. Norton's headset was filled with distraught voices now. People wounded. People burned. People dying. Chou was shouting orders both into his radio and to the men around him. They were pouring out of the Ozzie, rescuing their fallen colleagues and dragging them to cover.

Another barrage of rockets slammed into the American position, and into the Kazak and Tajik camps as well. More explosions. More cries for help. Norton was craning his neck to see through the sudden storm of flames and smoke below him.

Where the hell was Amanda?

A third barrage of rockets went by—and then Norton finally swung into action. It was obvious now that whoever planted the fake shuttle pieces deep in the crater had done so with two motives: to distract the U.S. in the real search for the shuttle, and also to lure them and the other indigenous special-ops units up here, to the top of the world, where they could be destroyed by the high-tech Hokums.

It was a brilliant plan. But that didn't mean Norton had

to stand still and allow its faceless mastermind to triumph so easily.

Not without a fight.

"How much ammo you got left up there?" Norton yelled forward to Delaney.

"Exactly one hundred and three rounds," was the hasty reply. "How much juice we got left?"

"About one quart short of the bingo," Norton replied. "And not a drop to spare."

He looked over his shoulder. Another half-dozen Hokums were coming over the mountains to their east. They would soon join the six choppers already attacking them.

"Okay, enough of this bullshit!" he yelled into his microphone. "Crank up that popgun, Slickman. We're going hunting. . . ."

It might have been at that moment—that exact point in time—that Norton truly became a chopper pilot. Before, he'd always thought of himself as a fighter jock stuck in a chopper. But now a switch had been thrown. A button had been pushed. He jammed the Sea Cobra's throttles to full and broke out of his funk and hover.

It was time to go to work.

A pitch to the left, and suddenly a Hokum was right in front of them.

"Go for the fucker's cockpit!" he screamed up to Delaney.

But Delaney was way ahead of him. He let loose a precise, if economical, burst of eleven cannon rounds and vaporized the Hokum's canopy—and the man inside. The chopper went end over end, then began a long fiery plunge into the crater below.

"Well, that was easy," Delaney exclaimed.

"Yeah," Norton replied. "One down, about a hundred to go."

The next thing he knew, Norton was twisting and turning the agile Sea Cobra all over the sky. It seemed like everywhere they looked, there was a Hokum, either hovering and firing or moving very slowly in order to throw ordnance into one of the eight encampments. It was really just a case of point-and-shoot for the American chopper pilots—Norton was doing the pointing and Delaney the shooting. They had two more Hokums bagged before the attackers even knew what hit them.

But the element of surprise and craziness could only last so long. Norton and Delaney knew the end was near when two air-to-air missiles went whooshing by their nose. They'd been fired by yet another Hokum, one that had just joined the fray and had gained their six o'clock. For the two ex-fighter pilots, used to such dogfight niceties as threat-warning radar and Sidewinder missiles, the near-miss was a huge wake-up call.

This thing was getting serious. . . .

Norton rolled the Sea Cobra over and went screaming back down into the crater. This action saved them from being hit by a follow-up barrage of air-to-airs, but did little for their personal well-being. The g-forces were bone-crushing.

"Hang on, partner!" Norton yelled as he recovered flight and started climbing out again. Another unsuspecting Hokum came into their sights. He was hammering away at the Tajikistani camp. No matter. Norton felt a shared brotherhood among the Paswar veterans now. A fraternity of misery. Delaney let loose a barrage from the chin turret that blindsided the Hokum. The cannon rounds practically split the chopper in two before sending it on a long fiery plunge down.

"It's going to get very crowded down there," Delaney remarked.

Another Hokum came into view. Norton wasn't hesitating a moment, wasn't slowing down, was barely paying attention to his flight controls. He was flying on pure adrenaline now. He was driving the Sea Cobra not like a chopper but like an F-15 fighter jet, all speed and fury and balls—and the Hokum pilots just could not deal with it. Another barrage from Delaney, another Hokum went down. Another bogie gets caught in their sights. Fire the cannon, another mook goes into the hole. It went on like this for an entire minute, an eternity in air combat time.

But after nailing seven Hokums, it became apparent that they had a problem. A big problem.

Delaney had run out of ammo. And because of the extra-full tanks they were lugging around with them, the Sea Cobra had nothing left to shoot.

"Now what?" he yelled back to Norton.

Before Norton could reply, there was a tremendous explosion off their left wing. He instantly pitched right, but not before the Sea Cobra had taken a mortal blow from a high-explosive air-to-air missile. Suddenly, the fact that they were out of ammunition was moot.

They were too busy being shot down. . . .

Delaney started yelling right away: "You got it, Jazz-man? Hang tough! It's a long way down—and a real long climb out!"

But Norton couldn't reply. He was using all of his strength trying to keep the copter level and under control. But it was no use. They'd been hit badly in the number-one engine—if they had been flying an Army Cobra, they would have been well into their death plunge by now. But even though they still had one engine running, the torque from its sudden overload was throwing them all over the sky.

Norton wrangled the chopper back under some control,

but time was clearly running out for them—as were their options. They couldn't fly level, they couldn't steer left or right. They could only go straight up.

So up they went.

Past the crater lip. Past the surrounding mountaintops. High enough to see the embattled American camp through the smoke and fire. The Sea Cobra was shaking very badly. The cockpit was filling with smoke. They were on fire. Yet they kept on climbing until they were a half mile higher than the highest peak.

That was when Norton did something that saved their lives—he killed the remaining engine.

The Sea Cobra began shuddering so violently now, Norton could feel his bones begin to rattle—not a good sign.

But then, just as suddenly, everything became calm again. The copter leveled out; a trick he'd first used in their previous mission had worked again.

Even without the engine, the Sea Cobra's rotor kept on spinning, as he knew it would. They were still on fire— and up very high. But not for long.

He pointed the nose of the chopper toward the American camp and crossed his fingers.

Then they started to drop.

Norton had his hands gripped so tightly around the controls, he imagined he could hear his bones cracking. Down through the clouds they went, through the smoke. Delaney remained silent. Norton could see him holding on, braced for whatever was about to come.

And whatever it was, it was coming fast.

Suddenly the American camp filled their field of vision. They were coming down very, very rapidly. Still, they could see the camp was awash in flame, burning debris, smoke, blood, and melted snow. A bad crash now would only add to the problem.

But Norton was not intending to crash.

Not completely anyway.

They were about two hundred feet above the crater lip when he finally yanked back on the controls with all his might.

Just one last time, he began pleading with the Cosmos. *Save us, just one last time.*

And for some reason, the Sea Cobra responded—it pulled up and went level right before they passed what was left of the tree line. They hit just a second later, coming down like a car dropped from a ten-story building. The Sea Cobra bounced many times before it fell over, its rotors digging mightily into the hard ice. Finally, they snapped off completely and went whizzing out over the crater.

Then the Sea Cobra burst into flames. Norton popped the canopy and dragged Delaney from his seat. His boots were on fire. They hit the ground and just started rolling. There was so much melted snow and ice in the camp by now that it extinguished their flight suits in seconds.

So much commotion was going on around them, hardly anyone noticed that they had come down. They got up and scrambled into the ice trench, where about a dozen Team 66 troopers had taken cover. Norton was shaking from head to toe. He was burned, he was battered. He was bruised all over.

But he was still alive. And so was Delaney.

At least for the moment.

For not two seconds later, another Hokum whooshed overhead, its cannons blazing.

"Christ, don't these guys ever give up?" Delaney yelled into Norton's ear.

"They must be getting paid by the hour!" Norton yelled back.

The Hokum pilots' attack was relentless, but this didn't

necessarily mean they were experts at what they were doing. The Hokum was a high-tech machine, but not exactly
a peach to fly. This particular Hokum's first pass over the
burning American camp did little more than make a lot of
noise. Though the streams of cannon fire sprouting from its
underling gun pods were fierce, their only accomplishment
was to shear off the side of the nearby rocky ledge, sending
hundreds of hot sparks and flint in every direction. Still, it
only added to the pandemonium inside the camp.

And within a few seconds, the Hokum had turned and
was bearing down on the encampment again, its sights set
on those huddled in the ice trench.

"He ain't aiming at rocks this time!" Delaney yelled.

The Hokum let loose a stream of rockets. Suddenly the
middle of the American camp was lit up again with dozens
of fiery explosions. The noise was horrendous; the flashes
blinding. Still, many of the Team 66 troopers in the trench
were firing their rifles back at the attacking copter. But the
Hokum was moving too fast for any of the return fire to
do much good.

It pulled up again and turned for a third pass.

"We might be kind a screwed now!" Delaney yelled,
again in Norton's ear. "I mean, we survive a crash, just to
get killed like this? Man, that sucks. . . ."

But Norton wasn't listening to him. He was looking
everywhere through the smoke and flames, desperately trying to find Commander Amanda.

But she was nowhere to be seen.

The Hokum swooped down on them again, ready to deliver its knockout blow. That was when one of Chou's men
suddenly jumped out of the trench and ran to the middle
of the blazing camp. He had a portable SAM launcher on
his shoulder.

"Well, now, there's a crazy fucker!" Delaney yelled.

The man was standing completely exposed, pushing the SAM launcher higher and peering through its aiming device, trying to get a fix on the attacking chopper—even as the aircraft was bearing down on him.

Though he knew it would do little good, Norton picked up a nearby M-16 and began firing at the Hokum. Others around the camp did too. The Hokum was now screaming directly at the man with the SAM, its gun pods flashing wildly. But even though a small storm of tracers was streaking by him, the trooper with the SAM stayed cool. He acquired a good lock on the Hokum and let his missile go.

It went off with a whoosh and a shaky trail of gray smoke. Rising even as the attack chopper was in its dive, it met the Hokum about 250 feet above the southern edge of the American outpost. The tiny SAM got sucked right into the Hokum's right air intake. There was a huge explosion, and the Hokum seemed to stop in midair. The flash was so bright, it blinded Norton for a moment.

"Son of a bitch!" Delaney was yelling. "Now, that fucker worked as advertised!"

By the time Norton could see again, the Hokum was turning over on its left wing. It came down hard, its top rotor hitting the ground and causing the flaming helicopter to cartwheel across the camp.

The stricken aircraft went right over Norton, Delaney, and the dozen or so Team 66 troopers. It slammed into the ground a second time, bounced up again, and then came down in another blinding explosion. And then another. And another.

"Yes! Yes! *Fuck you!*" Delaney was yelling.

But this was not a good turn of events. Norton had to shield his eyes from the glare. When he looked up again, he felt his heart sink to the ground.

The Hokum had come down, all right—directly on top

of the Osprey. The combined explosion had utterly destroyed the big American aircraft.

A sudden silence descended over the camp as everyone realized what had happened. The brave Team 66 trooper had undoubtedly saved them all. But as a result, their only means of transport had been destroyed.

Suddenly Chou was behind them. He was yelling: "Everyone was out! Everyone was out!" meaning no one was inside the Osprey went it was hit.

But Norton and Delaney barely heard him. They were up on their feet and running a second later. Both had the same idea.

They plunged directly into the fiery wreckage, using their thick arctic gloves to push aside the pieces of burning metal and plastic. With all the flames and smoke, those back in the trench could not see what they were doing. But after a few seconds, the two pilots reemerged. And they had a body with them.

Or at least it looked like a body. It was bloody from head to toe, and was still burning in places. It was flopping around like a life-size rag doll as the two pilots dragged it across the snow. Finally, they dumped it in a heap right next to the trench,

It was the Hokum pilot. He really was bleeding from one end to the other, with many compound fractures and horrible burns on his face and hands.

Nevertheless, Delaney grabbed him by the collar, ready to mess him up even further.

"What's the story here, asshole?" he screamed at the dying man. "Who paid you to do this?"

The man just shook his head. His jaw was broken and he could hardly move his lips.

"Maybe he doesn't speak English," someone said.

"They *all* speak English," Delaney roared. "And if it's

the last thing I do, I'm going to find out who sucked us in to come to this place, just so we could die, like this. . . ."

He turned back to the man. His helmet had actually melted onto his skull, that was how hot the fire had been from his crash.

Delaney gripped his collar even tighter. The man wailed in pain.

"Spill, dude!" Delaney yelled. "Or we'll keep you alive!"

Now that was a horribly dark threat. There was little doubt the man *wanted* to die. Too many vital things were either hanging off him or oozing out of him.

At that moment, Commander Amanda suddenly appeared out of nowhere. Norton was so relieved to see her alive, he nearly peed his pants. Even in this desperate moment, he could feel his heart start to thump just at the sight of her.

"Your intentions are correct, Major," she said to Delaney after surveying the scene. "But your methods seem ineffective."

She took her helmet off and let her hair fall around her shoulders. She looked down at the man, her face softening. He stopped twitching about, and stared back up at her. Even in his last few breaths, he knew he was in the presence of considerable beauty.

"You speak English?" she asked him softly, sweetly. "Can you understand me?"

The man nodded. Perhaps he thought he was seeing an angel, Norton mused.

She reached out and touched his face for a moment. The man seemed to melt away.

"I will make a deal with you," she said, pulling a bright yellow, prepackaged hypodermic needle from her pocket. It contained a massive dose of morphine.

She showed the man the needle; he knew what it was.

"Tell us," she said simply, "and you'll soon be in paradise."

The man thought a moment, then nodded.

Commander Amanda found a spot on the man's twisted, leaking torso that had not been shattered in the crash and slowly injected the super painkiller into him. All the while she stroked his head and kept smiling sweetly. The men around her remained motionless, watching the frozen little drama.

Finally, the injection was complete.

She leaned in a little closer. "Tell us," she urged him in a whisper. "Tell us now."

He began to sputter something. He was an Arab, so his English was hard to understand. But finally, he was able to put together a fairly coherent sentence.

"Look . . . for a man . . . without a bride," he said.

Then he laughed, displaying a mouth full of cracked and bloody teeth.

Then he died.

Everyone remained perfectly still. Finally, Delaney covered the man's face with a handful of snow.

Norton looked over at Commander Amanda. The smile was gone; she was on the verge of tears.

" 'Look for a man without a bride'?" she said. "What the hell does that mean?"

Suddenly time started moving again; the battle began swirling around them once more.

Chou started yelling: "More bogies incoming!"

A half dozen more Hokums swept down on the crater. They began firing rockets in every direction, pouring even more fire into the already decimated encampments.

Total confusion reigned once again. One Chinese chopper, hiding during the brief lull, tried to make a run for it. It went right over the American camp before being blown out of the sky by a Hokum air-to-air missile. Two gunners near the Pakistani position began blazing away at the attackers with an ancient AA gun. They were reduced to bloody bits by rockets from at least three of the mysterious gray choppers. Someone in the Kazak camp tried firing a rocket-propelled grenade at one of the Hokums. The gunner was literally vaporized by the return fire.

Now the entire top of the crater was ablaze with wreckage, burning fuel, burning bodies. The smoke rising up into the pristine crystal-clear sky, the cries of dying men echoing around the crater walls—suddenly it became too much for Norton to take. He actually heard something snap inside his head. Then he went a little nuts.

What happened after that would always remain a blur.

He recalled picking up one of Team 66's huge machine guns and, straight out of a bad war movie, running up to the lip and blazing away. He recalled seeing Delaney and a few of the Team 66 guys up on the ledge with him, firing at the swarming Hokums. He recalled thinking the sky itself was on fire—and that smoke had replaced the air they were breathing. His ears were bleeding, there had been so many explosions. People were shouting, crying, screaming behind him.

And beneath his feet—the ice started to groan again.

A Hokum veered right for him. Norton never stopped firing the huge gun. He saw rockets go off the Hokum's rails, saw them coming right at him. He never moved. The rockets streaked by him. He could feel their heat. Still, he kept firing. The Hokum got closer. It was coming on very fast, but to Norton's mind it was actually moving in slow motion. Hanging in the fiery air around him. Suspended. Like a big fat target.

He kept firing. . . .

Then, in the next instant, it was gone. A white-hot explosion took its place. A storm of debris came right at him. He heard someone scream for him to get down, but he couldn't move. Something hit him square on the head—it was a tire. A piece of metal clipped his knee. He fell over on his back, dropping the gun. Though his ears were filled with blood, he could still hear the muzzle sizzle as it hit the snow.

A cloud of fire and smoke went right over him. Blood began trickling into his eyes. The ice below him groaned again—this time it was very loud. Another Hokum streaked overhead. People were scrambling all around him. Some Team 66 guys were hurt. Some were dying. Somehow Norton retrieved the big machine gun and began shooting straight up in the air at the Hokum. The gray chopper was so close, he could see his bullets bouncing off its heavily reinforced underbelly.

Go for the blades. . . . he heard a voice whisper in his ear. *Shoot at the blades!*

He turned, and realized that Commander Amanda was lying in the snow right next to him. She was feeding the ammunition belt into his big smoking machine gun. Another explosion went off very close by. He saw Delaney out of the corner of his eye—he was firing a shoulder-launched SAM at yet another Hokum. More explosions, more fireballs. The ice beneath him was literally moving now—and groaning so loud, it was making his punctured eardrums hurt even worse.

He looked up to see that he was suddenly shooting into empty space. The Hokum was falling off to the side, its tail section on flame. He'd shot it down—or at least he thought he had. He reached over and pulled Commander Amanda closer to him. She did not resist. Another explosion went off, not twenty feet away from them. He pulled her even closer; she held on to him tightly. He saw Team 66 guys being carried over him. Blood was dripping everywhere. The ice groaned again. . . .

And suddenly . . . he was looking not up but down. And the ice was literally moving beneath him. And the noise in his ears sounded like the entire Earth was cracking open. He saw blood and ice mixed together—and suddenly Amanda was not there anymore. He looked down and saw only snow below him—he was looking straight into the crater, but all he could see was snow. Bloody red snow. And in his hand was a glove. Amanda's glove. The ice around the American station had cracked open. It was falling in on itself. Norton was teetering on the very edge of it, looking down, with her glove still clutched in his hand.

And she was gone.

Just like that . . .

The next thing he knew, Delaney and Chou were trying to drag him back from the newly created precipice. But he did not want to go. *He had to go after her!* He had to jump into the snowy abyss and bring her back up with him.

"C'mon, Jazz, we gotta go!" Delaney was screaming.

Go? Go where?

He wasn't going anywhere without her.

"Jazz . . . C'mon!" Delaney was yelling directly into his right ear, but Norton could barely hear him. Finally, they started dragging him away from the edge. He had snow in his mouth, in his eyes, his ears, his lungs.

Go? How could they go anywhere? They were trapped here. Both their aircraft were gone. And she was gone too.

Hands were all around him now. Gunfire and smoke still filled the air. His ears were hurting him—everything was so loud. He could barely see as well, there was so much blood in his eyes. Or were those tears? Now he was on his back again. Someone was tying something around his shoulders and legs. Suddenly he was being lifted up. . . .

He forced his eyes to open, and what he saw was a helicopter hovering over him. He was being pulled up into it.

And the strange thing was, this helicopter looked just like
a big banana.

16

Stikkala, Greece

The place was called the Plain of Meteora.

It was a long, flat stretch of land, located about 250 miles northwest of Athens and just outside the small village of Stikkala.

In 322 B.C., a battle was fought here between two mercenary armies; one was employed by Athens, the other by its enemies. This minor clash was notable for one curious reason. Early in the battle, the Athenian mercenaries had managed to completely surround their opponents. As the attackers closed in from all sides, the soldiers caught in the doomed formation were gradually squeezed into an ever-shrinking, frighteningly crowded box. With absolutely no hope of escape, the soldiers at the center of this box became so crazed while awaiting certain death, they dug holes in the ground and stuck their heads inside. There they stayed, while the one-sided battle raged on for more than three hours, until they too were finally slaughtered.

The Plain of Meteora was much more peaceful now. Acres of long, flowing greensilk grass, a few dozen groves of fig trees—and one very large windmill.

Towering over the landscape at more than fifteen stories high, this windmill was not of the Dutch variety. In addition to its great height, its vanes were covered with sails, which, in their day, had made the mill's grinding assembly turn very fast.

The structure had been abandoned for years now, its wooden gears long past repair, the sails worn and shredded. Although it had been renovated as a tourist attraction in the late 1980's, the rebirth had been short-lived.

"Who the hell would come to Greece to see a windmill?" Gene Smitz thought. "Except me, of course . . ."

He was sitting on the front bumper of a Panhard VBL armored car at the moment, slurping a cup of thick, black Greek coffee. The stuff tasted like highly caffeinated jet fuel, but that was okay with him. He was now approaching eighty-four hours without sleep. If he wanted to stay awake, he would need as much of this stuff as he could get.

The armored car was one of six that were now surrounding the windmill field. The vehicles belonged to a Greek special-operations group known as the Spikos Brigade—or in English, "The Spikes." They were providing the muscle for this phase of Smitz's strange, quixotic mission.

He had come to this place solely on information he'd beaten out of the man captured in the downtown Rome raid just a few hours before. He'd come to call the man with the red baseball cap "Big Brains," but the nickname hardly applied. A dunce cap would have been a more appropriate chapeau for this character. Even Il Lupo had described him as "terrorist-lite."

Big Brains was a guy of quasi-Arabic background with

connections to some terrorist underlings who knew how to
fly blimps, specifically the stolen soda-pop blimp. Though
he'd played the role of lookout during the theft, he knew
very little about the people at the top of the organization
or why they'd needed a blimp.

However, as his beating became more severe, Big Brains
did reveal the gist of a conversation he'd overheard during
one planning session. He claimed his shadowy bosses had
set up a "spacecraft mission-control center" somewhere in
Greece. A few more whacks to the head, and out popped
the bizarre piece of information that this control center was
hidden inside a "really big windmill," one as tall as an
office building. A quick check with Greek Army Intelligence told Smitz that the only "really big windmill" in all
of Greece was here, at Meteora.

Smitz flew to Greece aboard his personal hypersonic SR-
71 taxi, a ride that went by so fast, he didn't even have the
opportunity to close his eyes, never mind take a nap. So he
daydreamed during what amounted to a twelve-minute dash
across the Adriatic. He just wanted to get this mission over
with, and then go somewhere so far away, even the CIA
couldn't find him.

That is, if such a place existed.

It was early morning now. The fog was thick on the field.

Smitz finally got the signal from the Spikes' CO that all
was in readiness. The six armored cars drove slowly up to
the windmill and parked in a tight ring around it.

Smitz climbed out and checked his weapon. It was still
loaded, though at this point he was so tired, he wondered
if he had enough strength to pull the trigger if he had to.

He and six Spikes went through the door of the huge
windmill. It was basically hollow inside. However, there
was a long spiral staircase that led to the top, where he'd

been told the "secret mission-control center" was located.

So up they went up, taking each step slowly and carefully. It turned out to be an exhausting climb for the CIA agent. He was bathed in sweat even before they'd made it to the halfway point.

"Why don't these guys hang out in cellars?" he mumbled to himself.

Finally, they reached the top floor. There they were confronted with what seemed to be a sizable enclosed space, located on the other side of a wooden hatchway.

"Same day, different door," Smitz said aloud.

He didn't think this situation needed any door-splintering heroics like the last one, though. His instincts, and mostly his nose, were telling him that no one was on the other side of the hatch.

He toed open the door, pistol up just in case. One look inside the room and he felt his stomach drop to his feet.

Based on what Big Brains had told him, Smitz had expected this place to be packed with tons of high-tech equipment. Computers, tracking screens, consoles—just like a mini mission control. And why not? If Big Brains was to be believed, this place was supposed to be nothing less than a clandestine orbital tracking station, possibly one that was powerful enough to bring the secret shuttle down from space.

But all he saw inside the room was an ancient PC and a large rusting satellite dish of the type used for TV reception fifteen years ago.

He stood there with the Spikes, and felt what was left of his energy drain out of him.

What a wet dream this turned out to be. . . .

Then a cell phone began to ring.

Smitz was not carrying—however, all of the Spikes were. The six soldiers checked their cell phones. Finally, one held his up, and with some embarrassment, flipped it open and had a quick conversation.

"Who is it?" Smitz asked him sourly. "Your wife or your girlfriend?"

But the man just shook his head—and then passed the phone to Smitz.

"To telefonia enai yea sena," he said. "The telephone is for you."

Smitz looked at him for a long moment. Who would be calling him on this guy's phone?

"Must be *my* girlfriend, I guess," he stammered.

"She has a man's voice if it is," the soldier replied in broken English.

Smitz put the tiny Nokia up to his lips.

"Pios enai?" he said.

"Hey, that's pretty good, Smitty. Perfect Greek—just got to lose that Boston accent . . ."

Smitz recognized the twang right away. It was the guy in the mysterious gang of seven who usually did the talking. Smitz had taken to calling him the Voice.

He turned to the Spikes and told them in Greek: "Is it time yet to catch a smoke?"

Still smiling, the soldiers took the hint and went back out the door, closing it behind them.

Smitz returned to the phone. "You're calling to tell me I can go home, I hope?"

"You know better than that, Smitty," the Voice replied. "I see you're in the windmill?"

"I am . . . and I feel like I puked in an elevator. I really thought we were on to something here. But I was expecting something more elaborate than this—you know, like from a spy movie? But I really doubt that anyone would be able to pull a shuttle down with this rinky-dink crap."

Smitz scanned the bare room again.

"I mean, there's nothing here but an antique PC and a giant sat dish."

"Step a little to the left will you, Smitty?" the Voice requested. Smitz did as asked, too tired to even think about why.

"My God, you're right," the Voice finally said. "Are there even any power sources up there?"

Smitz checked the floor around the desk holding the computer. There were two electrical cables running behind it. He blew the dust off the computer itself. The unit was an ancient Commodore, the Model-T of PCs. It had a bunch of doodads taped to the monitor, devices he was sure allowed access to the Internet. But the modem was so old, it was the size of a bread box.

"There is power here," he finally reported.

"Well, then, see if you can get that rig turned on," the Voice suggested.

Smitz found the power switch and threw it. Amazingly, the computer came to life. The screen took forever to warm up, but once it did, it displayed an index of documents. The print was small, and the index language downright archaic—but Smitz had grown up with a Commodore. He knew his way around these old crows.

He pulled down and began reading the documents. Strung together, they appeared to be a blueprint for hacking into a worldwide net of shuttle-tracking computers.

Yet . . .

"This thing couldn't possibly have enough juice to pull a shuttle down," Smitz said into the phone. "Could it?"

"Apparently, it's not that hard to do," the Voice replied. "But there's really only one way to find out."

"And how is that?"

"Better pull up that chair, Smitty," the Voice said. "I think we're going to be here awhile."

It took more than an hour and a half, and lots of keyboard punching, but eventually—miraculously, even—Smitz was able to drag enough data out of the PC's primitive hard drive to piece together a rather complex puzzle.

The Voice had stayed on the line with him the entire time.

"From what I can conclude," Smitz said wearily, "they *were* able to manipulate the shuttle from here, that is, if they did everything just right."

"Can you tell how?" the Voice asked him.

"It's a guess," Smitz replied. "But it looks like they were able to get enough information from unclassified NASA stuff on the Web to hack into your own little secret space kingdom.

"Once in, they cracked your code and beamed up commands to your shuttle via this ice-cream dish here. It appears they were waiting here for some time to pull this off. There are files in here documenting all the upcoming NASA shuttle launches. Could be they locked onto yours, thinking it was one of the civilian shuttles."

"And they did it with out-of-date hardware thinking that we wouldn't be keyed into such old junk—making them almost impossible to track before the fact," said the Voice.

"Low-tech beats high-tech," someone in the background said.

"Maybe your friends at the NSA should reconfigure their systems to pick up old Commodores," Smitz said, unable to resist the urge to rub it in.

"The NSA doesn't even know we exist," was the ominous reply.

Smitz went on: "Whoever did this was able to send encrypted commands to your orbiter at pretty regular intervals following all of your comm satellite bounces. Once they hacked in, they hid bits of information inside your regular telemetry stream. Eventually, this overloaded your C/drives and corrupted the authentic systems. When that happened, all their stuff just took over. Killed the communication tracks. Overrode the command computer. Started the re-entry sequence, and . . ."

"And down she came," the Voice said, finishing the sentence for him.

"Like a ton of bricks," Smitz confirmed.

There was a long silence. Smitz could hear murmuring in the background. The connection was so crisp, it seemed like the gang of seven were in the next room.

Then another voice spoke: "Is there any way you can tell *where* the shuttle came down?"

Smitz did some more keyboard punching, but came up empty.

"I can't find any tracking data once the shuttle reentered," he told them. "They either did it somewhere else, or had a good idea where it would come down before they even started all this."

Another muffled silence as the seven ghosts conversed among themselves.

"There are some things we can't see, Smitty," the original Voice said, coming back on. "Is there any chance the whole setup there might be a ruse? Something thrown together to lead us off the track? I ask only because information we've just received indicates that whoever is responsible for all this might have, shall we say, an *unusual* sense of humor."

"Well, I'm too tired to laugh," Smitz replied. "But I can't imagine what I'm looking at as being anything other than authentic. Crude, but authentic. I mean, if it were a setup, then those responsible *would* have filled the room with new equipment—just to make it more believable. They certainly wouldn't have used this old stuff."

He studied the index of data on the screen now. He brought up one very pertinent file. "Need more proof?" he asked.

"Yes," the Voice replied.

"The name of this shuttle," Smitz said, reading off one hacked document. "It's top secret, I assume?"

"It is," was the reply.

"Is it 'the SSMT-*Avenger*'?"

A very long pause.

"Yes, it is," the Voice finally replied.

"Well, at the very least the people who set up this rig knew that—and from what I can see, they knew a hell of a lot more. It might look like the equivalent of a guy going to the moon on a firecracker, but I'd sure start checking the files for any disgruntled NASA employees you might have roaming around. Or maybe even someone closer to your own backyard."

Another long pause. Five minutes or more.

"We really have our work cut out for us now," the Voice finally said. "Or I should say, *you* do."

"I figured that," Smitz replied with a yawn. "What's next?"

"Well, thanks to you, at least we know *how* they did it," the Voice replied. "Now we've got to find out *who*."

"You don't have any ideas? Any clues?"

"We have suspicions," the Voice said.

More mumbling in the background.

"But in any case," the Voice finally went on, "it's time for you to get going again."

"Where to this time?" he asked, dreading the reply.

"Get back to your taxi," the Voice replied. "The pilot will have updated orders waiting for you."

Smitz checked his watch. The SR-71 was cooling its jets at a Greek military air base about thirty minutes away.

"What should I do about this place?" he asked the Voice.

More discussion in the background. "Put a few bullets into the back of that thing's head," was the reply. "Then get moving! We'll be in touch."

"Wait!" Smitty yelled. "I've been on this guy's cell phone for almost two hours. The cost of this call will be enormous. What should I tell him?"

Smitz could hear the seven men discussing this.

Finally the Voice said: "Tell him to send us the bill."

17

Aboard the *Bataan*

Captain John Currier was working out in the ship's weight room when the flash message came down from the bridge. Two unidentified aircraft were approaching the *Bataan* from the northeast. There had been no radio contact with the aircraft. No indications who they belonged to. But they seemed to be heading right for the ship.

Currier immediately contacted the ship's Air Boss. What was the current state of the deck? Clear, except for two Harriers up top warming their engines for a maintenance check. They could be airborne inside of ninety seconds.

Currier had to think a moment. This was not a typical situation for the *Bataan*. Usually the amphib ship sailed in the company of other vessels whose mission was to secure the airspace above the fleet. But with the *Bataan* now going solo, it would have to deal with this matter alone.

Currier's first instinct was that the two approaching aircraft were the Osprey and the Sea Cobra, returning from their top-secret assignment. Currier had been in the dark about their mission when the special-ops team departed the day before, and nothing had changed. He'd received no communiqués, no messages, no further instructions of any kind. He had remained at his present station as ordered, doing long, slow circles about twenty-two miles off the coast of Pakistan.

So, were these hostile aircraft coming toward him now? Currier's gut told him no. But if the bogies *were* the special-ops team, why hadn't they contacted the ship?

Currier couldn't take any chances. He dispatched the two Harriers with orders to intercept and identify the incoming aircraft. That done, he ordered the rest of the deck cleared and the ship called to general quarters.

Then he headed for the bridge.

The jump jets intercepted the bogies five minutes later about seventeen miles northeast of the *Bataan*. The Harriers' flight leader transmitted a code back to the ship that indicated the bogies were not acting in a threatening manner.

Then he added: "Wait till you see this."

A crash team was out on the deck of the *Bataan* when the two specks came in view about ten minutes later. They were being tailed by the Harriers, both jump jets flying in a ninety-percent vertical translation mode in order to maintain an airspeed low enough to pace the slower aircraft.

It was soon clear that the two bogies were helicopters. But few of those on the *Bataan* had ever seen choppers quite like these. Not only were the aircraft twice the age of many of the ship's sailors, when these copters were first built, many of the sailors' *fathers* had not yet been born. They looked like they'd flown right out of the early fifties.

It was the Kyrgyzstani Flying Bananas, of course. Limping along, running out of fuel, and perilously overloaded. Up on the bridge, Currier watched the old choppers through binoculars as they began a ragged circle around the *Bataan,* the Harriers in slow pursuit. These things were real egg-beaters. They had country markings splashed all over their fuselages and rotor housings, but Currier was still at a loss to identify them. Their windows, however, had been plastered with makeshift American flags. Currier would later learn these flags were made from strips of blue uniforms, white stretcher sheets, and bloodred bandages.

It didn't take a genius to know that this *was* the special-ops team returning from their mission, albeit in a very unconventional manner. But what the hell had happened to them?

Both choppers completed a noisy, smoky circuit of the ship, then began a very shaky landing approach, one behind the other. It was a calm day, the seas were placid, and the air was motionless, all of which should have worked in favor of the copters' pilots. Still, both helicopters came down like heaps onto the deck of the *Bataan.*

No sooner had they stopped bouncing when the strange aircraft were surrounded by heavily armed Marines. The rear door of the first Banana slammed opened. The first few people to stumble out looked like aliens stepping onto Earth for the first time. They were obviously soldiers; Huns in modern uniforms and bearing arms. The Marines closed in, weapons at the ready. Finally a familiar face bounded down the ramp.

It was Slick Delaney. He looked like he'd just crawled out of a car wreck.

He grabbed the first Marine he could reach and yelled: "Get your corpsmen out here! We got a lot of people hurt bad!"

•   •   •

Thirty minutes later half of Team 66 was gathered in the same cramped cabin where they had been briefed for the ill-fated mission just twenty-four hours before. The room was not as crowded this time.

Some of the troopers were nursing cups of hot coffee. Some were just staring blankly into space. All were trying to get the warmth back into their bones—and keep those same bones from rattling. No one was talking.

This was not their finest hour, and they knew it. Through no real fault of their own, they had nevertheless failed their mission, at a cost of twelve wounded; eight seriously, two mortally. They'd also lost the Ozzie, which, counting all of the whiz-bang crap on board, cost at least $80 million. Add one brand-new Sea Cobra, probably priced at $20 million, and they were looking at $100 million fiasco.

Sitting by himself at one end of the table, Chou was barely coherent. Now that they were back, any memory of the Paswar seemed like a bad dream. But whenever he closed his eyes, he could still see the blood on the snow. Could hear the cracking of the ice. Even smell the exhaust from the Hokum's smoky engines.

In ten years of leading this special-ops team through some very rough duty, this one had been the worst.

Many times over those ten years he had wondered, given his team's sterling success record, just what it would take to break them up. There was only one probable answer: for them to fail a big assignment. The mission to the Paswar had fulfilled that in spades. In the special-ops business, no matter what the circumstances, deep-cover combat teams usually lived only as long as they were successful. No one wanted a Spook crew who had stubbed their toe, never mind one that had fractured both legs, and taken a kick in the balls to boot.

Cold, exhausted, depleted, Chou was convinced of just one thing at this point: After what had happened in the past twenty-four hours, there probably was no more Team 66 to disband.

It had already fallen apart.

Slick Delaney had somehow found his way up to the bow of the *Bataan*.

He was sitting on the leading deck now, looking over the railing to the warm waters below. He had meant what he'd said right before the roof fell in on them at the top of the world. One way or the other, he was leaving the spy business. The only question was, how best to do it.

The ideal scenario would be if the CIA just allowed him to resign. That was a possibility. Though, in these dark moments, he'd convinced himself it was more likely he'd be thrown in prison for life. He knew way too much about the CIA's downside—especially the absolutely fucked-up way it ran its overseas special operations. From their point of view, it would be foolish to let him roam the streets, a loose cannon on two legs. They could kill him, of course, but Delaney hoped that stuff only happened in the movies. Besides, the Russians sent guys like him to the Siberian *gulags,* not because it was more humane than murder, but because it was literally a fate worse than death. He knew the CIA was no better.

So which would it be for him?

He took in a breath of the salty air. The water below was the exact color of whiskey. Delaney could have drunk a gallon or two of sour mash right now, not that it would do him any good. The mission to the Paswar had been a disaster. He had come closer to death than ever before, and had not liked the feeling. Had the Kyrgyzstanis not come when they did, and had the Americans shot at them instead of quickly accepting their offer of help, he'd still be up there, lying in the snow, frozen, bleeding. Or even worse, locked inside the ice forever, just like . . .

He shook these thoughts away and tried to breathe deep again. There was only one consolation in all this. It was a selfish one, but it was probably the only thing stopping him from going over the side right now.

And that was, no matter how much he was hurting inside—about what happened, about what he'd had seen up there and who came back and who didn't—he knew that somewhere belowdecks, someone else was feeling a whole lot worse.

Jazz Norton remembered very few things about the flight back.

It took what seemed like forever; that much he knew. And the ride had been noisy and the helicopters seemed on the verge of falling apart at any minute. Two dozen individuals, five of them seriously wounded, squeezed into a space meant for half that number—it was simply a miserable experience. The real mystery was how the dangerously overloaded Kyrgyzstani choppers had ever made it back over the towering Paswar peaks in the first place.

Unconscious and bleeding, he'd been stuffed into a crawl space up near the flight deck of the second Banana. It was about an hour after they'd evacuated the Paswar when he woke up the first time. Frozen, his head still bleeding, his right kneecap swollen to twice its normal size, he'd been pulled out of his coma by the wails of the wounded troopers around him. Some crying. Some dying. For one terrifying moment, he thought he was still back up on the crater.

Mercifully, he lapsed back into a stupor, this after waving away one of Team 66's medics. He didn't need him; there were other people a lot worse off than he was. He just wanted to stay curled up in the smallest space possible and let the racket of the old helicopter drown out the misery of those around him.

When he woke up the second time, the helicopters had touched down, near a small Pakistani village called Shu-jaadpur, he would later learn. Looking through the open side door, he saw the operator of a small village petrol station being made to fill their empty gas tanks with low-grade, low-octane gasoline—while at gunpoint. Norton might have laughed a little madly at that point. What better way to end this mission than with a gas station stickup?

He woke up the third time, for good, just as the two copters crossed over the coastline. How the Kyrgyzstani pilots had been able to navigate so precisely over snowy mountainous terrain and thick jungles, he would never know. They had apparently zigzagged their way south, flying very low and avoiding at all costs the route taken by the Americans on their way up. The reason for this was simple: That no Hokum had pursued them while fleeing from the Paswar was miraculous. The last thing anyone wanted was to run into any of the high-tech gunships on the way back to safety. Somehow the two Flying Bananas had made the trip unscathed and undetected.

He was able to open his right eye just wide enough to see the *Bataan* off in the distance, looking like the floating city of Oz in the hazy afternoon sun. He lay back and shivered through the final approach and landing. Once down, he did not move or make a sound until all of the other wounded people were carried from the Banana. Only then did he get up and limp off the old chopper under his own power. The ship's medical personnel took one look at him, pushed him onto a stretcher, pumped him full of painkillers, and brought him here, to the auxiliary sick bay, now to suffer alone.

He was in shock. He was sure they all were. The bitter cold. The sleepless hours. The adrenaline rush. The horror they'd seen up on the mountain. All the qualifying factors were there.

He was also coming out of a major case of denial. Despite his injuries and those of the people around him, during his waking moments on the long ride back, he'd somehow managed to convince himself that everything wasn't as bleak as it appeared. He'd chosen to believe that everyone had been saved and everyone would be okay and they'd all make it back to the *Bataan* to live and breathe another day.

But now this grim fantasy was draining out of him faster than the painkillers. Reality was rushing in and it wasn't pretty. Some things were still fuzzy—but some were not.

One thing he knew for sure: Not all of them had come home.

The door to the small auxiliary sick bay opened and Captain Currier walked in.

He took a long look at Norton. "Do you feel as bad as you look?" he asked.

"I don't know," Norton replied, mumbling through swollen lips. "How bad do I look?"

Currier put a legal pad and a pen down on Norton's gurney.

"I thought you might want to get your thoughts on paper, before any more time passes," he said. "They'll be all over you about this one, I'm sure."

Norton knew the Navy officer was right. Once the entire bucket of shit hit the fan, he could see himself getting debriefed on this disaster for weeks, if not months, or even years.

"I appreciate your help, Skipper," Norton told him. "And apologize for any trouble we might have brought down on you. You know how these things go. The guilty take cover and the search for the innocents begins. They'll probably want to put you on the griddle too."

Currier waved these concerns away.

"Let them," he said. "I told you before, once this cruise is over, I'll be sailing a desk. Being hammered by your bosses has to be better than that."

A corpsman appeared, checked Norton's multitude of bandages, pronounced him still among the living, and then left.

"Well, I suppose I should go make sure our friends from Kyrgyzstan are being properly attended to," Currier said once they were alone again. "Judging from the looks of things, I'd say you guys owe them at least a couple cases of scotch—if they drink scotch, that is."

Norton lay back down and resumed staring at the ceiling.

"I could use a case or two myself," he murmured.

That was when Currier closed the sick bay door and sat in a chair across from Norton's gurney.

He lowered his voice. "Stop me if I'm out of line here, Major," he began. "But as captain of this ship, I've got a thousand people under me, and that means I've become an expert at reading the human condition. And you, my friend, are a mess."

"No need to sugarcoat that, Skipper," Norton replied.

"And you're a mess not just because your mission went belly-up. You just look like you've got some unfinished business to take care of. *Personal* business . . ."

Norton sank deeper into his stretcher. This might not be the conversation he wanted to have right now. "I think you've got me at a disadvantage, Skipper," he mumbled.

Currier pulled his chair closer. "Look, I'm not privy to where you guys went and what went on when you got there. I don't know your specifics. But I can count. And I know you came back with one less person than you went out with."

He paused.

"The girl didn't make it, did she."

Norton closed his eyes tightly. "No, she didn't."

"And the people responsible for that are still out there?"

Norton nodded painfully. "They sure are."

Currier paused again. He was choosing his words carefully.

"Well, then, let me tell you something," he said finally. "I'm almost forty years in the Navy. My first duty was with the Riverines in Nam. You know, running gunboats up and down the Mekong? We got in a shitload of scrapes and we took a lot of casualties and there were times when we had to leave before we could get the guys who got our friends. Some asshole lieutenant commander somewhere would make a decision from his nice cozy air-conditioned billet, and we'd be withdrawing before we did what we were supposed to do in the first place. Whenever that happened, we looked just like you and your guys look right now.

"Unfinished business, Major. It can eat away at you for a very long time. Maybe forever. Take it from me, I know. Now, God help me, I've been married twenty-two years to the greatest woman on this planet—but someone has deprived us. You, me, the whole world has been deprived of that girl. And not just because she was one of the most gorgeous creatures I have ever laid eyes on. She was a special person—and you knew it the second you saw her. She was young, bright. Her whole life ahead of her . . .

"Now, I'm not someone who gets all warm and fuzzy after a tragedy. Just the opposite: I'm actually a big proponent of revenge. It's not pretty, but it does help you sleep better at night. So I'm going to impart a little bit of unsolicited wisdom here. If there's a chance that whoever is

responsible for her death will get away with it, then somehow, someone should try to even that score. It won't bring
her back. But I'll guarantee you this: The whole world will
be better off. Especially you, Major Norton. *You* will feel
a whole lot better when you think of her, which I'm guessing will be just about every day. For the rest of your life."

Norton was getting pissed. Who was this guy to come in
here and rip the Band-Aids from his wounds like this?

"Begging your pardon, Skipper," he said acidly. "But
how is it that you're such an expert on how I feel?"

Currier reached into his jacket pocket and pulled something out.

"Because you were holding this so tightly when you
came aboard, my corpsmen nearly had to break your fingers
before you let it go."

He handed it to Norton. It was Amanda's glove.

Dead silence between them. A helicopter was lifting off
up on deck.

"Now, I've notified Langley that you've returned," Currier finally said. "And the flash message I got on their return
bounce said that I was to impound all of you and sit tight
for further orders. That tells me that whatever went down,
you guys will probably take the fall.

"However, it so happens that this flash message was,
well, scrambled in transmission. We have requested they
resend it. That will take at least a half hour. Until I get that
clarification, I must abide by my original orders. And they
were to provide you with access to any means and equipment this ship could offer, including aircraft."

He looked Norton right in his swollen eyes.

"That offer still stands, Major. But I wouldn't waste any
time deciding what you want to do with it."

With that, Currier got up and left the room without another word, leaving the door open behind him.

• • •

Thirty minutes later, still battered and bandaged, Norton limped his way up to the *Bataan*'s flight deck.

It was late afternoon now. The sun was a brilliant red ball sinking slowly in the west, turning the water around the amphib ship a bright golden yellow.

A lone Harrier jump jet was sitting at the far end of the deck. Its engines were warmed up; it was ready to fly. A deck crew was just finishing topping off its fuel tanks.

Norton made his way to the aircraft, realizing as he drew closer that this Harrier was actually a variant of the standard Marine Corps Sea Harrier. This was an AV-8F model, a two-seater. And someone was already sitting in the rear seat.

It was Delaney.

"What the hell do you think you're doing?" Norton shouted up to him.

"Same thing you are, Jazz," Delaney yelled back.

"Is that right? And how do you know what *I'm* doing?"

Delaney was able to lower the engine scream to a manageable whine.

"Because we think alike—and we both know this thing was screwed up from the start," he replied. "You remember what happened during ArcLight. The empty base. The decoy airplane. All that bullshit back then was a diversion. Something thrown in to fuck us up. Why? There was only one reason why. Because we were getting too close.

"So I figure that's what's happening here; like Yogi Bear says: 'It's déjà vu all over again.' Look at it this way. Supposedly the CIA has people all over the world looking for this shuttle—the real one, right? Now, do you think any of them found a decoy at their point of search? No freaking way. I'll bet my life on it. Why would anyone go through all that—attracting all that attention—if they didn't have

something to hide? Something close by? No, we got close—
and so did all those other chopper troops up there. And
they tried to grease us all. And if it wasn't for Attila and
his friends, we would have never got out. But that doesn't
change the fact that what we were looking for is down there
somewhere—not *where* we were. But close by. Just like
ArcLight."

"So this is a call to duty for you?" Norton asked him.

"I guess," Delaney replied. "Ain't it for you?"

Good thing there weren't two Harriers warming up on
the deck, Norton thought, because they probably would
have flown in two different directions.

Or maybe not . . .

"So what do you have in mind?" Norton asked Delaney.

"Like I said, same thing you do," Delaney replied "That
we go back."

"Back? To the Paswar?"

Delaney shook his head. "What are you. . . . still high on
painkillers? No fucking way I'd go back there! But we
don't have to. I think the place to look has been right in
front of us all this time."

Norton thought about that for a moment, and then he
smiled—it made his entire body ache.

"Yeah, I think you're right," he said.

18

Kuri-fa, Turkey

Gene Smitz had been sitting inside the blue and white stretch limo for more than an hour.

It wasn't bad for a government car, even if that government was Turkey. Air-conditioned, supplied with ice water, stale sandwiches, cold tea, even a small TV. Pretty luxurious in this part of the world. But it didn't have a bed, and that was what Smitz needed the most at the moment—the opportunity to sleep, perchance to dream.

The limo was parked just inside the gate of an abandoned military base located near Kuri-fa, a tiny village in the most southeastern part of Turkey. The SR-71 Blackbird was waiting on a runway nearby, its pilot sitting motionless inside the cockpit. Ever at the ready to serve as Smitz's personal hypersonic taxi boy.

Either that or he was asleep.

Parked next to the limo was a van full of Turkish state

security police, their engine running in the growing rain.

Everyone here was waiting for a Russian.

He was already an hour late.

The orders waiting for Smitz when he returned to the SR-71 back in Greece had been maddeningly simple: Someone inside one of Russia's intelligence networks had located a guy who knew a guy who knew *the* guy who had stolen the soda-pop blimp. If the theory was correct that whoever stole the blimp was the same person who stole the space shuttle, then the name of this perpetrator was an extremely important piece of information.

So Smitz had rushed here, to frontier Turkey, to get a name from a Russian.

Smitz was standing outside the limo, in a steady rain, taking his third piss of this latest ordeal, when he heard a small jet approaching the airfield.

The Turkish guards heard it too. Four of them alighted from their van and smartly took up positions around Smitz's limo. The small Russian-built business jet landed and taxied over to the entrance gate. Smitz zipped up and climbed back inside the limo. He checked the ammo clip in his massive handgun, and then slipped the weapon under his right ass cheek. He knew he could get the gun out and firing in about two seconds if he had to.

Through the rain-splattered window he watched a single passenger climb out of the Gulfstreamski. He was a big man, tall and wide; the airplane recoiled when he finally stepped off of it. Smitz was about one third his size. He pressed his weight onto his gun. Yeah, it was still there.

The man waddled over to the limo, waving his credentials in the rain. Smitz nodded to his driver, who signaled the two guards closest to the limo. They frisked the man, then opened the door and let him in.

The man slipped into the seat beside Smitz with ease. He was a Russian, all right. Unruly beard, face full of moles, bad teeth, bad haircut—but a really nice overcoat. Smitz had met a hundred of these guys.

"So, you got the name?" he asked the man.

"I do not," the man declared in thick, broken English. "I have something better."

Smitz was instantly livid. His right hand reached for the gun.

"Why are you here then?" he asked the Russian harshly. "Just to waste my time?"

The Russian just smiled.

"You must learn to listen a little more closely, my friend," he replied. "I said I have something *better* than the name you seek."

"What could *possibly* be better than the name?"

The Russian flipped open his briefcase with some flare. He took out a clumsy, oversized industrial-strength laptop. It looked like it was more than a decade old, yet it seemed to be this man's pride and joy.

He had a slightly more sophisticated telephone modem attached, and with a gleam in his eye, began connecting everything together. Smitz waited impatiently as the laptop's screen turned six different colors before it finally blinked to blue and flashed the magic Russian word: *"Gotov!"*

"Behold, it's ready," the man said, as if he'd just made a great discovery. "Isn't our technology wonderful?"

That did it for Smitz. He pulled out his pistol and shoved it into the Russian's face.

"My friend, I am in a hurry . . . and that means we have no time for games."

The Russian never lost his smile. "You want to know what is better than a name?" he asked. "How about a photograph?"

"A photograph? Of who?" Smitz asked.

"Of the one you seek," the Russian replied. "My people talked with your people, and your people said that if you saw this barbarian's picture, then all the answers would come to you. Your mission would become easier . . . and I think that's a direct quote."

Smitz was much too tired for this—his choices were to either shoot the man or go along with him. And frankly he was too exhausted to pull the trigger.

So he put his gun down and said: "Okay, show me the picture."

The man let out a jovial "Ah!" Then he began pounding on his laptop. After much clattering and beeping, a linkup was established and he started to download something from somewhere. Smitz read the screen timer. It said the download would take more than twenty-five minutes. Even for a Russian-made coal-fired portable computer, that seemed like a very long time for a simple JPG or GIF.

"What are you downloading exactly? It's just a photo image, right?"

"Yes, it is."

"Then why is it going to take so long?"

"Because," the Russian replied, "it is a very big picture, of a very big man."

19

"Who knew it could rain this much in Hawaii?"

It was a good question. At the moment the rain was coming down so hard on the island of Oahu, the deluge was approaching biblical proportions.

"I mean, I didn't think it rained out here at all," Marty Ricco went on. "Think the travel agents have been lying to us all along?"

"I wouldn't doubt it," Gillis replied.

It was now early evening. The pilots were sitting in the cockpit of the 747, drinking really bad coffee and listening to a local jazz radio station. The trip over the Pacific had been uneventful. It had taken just under seven hours, a drop in the bucket for veterans like them; they'd flown eighteen-hour in-theater refueling missions in the past without blinking an eye.

The jumbo jet turned out to be a breeze to fly once they

got some air underneath it. They had proceeded with the flight plan already set into the airplane's computer, and did everything they could to mimic a typical airliner. This included responding promptly to the various weather and traffic stations and hailing air carriers passing them in the opposite direction. The experience wasn't that much different from flying their old KC-135 tanker.

Some things they weren't used to, though. Getting slotted into the landing pattern over Honolulu Airport was like trying to enter a Massachusetts traffic circle at rush hour. They were stacked up for nearly an hour before finally getting the okay to land. Just as they began their descent, it had started to rain.

They had seen the black storm clouds off on the western horizon, but never did they think they would move in so swiftly. No sooner had they touched down than they found themselves in the middle of the worst rainstorm to hit the islands in decades.

As promised, an airport vehicle had met them when they finally came down. But following the bright yellow truck proved more difficult than they could've ever imagined, so dense was the downpour. Finally, they picked up its trail again and rolled to the end of the airport's most isolated taxiway.

And here they had sat now for almost two hours.

Waiting.

"I actually think this might be a typhoon," Gillis was saying now as the rain continued to beat without mercy on the airplane.

"Typhoon? Doesn't that mean a tidal wave is coming?" Ricco asked with some alarm. "I mean, we're right on the ocean here. It would wipe out this place in a minute."

Gillis just shook his head.

"Don't worry," he said. "We ain't that lucky."

Evening turned to night. The coffee got worse and the radio station faded out.

Finally they saw two vehicles approaching. One looked like a rental car; the other was a motorized stairway.

Both stopped at the rear of the 747. Hatches were opened, then slammed shut. Soon Gillis and Ricco could hear someone climbing up to the cockpit.

They had been told to expect someone named "Ginger," but both pilots had assumed that was just a code name. They had assumed wrong.

Ginger was a knockout. She was petite, small-breasted, and indeed a redhead this week. She wasn't dressed like a Spook. Bikini top, cutoff jeans, bare feet. Gillis and Ricco had more than forty years of married life between them. Neither one had ever strayed, but like any guy, both had done a lot of looking. But they had never seen sex on a spoon like this.

Ginger was all business, though. She sat in the cockpit's jump seat and handed them four computer disks, along with instructions on how to download the information into the 747's flight computer. Then she passed them each a printed version of their orders.

The two pilots read over the mission specs and did a simultaneous groan.

"Transit to *Diego Garcia*?" Ricco grumbled, reading the first paragraph of orders. "That's in the Indian Ocean, for Christ sakes."

" 'Unless diverted en route,' " Ginger said, reading the orders more carefully. "And if I were a betting person, I would say you won't get more than two thirds of the way to Diego Garcia before you are diverted."

"That's still a hump from here," Gillis said.

Ginger just shrugged. "Write a letter to your Congressman," she said. "I'm just the messenger."

Both pilots finished reading the mission text, and discovered that the answer to their biggest question wasn't even mentioned.

"This tells us what to do, what route to take, how high to fly," Gillis said. "But it doesn't say what we're supposed to pick up if and when we get to where we're supposed to be."

"I can't help you there," Ginger said, lowering her voice. "But I can tell you that all this has to do with a space shuttle that's gone missing. It's down somewhere in Southwest Asia and they are still looking for it apparently. They thought they had located it earlier today, but last I heard, that was a false alarm. Once they do find it, though, that's when you guys will be called in."

The pilots just looked at each other. "Missing shuttle?" Ricco said. "What's that have to do with us?"

Ginger smiled sweetly. "You'll be part of the recovery effort, I guess."

Gillis was shaking his head. "Did you see what's down in our cargo bay?" he asked her.

She nodded toward the rear of the plane.

"Yeah, I sure did," she replied. "What the hell is that thing for?"

"*That's* what we'd like to know," Gillis said. He felt a sudden fear bubble up inside him. Could someone, somehow, somewhere along the way, have fucked up their part of this mission, thinking—could it be possible?—that *they* could pick up a space shuttle with the Sky Crane? It didn't make sense. But after dealing with the CIA Special Foreign Operations branch for the past two years, he knew anything was possible. In fact, the more fucked up, the more likely.

Gillis expressed this fear to Ginger, but she made it go away with a wave of her hand.

"This much I *can* tell you," she said. "They're not expecting you to lift the shuttle. I mean, they're not that out-to-lunch."

"But if not the shuttle, then what?" Ricco asked her.

She didn't reply. Outside, it seemed like the rain was letting up.

"I think you guys better get going," she said instead.

20

It was called Sharpur-say.

It was a ten-mile stretch of high desert plain located in central Pakistan. An enormous mountain range spread out like jagged white teeth across its northern horizon; along its southern edge ran a series of flat-top hills, many with thick trees running down their banks.

One of these hills was the place code-named Exxon One. Three hundred yards from its base, the huge wedding tent still stood, several hundred cars still parked around it.

Besides the sound of the wind blowing through the seams in the tent, it was quiet on the Sharpur-say.

But not for long.

The two-seat Sea Harrier arrived in the area just after sun-down. It was a crystal-clear night, stars blazing, no moon. Staying low, avoiding any large population centers, the jump jet had made the trip in under two hours.

The mood on the ride up had been somber. The pilots

barely spoke, and when they did, it was limited to the operation of the aircraft. They were both tired, battered, and still pissed for being made suckers again. There really wasn't that much to talk about.

They did have a plan, however, one hatched right before takeoff.

Three things had led them back to the Sharpur-say. It was here they'd seen the shuttle's likeness scrawled into the ground. Then there were the Hokum pilot's last words; his reference to a man without a bride evoked an image of an empty wedding tent. Combine all that with the similarities between this nightmare and the ArcLight mission, especially setting up a dummy target close to the real one, and, well, all the arrows just seemed to be pointing to this place.

There was no such thing as an inconspicuous approach in a jet aircraft—but that was the whole idea. The pilots did not employ any means of stealth upon their arrival. Covertness was not the purpose here. Just the opposite—on this moonless night, they were aiming to wake the dead.

It was a reckless thing to do. Norton knew that. He had always prided himself in being meticulous when flying a combat mission. Attention to details and planning for contingencies were what usually kept you alive during combat air operations. That simple formula had worked for him in his ten years of doing a very dangerous job.

But this, what he was doing now, it was simply reckless. There was no better term for it. And it was so unlike him, in some ways, he felt like he really wasn't doing it at all, that it was not real. But the triple-ace-overhand knot tied up in his stomach—now *that* was real. So was the Size-4 Navy-issue Polar Environment Glove/Female from which he just could not unwrap his fingers. The world was not fair; it was as simple as that. Who lived and who died—

not fair. Good or bad, who succeeds and who fails—not fair. His eyes had turned dark, and so had his heart. In that state of mind, recklessness felt like a virtue.

So it was that he came roaring out of the south, flying so low over the wedding tent, the ground around it shook. He peeled left, exited by way of the western end of the plain, turned up and over, and came back again. This time he rocketed over the hill where they had refueled on their way up to the Paswar a million years ago.

Putting the jump jet on its left wing again, he turned another 180 and roared back over the tent. Another twist, another turn, and he was streaking above the hills again. Back and forth they went. The noise they were making was absolutely earsplitting. He went so low over one group of parked cars, he broke dozens of windshields and set off scores of car alarms. Another pass over the hills was so shallow, the jet exhaust burned the tops of the sloping trees.

All the while, Delaney was holding on for dear life and trying to keep a good reading on the ground via his helmet-mounted NightVision scope. Had this jump jet been a TAV-8BF—a sort of a Forward Air Controller for the Marine Corps—then his backseat position would have been packed with the latest in ground-threat-warning devices, including SAM detection, defensive ground-mapping radar, infrared capability, and electronic-signal-interception devices.

Trouble was, this bird was a lowly old trainer, unarmed and having none of this stuff. Not that Delaney could have run any of it anyway. No, for this he would have to rely on his own NightVision-enhanced eyeballs.

Ten minutes of very noisy flying back and forth went by, yet all remained still on the Sharpur-say.

This in itself was strange. If the tent was here for a week-long Pakistani wedding party, then where were all the people? And if there were no people on hand, why were all the cars still here? Even if everyone was asleep inside the tent, the bombastic flying would have sent them shrieking from their beds by now.

Finally, Norton pulled up and put the Sea Harrier into a hover right above Exxon One.

Delaney spoke: "Hate to think we're just wasting gas here, partner. But if there is anyone down there, they're either deaf or they know how to hide, real good."

Norton was thinking the same thing. They were trying to flush some quail here. And few things were worse for a soldier on the ground than the scream of a jet fighter going right overhead. The noise alone could drive you crazy, make you do stupid things. That was what Norton was hoping for.

"Just give it a few more—"

Suddenly, Delaney's NightVision goggles lit up.

"Holy Sheet!" was all he was able to say.

In an instant the night was lit up like day. SAM missiles, AA rounds, machine-gun fire . . . suddenly tons of this stuff was coming up at them.

"Bingo!" Norton was yelling. "I knew the mooks would give themselves away!"

"Okay, so we proved someone *is* down there!" Delaney screamed back. "Now let's get the hell out of here!"

But it was already too late for that. Indeed, Norton's plan had worked too well. The barrage that hit them was so intense, so concentrated, there was no way they could have avoided it. One missile severed their right wing and kept on going; another impacted on the tail. A 22-round cannon barrage tore through their nose and killed all the electronics on the plane. It was only because Norton had begun to accelerate away just as the AA fire hit that the Sea Harrier didn't blow up right then and there. But the wounds were mortal ones. There would be no fancy flying now like up in the Paswar. They were going down, fast. . . .

"Should we punch out, Jazz?" Delaney was yelling up to him.

The old fighter pilot maxim said: If you have to ask, then it's already too late to eject.

That was the case now.

Norton yelled back to him: "Let's stay with it."

Somehow Norton was able to keep the crippled jump jet airborne long enough to get out of the vertical mode and put them back over the flat plain. Then he slammed the exhaust thrusters back to vertical in a last-ditch effort to blunt the impact when they hit the ground.

But when they hit, they hit hard. The Harrier slammed into a small ravine about two hundred yards from the line of hills. At least they went in feet-first; the landing gear snapped off and the crooked nose bored three feet into the hard sand. But there was no fire. Norton blew the canopy an instant before impact, sparing them most of the concussion. Dazed and cut about their faces and hands, he and Delaney were still able to scramble out of the wreck, rifles in hand, and dive for the relative safety of a nearby ditch.

"Man, are the Marines going to be pissed at you," Delaney gasped, out of breath. He began checking himself for any broken bones. "Busting two of their aircraft? In just two days? They'll eat you alive. . . ."

"They'll have to find me first," Norton told him.

The wind was howling fiercely; they could still hear sparks and pops coming from the downed Harrier. Other than that, though, it was completely quiet.

Norton peeked up over the top of the ditch. "Are you convinced now that there's something screwy going on around here?" he asked Delaney.

"Well, getting shot down sold me on that concept," Delaney yelled back. "Just don't tell me you did all this on purpose or I might have to kill you right here. . . ."

Before Norton could reply, the night exploded in gunfire again. This time it was tracer bullets and rocket-propelled grenades, lots of it, going right over their heads. Luckily, the streams of fire were being directed at the jump jet. Dozens of rounds had already perforated the fuselage.

"Well, it's official," Norton said. "We're looking at a long walk home. . . ."

"Yeah, and don't forget that swim too," Delaney reminded him.

They were lying as flat as possible in the muddy wet ditch, bullets and shrapnel whizzing just inches above their heads. One wrong move in any direction might be their last.

"We gotta move, partner," Norton said, "before these guys realize we ain't still inside the plane."

"If you got a plan, I'm all ears," Delaney replied. "—If I still *have* any ears, that is."

Norton peeked over the top of the ditch and back toward the Sea Harrier.

"How much gas would you say we had left in the rig?" he asked Delaney.

"Hundred gallons or so," Delaney replied through a mouthful of dirt. "But if you're planning on flying out of here in that thing, I think the ride back might be a bit bumpy."

Norton wasn't listening to him. He turned himself around until he was facing the horribly battered jump jet.

"These guys have hit everything *but* the fuel tanks," Norton said.

"And that's a bad thing?" Delaney replied.

Norton managed to raise his M-16 out of the ditch and

with the NightScope turned on, keyed in on the Sea
Harrier's right-side underwing fuel tank. He squeezed off
nine rounds—nothing. On the tenth one, the fuel tank blew
up. The explosion was tremendous; the fireball rose two
hundred feet in the air. It was so spectacular, it halted all
of the gunfire from the hill.

Which was just what Norton wanted.

For no sooner had the aircraft blown up than he and
Delaney were out of the ditch and running as fast as their
injured legs could carry them, deeper into the night.

21

"Okay, what have we got?"

"You mean, what have we got *left*."

"Just read 'em off . . . can you see anything at all?"

"Yeah, it's okay. Looks like we've got scrambled eggs and Tang. Hash browns and Tang. Meatless lasagna and Tang. Beef stew and Tang."

"Jessuzz, you got any Tang?"

"You know what, I *hate* Tang. I've *always* hated Tang. Why the fuck is everyone so hung up on the fucking Tang? Is there a law somewhere that says you can't go into space unless you've got an assful of Tang?"

"I don't think NASA even uses it anymore. . . ."

"That's not my point, asshole. . . ."

"Relax, will you. . . . You might have to get a liking for this stuff before this thing is over. Pretty soon it will be all we have left."

"Are you telling me to relax? Well let me tell you

something. *You relax.* And shove that Tang right up your ass. . . ."

"Yeah? You first!"

The four astronauts all took a deep breath, let the moment pass, and then calmed down.

It was not the first argument they'd had in the past seventy-two hours. And the way things were going, it wouldn't be the last.

They were cold, they were dirty, and they were beginning to smell. None of them had had a decent shower in nearly four days. They had no toothbrushes, no toothpaste, not even a bar of soap. Their spacecraft barely had a toilet, and it was so small and hard to use, a Winnebago owner would laugh at it.

The reason for all this was simple: Their spacecraft, SSMT-*Avenger*, was not a typical space shuttle. It had very few comforts of home.

The *Avenger* was smaller than the NASA shuttles by about a third. Though it looked almost identical from the exterior, it was a very different flying machine on the inside. The *Avenger* was basically a cargo bay with wings. There was no mid-deck as on the civilian shuttles, no lower berth, storage compartments, science bay, or designated sleeping area. The SSMT was a no-frills affair. It really had only two missions: It could lug spy satellites into orbit on very short notice, and with the same amount of haste, rescue any spy satellites that had somehow lost their way.

This latest flight—the disaster that had started just one hour after they'd been hustled out of the strip joint—had been an exercise of the second kind.

"How about the guy in back? Think he has anything better to eat than this crap?"

"I don't think he eats. . . ."

"Or sleeps. Or breathes . . ."

"Well, I'm sure he bleeds—so when it's our time to go, he'll be going too."

Except for the thinnest sliver of light coming through the main hatchway, it was pitch-black inside the shuttle cockpit. They had mistakenly deployed their emergency windshield blast protectors upon reentry; the panic aboard the spacecraft at the moment of unexpected descent was truly mind-blowing. They were all convinced they were about to burn up. Once they'd touched down, surprisingly in one piece, the electrical system shorted out and the blast protectors stayed locked in place. This not only made it very dark inside the spacecraft, it made it nearly soundproof as well. They'd been shut up all this time, without any idea where they were, or what was going on around them.

They knew they were being held hostage, however—that much had been made clear to them by the two men who came banging at the side hatch just a few minutes after touchdown. These men were Arabic, well-spoken, well-dressed—and heavily armed. They explained that it would be best if the astronauts left the shuttle, as many explosives were being placed around it, to be detonated if negotiations between the U.S. and the hijackers failed. The men claimed, convincingly, that the shuttle was surrounded by hundreds of heavily armed fighters and that its location was so well hidden, "no one can find you." What's more, complex diversionary actions had been enacted, leaving the immediate area free of any potential "special-operation rescue attempt," at least for the time being.

From this point of view then, the astronauts had no other choice but to abandon the shuttle.

But the astronauts could not do this, for several reasons. First of all, they were military guys, three of them were Navy, and it was considered poor form to give up the ship. But even more important, they knew they could never leave

the *Avenger* as long as the cargo they had picked up in
space—or "rescued" was the better word for it—still remained in the rear bay. If for some reason they got through
this ordeal alive, yet yielded what was in the cargo bay—
well, it would not be a life worth living. Their own government would charge them with desertion, convict them,
and have them shot—and not necessarily in that order. That
was how important they knew their cargo to be.

So, leaving the *Avenger* peacefully was not an option.

They had one thing working in their favor, though, and
it was an unexpected advantage. It was clear that however
the hijackers had done it, they believed that they had
snatched one of NASA's shuttles, and not a top-secret military spacecraft. The astronauts quickly set them straight on
that score, and then informed them, falsely, that the shuttle
was itself loaded with high explosives, to be used in cases
such as this. They told the hijackers that if anyone was
going to blow up the space shuttle, it would be them, the
astronauts, and that they would do it at the first sign that
the hijackers were going to move on them forcibly. And if
the shuttle was blown up, the U.S. was unlikely to pay very
much for a pile of rubble. The remains of a spacecraft that
wasn't supposed to exist in the first place weren't worth
very much to anyone.

Hearing all this, the hijackers literally told them, "We'll
get back to you," and then departed, sealing the door shut
with acetylene torches shortly afterward.

That had been three days ago.

They hadn't been back since.

"You know, when you really come down to it, it's all his
fault. . . ."

"Whose fault?"

"The guy in the back, who the fuck else?"

"Jessuzz, don't start this again!"

"Wait a minute, just hear me out, okay? You forget that I was supposed to be married today. Remember? So, *ex-cuuuuse* me if my stress readings are off the board. . . ."

"I don't give a shit where your stress readings are. The guy in the back was just doing his job, just like we were doing ours when they yanked us out of the sky. You can no more blame him than any of us. . . ."

"Yeah—but if he hadn't fucked up in the first place, we wouldn't have had to launch so goddamn fast, and in my opinion, that means we wouldn't be in this situation right now."

"The quick launch had nothing to do with it—I've been through sixteen goddamn quick launches. There's nothing magical about them—you go up, you come down. Besides, these mooks didn't even know what they were snatching, never mind what's inside the cargo bay. It was either us or the next NASA shuttle that went up. In some ways, we're lucky it was us. . . ."

"That's bullshit, man. And you know it. The fact is, if the fucking guy in the back hadn't fucked up and got caught up there, or whatever the hell he did, then none of this would have happened. I think he should be made aware that we know this. . . ."

"You don't think he knows that already? Look, we briefed him on the situation and he's been sitting back there ever since. You think in these three days the thought hasn't come across his mind, 'Hey maybe I fucked up and caused this'?"

"I just think we should be sure of that fact. . . ."

"Okay then, *you* go back and tell him . . . and maybe he'll blast you with a ray gun or something. *Anything* to shut you up. . . ."

●   ●   ●

Light depravation is a strange thing.

It can throw off the body's internal clock, affect the senses of sight and hearing, even smell. It also makes it difficult to judge time accurately. A person deprived of light for any long period of time might think his heart was beating abnormally slow—or too fast. Seconds could seem like minutes—or minutes like seconds. After a while in the dark, time itself seemed to lose its timing.

Which was why the astronauts didn't know how much time had passed between the beginning of their latest catfight and the sounds of gunfire that suddenly came to them.

However long it was, one moment they were arguing, the next, bullets were pinging off the side of the *Avenger*. They could even hear voices shouting, which was strange because the shuttle was virtually soundproof. Then they realized the gunshots were coming from right outside the main hatchway. Someone was shooting the welds off the door.

"Damn, this is it! Those fuckers are coming in to kill us!"

They stood by helplessly as the people on the other side of the door kept firing weapons. Finally the last weld was shot away and the hatch flew open. Dull light streamed into the shuttle for the first time in nearly four days, temporarily blinding the four spacemen.

What they could see, though, were the outlines of two soldiers coming through the door. But these weren't Arab fighters. These men were wearing oversized Fritz helmets, American uniforms, and carrying M-16's.

As one, the astronauts let out a cheer.

"Yes! You're here to rescue us!"

But before the soldiers could say a word, one of them slammed the door shut and locked it.

And suddenly, it was dark inside the shuttle again.

Two flashlights flipped on. The astronauts looked at the soldiers and the soldiers looked at the astronauts. No one said anything for what seemed like a very long time.

Finally, one astronaut spoke. "You *are* here to rescue us, right?"

"Not exactly," Jazz Norton replied.

22

Somewhere over Turkey

Takeoff in the SR-71 was especially bone-crushing this time.

Though it was the fastest conventional aircraft in the world, the spy plane really wasn't the most efficient. Its great speed worked best at great heights. In fact the heat from these high-altitude dashes was enough to shrink the airplane by a significant factor, literally sealing its fuel tanks and any other seam found that was not exactly flush. On the ground the thing leaked like a sieve.

This didn't mean the plane couldn't go fast at, say, forty thousand feet, though. It didn't need a nosebleed to haul ass. But to attain a high speed at a lower-than-usual altitude, the plane really had to get a full running start. This meant throttles wide open for the most kick-ass takeoff possible. Thus the sensation of bones being crushed in one's chest, as all that scenery just became sort of a blur and you found your bootlaces somewhere up near your chin. It was enough to take your breath away. Or even stop your heart.

But Gene Smitz was used to all that by now.

This was either his fifth or sixth takeoff in the last twenty-four hours—he couldn't remember which, nor could he have cared less. Other things seemed unimportant as well. He hadn't eaten anything of substance in three days. He'd only showered once. He still didn't know his pilot's name or how much the man knew, or whether he knew anything at all. The eyeball-blistering takeoffs had become routine. Smitz would simply count to forty or so, the time it took the Blackbird to climb seven or eight miles. Then came that very pleasant feeling as the pilot eased off the throttles. Suddenly that blur became clouds and the yellow streak became the sun. And the heart resumed beating. And your breath returned.

And suddenly you were flying again. . . .

But Smitz had become so nonchalant to all this by now, halfway up in this ascent he'd managed to reach inside his boot and retrieve a long piece of pale yellow paper. It was the printout from the Russian's fat-lap computer. It had come down from the ethers as a GIF image and despite the shoddy equipment, the image had been high-quality. And just as Smitz's new best friend Dmitri had promised, it *was* a big picture of a very big man.

And Smitz knew him. His name was Azu-mulla el-Zim, or more simply, Zim.

Zim was the criminal mastermind behind the deadly ArcLight affair; it was his people who were caught flying the rogue gunship. He'd been involved in the Russian air-craft carrier mutiny as well, initiating the huge black-market arms deal that sparked the ship's takeover.

As soon as Smitz saw the photo printout, it all fell together. Soda-pop blimps? Stealing space shuttles? Money to burn? Of course Zim was behind it all. No one else in the world could pull off such a flamboyant stunt. The guy was right out of a spy movie.

Or maybe a horror flick.

He weighed close to six hundred pounds. He had a taste for fish eyeballs and young Asian girls. He had more money than God; Osama bin Laden looked like a Boy Scout, both in his terrorist activities and his bank account, compared to the Great Zim. But Zim was such a demented prick, neither Saddamn or the Iranian mullahs nor anyone else in the terrorist underworld dared to defy him. He was as crude and bloodthirsty as any of the world's most dedicated militants—times ten.

"A well-connected, overweight, sick, demented prick with a ton of black-market connections," Smitz had whispered upon seeing the photo for the first time. "An octopus with a hundred arms."

"I hear he also collects fine art," Dmitri had said. That was when Smitz had thanked his new friend and sent him on his way. They'd meet in Moscow for drinks when this was over.

At the moment, though, Smitz still had things to do.

Or at least he thought he did. . . .

Now cruising at forty thousand feet, and closing in on 1500 mph without breathing hard, the SR-71 didn't have a destination. Not yet anyway.

Smitz knew who was behind the whole shuttle-hijacking operation—but now what? He had to talk to the seven ghostly CIA agents to see what the next step should be. The problem was, they always got in touch with him—he had no idea how to contact them. He wouldn't even know where to begin.

This dilemma was solved not two seconds after the thought went through his head. One of the small TVs on the very rudimentary control panel in front of him blinked on. It slowly coalesced into the image of the seven spies looking out at him from their dark, wooden chamber again.

There were no salutations this time. As soon as Smitz was sure the seven men could hear him, he began rattling off the story behind the meeting with Dmitri and what the Russian had given them.

"Zim was the number-one asshole on our suspect list," the Voice told Smitz, coming through loud and clear on his headset.

"Well, we know he was able to build a tracking station which deteriorated the shuttle's ability to stay in orbit," Smitz said. "And when it came down, he hid it. What I'd like to know is, where does the blimp come in?"

"An elaborate diversion was apparently pulled on our main rescue team," the Voice told him. "Zim was able to draw them into a huge ambush up in the Paswar mountains, and came close to killing some of our best people—and friends of yours, by the way."

"Team 66?"

"And those two fighter jocks, Norton and Delaney, too. We think Zim's people used the blimp to plant dummy shuttle parts inside this crater way the hell up near the Himalayas. Your friends found fake nozzles, a fake wing, a fake tail. They were all made of plywood, but were probably too big to lug up there by helicopter."

"So this fucking nut *steals a blimp* to haul all that shit up there?" Smitz asked, amazed at the audacity of such a scheme.

"We're guessing he lowered the wooden parts from the blimp," the Voice went on. "And then had people put them in place. Plus, the reports we intercepted of strange aircraft in the sky near the Paswar—making us believe the shuttle had come down there in the first place—were obviously the blimp as well, probably trailing some kind of EW device made to mimic something more substantial."

Smitz was amazed. "I don't know whether this guy needs a psychiatrist or a movie agent."

"Probably both," the Voice conceded. "He's crafty and he thinks big. He can hire just about anyone he wants—pilots, policemen, eggheads. And let's face it, he accomplished what he set out to do. He misdirected a lot of our people up there at the most crucial point of the search, while at the same time, putting the shuttle under wraps and covering his tracks."

A burst of static interrupted the broadcast, but just for a moment.

"The cold hard fact is," the Voice went on, "Zim could have the shuttle just about anywhere by now. I mean, Delta Force, the 82nd, the SEALs, you name it. They are all standing by, ready to act—but they don't know where to begin."

Smitz said: "Can I lock up the movie rights for this one now?"

The Voice ignored his joke. "The key thing now," he said, "is that *you've* got to determine his location . . . like immediately."

Smitz laughed. "Oh, really? And how long has the CIA been trying to find this guy? To prove whether he was alive or not?"

"About a year," was the humbled reply.

"And now you want me, *just* me, to find him? In, what, the next twenty-four hours?"

"Truth is, we don't have twenty-four hours," the Voice said. "This thing is really moving in a strange direction.

There's a possibility that some drastic action will be taken once the damn shuttle is finally found."

Smitz was confused: "What do you mean?"

"Due to certain circumstances . . . there might be pressure to take the ten-dollar solution."

Ten-dollar solution? That was a Spook term for taking the easy way out. But in this case, Smitz didn't think he liked the translation.

"Are you saying that when they do find it, they're thinking of . . . bombing it? With our guys still on board?"

Silence.

Ten long seconds of it.

Then the Voice said: "That's one of several options."

Smitz said: "But can't they kill time negotiating with this guy?"

"There will be no negotiating with Zim or anyone else," the Voice said. "Even if he did contact the U.S., which he hasn't. At least, not yet . . ."

Smitz couldn't fathom what he was hearing.

Why was the CIA planning to destroy the shuttle once they found it? Was it simply fear of having to negotiate with a wacko terrorist like Zim? Did they believe the shuttle was so valuable they could not allow it to fall into his hands—or anybody else's?

That just didn't seem likely. True, shuttles were marvels of technology, but the whole concept was hardly so top secret that you'd be willing to kill your own people just to keep one safe. It *had* to be something else.

Then another thought came into Smitz's weary head.

"What's inside this shuttle anyway?" he asked the seven agents directly. "Is it carrying some kind of cargo?"

No reply.

"I mean, that's the only thing that makes sense," he went

on. "Is there something inside that's so important, you to want to blow it up in order to save it?"

Nothing.

"C'mon, you guys—don't you think after all the bullshit I've gone through that I have a need to know?"

At that instant, the TV transmission disappeared from the control panel screen, to be replaced briefly by an episode of *Star Trek*—dubbed in Arabic.

Smitz just shook his head.

"I guess I'll take that as a no," he murmured.

Off the coast of Pakistan

The ships came out of nowhere.

There were five of them—all U.S. Navy. They arrived just after midnight, surrounding the USS *Bataan* like a fast-moving fog bank.

There were two missile cruisers, the *Virginia* and the *Ticonderoga*; two destroyers, the *Arleigh Burke* and the *Thomas S. Gates,* and the missile frigate *Neponset.*

From the bridge of the *Bataan,* Currier watched the shadowy squadron of ships take up station around his vessel. He had not been informed in advance of their movements.

"Suddenly we've become very popular," he thought. "Probably not a good thing."

As it so happened, Currier was good friends with the skipper of the *Gates,* an old Navy classmate named Hailey Koosman. No sooner had the *Gates* come up alongside the amphib ship than Currier had Koosman on the phone.

"What's the buzz, Koozer?" Currier asked his friend.

"Someone thought you needed company out here," was the guarded reply.

"Well, we haven't exactly been lonely," Currier told him.

There was a short silence, then Koosman came back on:

"How are you fixed for chow, Bear? You overextended anywhere?"

Currier got the hint. "Actually, we're very low on dairy stuff," he replied. "Got any overflow?"

Another silence.

"I've just checked with my supply officer," Koosman finally replied. "And yes, we'll be glad to lend you some. See you in about a half hour."

Exactly thirty minutes later, a supply copter from the *Gates* was landing on the *Bataan*'s deck.

Koosman himself was the first to step off the hump chopper. Currier was waiting for him; they greeted each other warmly. While a deck crew helped unload barrels of milk from the copter, Currier and Koosman walked toward the end of the deck.

"I can't tell you much, Bear," Koosman said once they were safely out of earshot. "Only that we're loaded to the gills with Tomahawk cruise missiles—and we've got a target grid that takes in just about all of Southwest Asia. From what I've been told, the exact IP has not yet been established. But when it is, we may be called on to launch on it."

"Sounds serious," Currier replied. "We've had some special-ops guys pass through here recently. I imagine there's got to be a connection."

"I don't doubt it," Koosman agreed as they reached the end of the flight deck. "But if they're anywhere inside our target grid, they better get a move on real quick. Our missiles are loaded with Type-6 HE warheads. Are you familiar with them?"

Currier shook his head.

"They call them fake-nukes," Koosman revealed. "Incredible coverage, incredible power. If they make the call to us, and we launch, whatever they want us to destroy will be destroyed utterly. Take it from me, there'll be nothing left."

"Not good news for anyone caught out there in the rain," Currier said.

"Anyone good, bad, or ugly," Koosman confirmed. "They won't have a prayer."

23

One hour later

"So, now you know everything that's happened to us in the past seventy-two hours."

Norton tried to stretch his battered body within the cramped confines of the *Avenger*'s tiny cockpit—with little success. He'd been through a lot in the past three days, including almost being killed a few times. Still, he didn't envy the ordeal that the four military astronauts had endured. From believing they were seconds away from certain death when their shuttle inexplicably began falling out of orbit, to being stuck here, in near-total darkness, with little food or water, rising tempers, surrounded by hundreds of armed fighters, going on four days now. Not the best way to spend a weekend.

The irony was, of course, that he and Delaney were now stuck here with them. After they'd escaped the gunfire following their crash, the tent had been the only logical place to try for. Taking advantage of the confusion after the Sea Harrier was blown up, they'd found an unguarded pathway through the parked cars and into the tent itself. Finding the shuttle within had been almost anticlimatic. They had done what they had set out to do—but a lot of good it did them. They were now locked inside the big white coffin. In the dark. With something tied down in the cargo bay that was *so* top secret (Norton's wild guess earlier had been a good one), that the astronauts spoke of it only in reverential whispers. The place was starting to give him the creeps already.

"Well, that's our story," said the one astronaut who had done most of the talking. "Now, why don't you start off by telling us where the hell we are."

"Just outside of Nowheresville, Pakistan," Norton replied. "They got a big party tent covering the shuttle, and the tent is surrounded by about three hundred Mercedes Benzes. The hills to the south have a lot of guys with guns hiding in them. They made it look like a huge wedding. After they brought you down, they most likely had their cars go back and forth over your landing tracks, obscuring them from above. I guess we've got to give them credit. Once they put you under the big top, you disappeared from the eyes of the world."

Norton then briefed them on the Paswar disaster and why he and Delaney had chosen to come back to this place.

The astronauts were astonished.

"Well, whoever pulled this thing off must be fucking brilliant," the alpha astronaut said.

"Yeah, brilliant and ballsy . . ." one of his colleagues agreed.

"Brilliant, ballsy, and devious . . ." said another.

"Well, we don't have to start a fan club just yet," Delaney interjected, his voice a slow drawl in the dark. "This was not an entirely foolproof plan they've concocted. I mean, they've made it work so far. But there are some holes showing."

Norton clicked his flashlight on and illuminated Delaney's face for a few seconds. These revelations were news to him.

"Please, go on," he told his partner.

"It's simple," Delaney continued. "They've got this thing under this big tent. They've got the place surrounded. They've pretty much kicked ass on any special-ops groups who might be inclined to come to the rescue, if and when this location is found."

"Yeah, so?"

"Well, that doesn't mean people still aren't looking for this tin can," Delaney said. "I'm sure they've got spy satellites, eavesdropping stuff, overflights around the clock. After all the shit that went down with us, they're probably concentrating right on this very neighborhood. Where are we? South Asia?"

"Southwest Asia," Norton corrected him.

"Yeah, whatever." Delaney plowed ahead. "So, I think the first thing we got to do is let everyone know just where we are."

"And how are you going to do that?" the lead astronaut asked him.

"I've got a plan in mind." Delaney smiled in the darkness. "But to be honest with you, before my friend and I go back out there to get our asses shot at again, I think we need a little bit of goodwill . . . on your part."

"Goodwill?" the lead astronaut said. "What are you talking about?"

"In your cargo bay, you know, 'the thing.' The *top-secret* thing?"

"What about it?"

"Tell us what it is."

The astronaut just laughed. "Get lost. We can't tell you and we *won't* tell you."

Delaney was instantly ticked off. "We risk our lives to come save you guys, and you won't even tell us what's in the back?"

"I don't see you saving anyone, cowboy," the malcontent astronaut declared. "You were practically *chased* in here, for Christ's sake."

"We prefer the term 'tactical infiltration,' " Delaney sniffed.

"Besides," the lead astronaut said, "that thing in the back is worth a trillion dollars. You hear me? A *trillion* dollars. Can you imagine how classified something that expensive must be?"

Delaney was really getting pissed now. Norton knew his partner would have clocked the bitchy astronaut in a heartbeat—if he had been able to see him, that is.

"A trillion dollars?" Delaney shot back. "Are you trying to impress me here?"

"We don't have to impress you, Clem. All you got to know is that's important shit in the back. Nothing else in this world is worth more. . . ."

"Really. Well, how about your life, asshole?" Delaney salvoed right back. "How much is *that* worth?"

Suddenly another voice spoke.

"*I'll* make a deal with you," the voice said.

The six of them froze. Someone else was in their midst. A seventh person was in the dark with them.

"If you help save us, I guarantee you'll find out what we are carrying in the back."

Norton pointed his flashlight in the direction of the voice. The man was standing next to the door leading to the rear cargo bay. No one had heard him open the hatch, no one knew how long he'd been sitting in the dark with them.

But the real shock came when Norton's beam found the man's face. Norton recognized him. Tall. Nordic-looking. White flight suit. Keds sneakers.

"Son of a bitch," Delaney whispered. "I was wondering when you'd show up."

It was the guy who flew the super-duper secret airplane. The guy who had come to their rescue twice in their two previous missions.

The guy they knew as Angel.

24

The tent was big, but it was not seamless.

It was tied down in dozens of places, and some of the stakes holding it into the ground went almost three feet deep. But there were openings on each of its corners. Unguarded openings.

Norton and Delaney already knew this. They had evaded their pursuers after the Sea Harrier crash by sprinting through the opening on the tent's southwest corner.

It was there that both pilots found themselves now, crouched next to a tied-back flap, peeking out from behind the nylon, their NightVision scopes cranked to full power.

Strangely, there were no guards within five hundred feet of the tent. The few armed men they could see walking picket duty were way out beyond the last line of cars. The spacecraft was indeed surrounded—but the hijackers were giving it a wide berth. Why?

The two pilots thought they knew. There were dozens of wooden crates stacked under the spacecraft. Each was packed with hundreds of sticks of plain old dynamite. No need for anything fancy like Cemex or *plastique* here. With the dynamite wired up in an elaborate system of electrical cables and fuses, it was obvious the hijackers weren't bluffing about destroying the shuttle. Strike a match, throw a switch, or push a button—it wouldn't make any difference. It would all go up and leave nothing behind.

The problem was, an accidental gun discharge, a stray signal from a cell phone, a windblown cigarette butt—all of them would accomplish the same result. And then the hijackers' prize would be gone. So they weren't taking any chances. The closest any of the guards got to the shuttle was one thousand feet, or more than three football fields away.

This was why Norton and Delaney's escape into the shuttle had been almost effortless.

Getting out would prove to be more difficult.

Before taking up station at the southwest tent opening, the two pilots had done a quick survey of the shuttle itself.

During their hasty entry, they hadn't noticed several things about the spacecraft, including the stacks of dynamite. Now they could see evidence of a very rough landing. All of the shuttle's tires were flat and the right-side landing gear was twisted, giving everything a slight tilt in that direction.

It was also clear that this was not an ordinary shuttle. First of all, it was not white, but gray—almost camo gray. And its outer skin was made up of bigger, less numerous, heat-resistant tiles. It carried no ID markings or emblems of any kind. It looked a bit sleeker, a bit more modern than the orbiters in NASA's aging fleet, if slightly smaller. It had a definite military air about it.

The shuttle's nose was pointing due east, so from their present position, the pilots had a clear view of everything to the south and west. The hill they knew as Exxon One was right in front of them. It was alive with silent activity. Many of the armed hijackers appeared to be stationed on the hill, which was odd, because . . .

"Were they all hiding up there when we first bounced in?" Delaney wondered. "Or did they take over the hill after we left?"

It was a good question. Could all of these fighters really have been hiding when the Ozzie and the Sea Cobra had touched down on Exxon One way back when? Lying low so as not to blow their cover? The Sharpur-say was about halfway from the *Bataan* to the Paswar, the only reason it was picked as the refueling stop. If the armed fighters were already there, and they saw the two American aircraft coming, it must have caused a massive case of pants soiling. Of all the hills in Pakistan, the Americans had decided to land on this one. What were the chances of that? The relief when the two aircraft left must have been just as liberating. And maybe *that* was why the Hokums were waiting to ambush the American aircraft in the deep snowy river valley shortly after they left Exxon One. Or maybe they knew the Americans were coming all along.

But whatever the case, the armed men were now covering the infamous hill as well as all the high ground on either side of it. Burrowed into the tree-covered slopes, their weapon positions expertly hidden from everything except NightVision, some fighters were manning heavy machine-gun posts; others were equipped with rocket launchers and mortars. The pilots could also see APCs, and heavy mobile guns. There had to be at least a couple hundred caftan-clad fighters just in the hills alone.

"Man, these guys came to party," Norton said, scanning the multitude of gun positions.

"Yeah, I've seen this movie before," Delaney drawled. "And I don't recall it ending too well for the cowboys."

Norton checked the time. It was 0430 hours. It would be light soon. They had to get to work.

The plan was simple. The tent itself was the problem. If they were somehow able to get it off the shuttle, in one act, the hijackers' cover would be blown.

But how to do it? They couldn't dislodge or chop down the tent poles. That would only cause the tent to fall on top of the spacecraft, hiding it even more than now.

There was only one other way then. . . .

The wind began howling, as if on cue. Norton pulled a huge knife from his boot pocket.

"You ready, Slick?"

Delaney retrieved a gigantic knife of his own.

"Ready as I'll ever be," he replied.

To those armed fighters on the hill overlooking the vast plain, it seemed at first like the wind was blowing just a little harder than usual.

It was still the middle of the night for the small army of hijackers, and the majority of them were asleep at their posts. For them too, this had been a long and tiring affair. Most of the people up here were hired hands, Islamic fighters from northwest Afghanistan, the one part of that country the Taliban did not yet control. Their job was to guard the hijacked shuttle, while keeping a low profile themselves, at least until negotiations commenced with the U.S. This they had been able to do to near perfection since the *Avenger* was forced to land here three days before. Until tonight, that is.

The fighters had become used to the rippling noise made by the night winds buffeting up against the wedding tent. The sides of the enclosure were pulled tight nearly everywhere, but this did not mute the distinctive sound whenever the wind picked up to a healthy gale.

But now, suddenly this noise became louder. A *lot* louder. So loud it woke up those fighters still sleeping. Then came a sickening crackling sound. Almost like a huge tree toppling in the forest.

This brought most of the armed men up to the edge of the hill. They saw one end of the tent had been severed from its poles and was being lifted up by a huge gust of wind. Suddenly this gale got under the rest of the tent, and with a thunderous rip, blew it off its spars, sending it like a parachute into the night.

And just like that, the shuttle was bare-ass for all to see.

All hell broke loose in the hijackers' camp. Officers began running around, waking their men and screaming orders at them. In seconds, scores of fighters were running to their cars and in a wild, dusty scene, went screeching off after the tent, chasing it as it blew its way down the ten-mile-long plain.

What had happened? Had the tent ropes broke from simple wear and tear? Or had they been cut? No one knew. One company of fighters immediately ran down the hill, intent on attacking those inside the shuttle. But their officers called them back. There was no way they could take such an extreme action on their own.

Not without notifying the man behind this operation first.

The problem was, no one wanted to make that call.

There were seven unit chiefs on top of the hill; they were the closest thing the hijackers had to a command structure. They knew the change in the situation would not sit well with the individual who'd been financing this scheme all along. Yet they had to update him immediately.

These seven chiefs now gathered at the flattened spot located about halfway down the pathway that led off the hill. It was there that they had drawn, and then forgotten to erase, an outline of the purloined shuttle. Truth be known, the sketch had been drawn, even before the shuttle had left orbit, simply as a way of telling the hired fighters which direction the spacecraft would be pointing when it fell out of the sky to its unlikely landing spot on the Sharpur-say plain.

But by not brushing it out, they had tipped the Americans to come back here, looking for the missing shuttle. That was what the intruding jet fighter had been doing earlier that night—luckily the hijackers had managed to shoot it down. But there was no way any one of them wanted to tell that story to the man in charge either.

But now they had a *real* problem. The shuttle was undraped. Exposed. Out on the featureless plain, it stuck out like a sore thumb, even in the waning darkness. When the sun came up, it would be in full view of anything flying overhead, be it a recon plane or a spy satellite.

And this was not good.

So, the Great Zim had to be called. But who was going to do the dirty work? Who would break this terrible news to a man who shot his manservant of twenty-two years simply because the snake cream for his coffee had arrived a bit too warm?

Huddled now in the small clearing, stepping on the drawing of the shuttle, but still not rubbing it out, the seven chiefs solved this dilemma by deciding to summon the most insignificant, lowest-ranking fighter from each of their groups. When these seven men arrived at the clearing, six were immediately deemed too good-looking for what the chiefs had in mind and dismissed. The seventh man, a young fighter named Ahmed Qil, was then informed that he was about to become a communications specialist.

Qil's chief produced a cell phone. Zim's number was dialed and the cell phone handed to the young fighter before the first ring. Eventually the Great Zim himself came on the line, and reading from hastily scrawled notes, Qil delivered the bad news to the billionaire terrorist.

The return conversation was brief. The young fighter received a one-sentence reply and then the connection went dead.

Qil turned off the cell phone and then said: "The Great Zim himself is coming here. And he says he is bringing the two amigos with him."

The seven chiefs gasped as one. Each man felt his hand involuntarily go to his throat. This was not good news.

Qil's commander took back the cell phone, then drew a pistol from his belt and shot the young fighter in the head, killing him instantly.

Then he turned to his six counterparts and said: "If Zim and the two amigos are coming, then we will be joining this young martyr in Paradise way too soon."

25

Was it possible to dream at eighty thousand feet?

Going more than three times the speed of sound, so close to the edge of space that you could see the stars in the daytime, were a person's dreams too slow to catch up?

This seemed like a very intriguing question at the moment—but Gene Smitz would not get the answer. At least not anytime soon.

For the first time in more than four days, he'd actually started to nod off. To finally drift off into an uninterrupted slumber. He was still strapped into the backseat of the SR-71; they'd climbed nearly sixteen miles high, and were now doing the operation the Blackbird had been built for: high-speed recon.

And they had acquired a new destination. If Smitz's mission now was to find Zim, he figured the best way to do that was to look for the shuttle. Because wherever the hijacked spacecraft was located, the billionaire terrorist probably wouldn't be that far away. So, after hearing about the

ambush up on the Paswar, Smitz decided that was as good
a place to start searching as any.

They reached the crater not an hour after taking off from
Turkey. Just a bit drowsy at this point, Smitz was able to
watch the real-time TV broadcast of the images being re-
corded by the spy plane's myriad of cameras. The top of
the Paswar crater was still smoking in places when they
arrived. Wrecked helicopters, blown-up gun emplacements,
bodies—even from this great height Smitz could clearly see
the circle of destruction. The mayhem contrasted utterly
with the pristine high-altitude terrain surrounding the crater.

Some gray helicopters were in evidence around the crater
as well.

From there, they'd turned south.

Smitz knew a little bit about how Zim operated. During
the ArcLight operation, Zim had set up a dummy aircraft
that initially fooled the American strike team. But as it
turned out, the real gunship was actually very close by. If
that was the case again here, then Smitz was guessing the
shuttle might be somewhere in Pakistan.

It was at that point that his body finally began to turn on
him. Even though his brain was still processing information, everything below his nasal passages was falling
asleep. Whether Zim even knew what he had or not, those
deep in the U.S. intelligence community felt it was better
to destroy it than allow·it to fall into Zim's hands. It was
an ancient military theorem. As a last resort you destroy
something that is so valuable to you, you just cannot allow
it to fall into your enemy's hands.

So whatever was in the back of the shuttle, and how it
got there, was . . . almost . . . irrelevant now . . . because . . .

These were the thoughts that were going through his

mind when he leaned back, closed his eyes—and finally felt his eyelids start to droop.

And not a second later, the pilot's voice suddenly came over his headset.

"I think you should see this," was all he said.

Smitz was instantly jolted back to the real world. The main CRT screen on his control panel was coming alive. It was the live feed from the SR-71's infrared camera. It had detected a smudge of heat that hadn't been there just seconds before. Smitz stared at the ghostly image for a few moments, allowing his brain to fill in the spots not being shown by the heat-sensitive camera. Slowly but surely the image turned into a rough outline of a winged craft of some kind, long snout, with a roughly delta configuration.

"Son of a bitch, that was easy," Smitz breathed.

It was the shuttle.

Aboard the USS *Thomas Gates*

The flash message reached the destroyer *Gates* at 0515 hours local time.

The target grid for the anticipated missile attack had finally been narrowed to an impact point. All ships in the shadow force were told they should set their Tomahawk cruise missiles accordingly. They should be ready to launch anytime after 0550 hours.

Inside the ship's combat management center, Captain Koosman reviewed the message with his weapons team. The targeting process had already begun. Their ultra-high-explosive Tomahawks were being given last-minute systems' updates. As it turned out, the impact point was barely a quarter mile square. This gave the pending attack a historical aspect. If all five ships in the shadow task force were told to launch their full complement of Tomahawks, it would constitute the most concentrated cruise-missile attack ever.

"They want dust?" Koosman thought. "They'll get dust."

He was heading back up to the bridge when he was handed another message, this one from the officer of the watch. Some unusual activity had been spotted on the deck of the *Bataan*.

Koosman reached the bridge in time to see two strange helicopters in the process of warming up on the deck of the nearby amphib ship. Even without using his electronic binoculars, Koosman could make out a line of shadowy armed men boarding the ancient double-rotor choppers. No sooner were the troops on board than the two aircraft lifted off from the *Bataan* and turned north, toward Pakistan. Then engines obviously cranked up to top speed.

Koosman quickly had Currier on the phone.

"Hey, Bear? None of my business really—but what the hell *was* that?"

"The two aircraft we just launched?" Currier replied.

"Yes, of course," Koosman told him.

There was a short silence on the other end of the phone.

Finally Currier said: "How much time you got, Koozer? It's a long story. . . ."

26

Sharpur-say

It was right after sunup, just as the dull early morning glow began glinting off the newly revealed space shuttle, that someone came knocking on the spacecraft's main door.

Even as the astronauts dove for cover, Norton and Delaney had their weapons up in a flash. They took up positions on either side of the hatch. Then Norton toed it open. Two middle-aged men were waiting on the other side. They were both wearing suit coats and ties. One was carrying a briefcase; the other was holding a white flag. They appeared unarmed.

"Who the *hell* are you guys?" Norton asked them harshly.

In smooth Arabic-tinged English one man replied: "We are the lawyers."

Norton and Delaney looked at each other. *Lawyers?*

"Lawyers for who?" Norton asked them.

"Who cares? Let's just shoot them now!" Delaney yelled.

The two men smiled nervously. They were one of Zim's most prized weapons. They were, in fact, the two *amigos*.

But at the moment, they both seemed a bit confused.

"We were under the impression that there were only four people aboard," one said, doing a head count in the small cockpit. "How did you two gentlemen get here?"

"None of your business," Norton told them, pulling the two men inside the shuttle and getting out of the line of fire.

"So what do you want?" Delaney asked them sternly.

"We have been authorized to invite you to a negotiating session," one man said. "It is hoped this will be a constructive discussion between interested parties, one that might help resolve this current impasse."

"Oh, yeah? And who's running this love-fest?" Norton asked them.

Both lawyers began stammering a bit.

"Well . . . our client, of course," one finally spat out. "The gentleman who is responsible for your present situation."

"It really is in your best interest to come," the second lawyer added.

The pilots again looked at each other. Was this a good thing or not? They didn't know. Behind them the astronauts had come out of hiding. They didn't seem to know either.

"If they want to talk, maybe you guys should go talk to them," the lead astronaut finally said. "Me and my men are staying here, though. We ain't separating from our ship."

Norton turned back to the lawyers.

"What are the conditions for this 'negotiation'?"

"There are none," one lawyer said with a smile. "This offer is unconditional."

"So was Robert E. Lee's surrender," Delaney noted coolly.

"We're not going unarmed," Norton told them.

The lawyers had a hushed conversation.

"Nor would we expect you to," one said finally. "In fact, we encourage you to bring your weapons."

"I don't like the sound of that," one astronaut opined.

Norton said: "We get to bring our weapons *and* you guarantee that nothing happens to the other people on board here while we are gone . . . is that a deal?"

The lawyers conferred briefly again.

"Yes, it's a deal," one declared.

"And we ain't *signing* anything. . . ." Delaney told them.

Another conference.

"Okay, deal . . ."

A long silence.

"Do you accept then?" one of the lawyers asked.

Norton turned back to Delaney and the astronauts. They all knew that at any minute the pendulum could swing the other way and the hijackers might see the wisdom of just storming the shuttle, and killing them all, and then letting the chips fall where they may.

The question was, if the newly uncovered spacecraft was spotted, could a rescue force get here before the hijackers felt it was time to make their move?

More importantly, would "negotiating" buy some valuable time? Or simply waste it?

"I say we do it," Norton finally said. "Who knows, maybe they think *we've* got *them* over a barrel."

Delaney asked him: "Why in the world would they think that?"

Norton just shrugged. "I don't know. But if it wasn't true, would they have really sent the lawyers?"

• • •

They walked off the shuttle, the lawyers in front of them,
one waving his white flag, the other his briefcase.

The Sharpur-say plain looked a lot different up close in
the daylight. Bigger. Drier. More isolated, especially now
that the big tent was gone.

There were still no guards within a thousand feet of the
shuttle. Many of the cars were gone as well. But something
new had been added. Out beyond the first line of guards,
just in front of Exxon One, a big white structure had suddenly materialized. It was constructed of six prefab units,
elongated house trailers whose modular edges had been
bolted together, with a roof put on top. Norton and Delaney
had never seen anything like it. The structure had been
hauled into place by a half-dozen enormous trucks now
parked nearby.

Dome-shaped and adorned with Muslim-style details, the
structure looked like a palace. On wheels.

"A 'portable palace'?" Norton whispered to Delaney.

"That's what we call outhouses back where I'm from,"
Delancy drawled in reply.

There was a large group of armed men milling about in
front of this structure. Many were carrying heavy weapons.
Several mobile guns and ancient Russian-built BMP personnel carriers were also in evidence.

"A display of force," Norton whispered to Delaney.
"They're trying to intimidate us. . . ."

"Crazy kids," Delaney scoffed.

They reached the line of armed men. Each was wearing
a dirty white turban and an assortment of blankets as clothing. They looked tough, grim. Few had been to the dentist
lately. Or the barbershop.

The armed men made way for them grudgingly. The lawyers guided Norton and Delaney through this gauntlet, then

walked them up the twenty-step staircase that led to the front door of the structure.

This entrance was also heavily guarded. But the armed men stationed here seemed twice as big, twice as ugly as the other fighters around them. In fact, they were members of the Black Squad, one of the most feared terrorist mercenary units in the world. These men were glowering at Norton and Delaney's weapons, but did nothing to take them away.

At this point, the lawyers hastily shook hands with the two pilots, then signaled for their car. A gold Mercedes limo roared up with a screech, and the two *amigos* headed down the steps for it.

"Due in court, guys?" Delaney called after them.

"Something like that," one of them called back.

They climbed into the car and were gone, the Mercedes kicking up a storm of dust as it retreated hastily from the scene.

"Ain't that typical," Delaney breathed.

One of the huge guards opened the main door now and with a grunt, indicated Norton and Delaney should go inside.

"Thanks, Sunshine," Delaney told him.

The palace seemed twice as strange on the inside as it was outside. It was actually one large hall, with low, star-painted ceilings, and a huge revolving ball in its center that made the place look like a discotheque. There were luxurious couches and divans scattered everywhere; Oriental rugs ran from wall to wall. There were even some plastic faux columns, swirling colors of yellow and green, like something out of *1001 Arabian Nights*.

In the middle of the hall was a small mountain of pillows. Sitting atop all these feathers was the largest human being Norton and Delaney had ever seen.

He was huge, grotesquely so. He had a very fat, flat face, his features practically impossible to distinguish due to all the excess epidermis. He had the poorest excuse for a goatee on record. What's more, he was wearing a blue dressing gown, ladies' gloves, and a jewel-encrusted turban. He looked like a huge mealworm in drag.

"I'm guessing this guy has been eating nothing but macaroni and cheese since birth," Delaney whispered to Norton. "And that dress adds at least fifty pounds. . . ."

"Be cool, bro," Norton cautioned him. "Don't you know who that is?"

Delaney took another look.

Then it hit him.

"I'll be damned," he said. "Is that the Great Zim?"

"Know anyone else who tips the scales like that?"

"But I thought we greased this guy, you know, after we KO'd the ArcLight gunship."

"So did I," Norton replied. "And I'd say this might be his evil twin, but I don't think there's enough food in the world to feed two of them."

The enormous Zim looked down at them. His breathing was so labored, it sounded like he was snoring.

"So this must be the famous Jazz Norton," he said in a very bizarre girlish voice. "I've followed your career for years."

Delaney was immediately insulted. "Hey, I'm here too, pal," he said.

Zim looked down at Delaney and in a perfectly dismissive tone, said: "Oh, yes, hello, Tonto . . ."

Zim snapped his fingers and one of the huge Black Squad guards held out a bowl of grapes for him. At least they looked like grapes.

"For some reason I'm not surprised to find you two mixed up in this," Zim said in his weird singsongy voice.

"But really, shouldn't you both be drunk in a bar some-place?"

"Don't knock a liquid diet until you tried it, Tiny," De-laney shot back at him.

Meanwhile Norton was appraising the situation. There were fourteen Black Squad guards inside the room, ten standing on a platform behind Zim. Two flanking Zim him-self. Two more at the door. Others were probably looking in from somewhere else.

Though they'd been allowed to walk in with their weap-ons, Norton was sure he and Delaney would lose a shoot-out against the Black Squad gunmen. They all looked anxious to start firing right now. The only thing running in the pilots' favor was the size of this mobile royal com-partment. While expansive as these things go, it was nev-ertheless too small for accurate gunplay. Anyone could get hit if the bullets started flying in here, including Zim. And it wasn't like his bodyguards would be able to hustle him away at the first sign of trouble. The man must have weighed six hundred pounds, if not more.

Norton's conclusion: The guards might be reluctant to shoot first.

But there was an added complication here. A small port-able computer was set up right next to Zim's summit of pillows. On its screen was a 3-D image of the *Avenger*, dynamite packs in place. In the upper right-hand corner of the screen there was a red field with the words "Start Arm-ing Sequence" blinking inside. Obviously, this was the mechanism for detonating the explosives under the shuttle. In fact, Zim was twiddling with a remote-control device that appeared to be dedicated just to that event.

"Well, you wanted to talk," Norton finally yelled up to Zim. "So, talk."

Zim laughed and inhaled a small slimy greenish ball.

"Let's make it simple," he said. "Give us the shuttle peacefully and we'll let you go . . . with your throats intact."

Delaney laughed out loud. "Take a freakin' hike, big boy," he said. "Who do you think you're dealing with here? A couple of morons?"

Zim ate another grape-like globule. "Well, you must admit, finding yourselves in this position, you're not exactly geniuses," he said. "Unless of course you *intended* to get shot down last night . . . which would make you absolute fools."

He bit hard on another greenish ball. The squish alone told Norton it was probably not a grape. A fishy odor was slowly filling the room.

"Look, let's cut the crap," Norton said. "You wanted us here—so here we are. Now what?"

Zim began chewing very noisily. The fishy smell was stronger than ever. "Well, this is the part in the movie where I threaten you into doing what I want, I guess."

"Why bother with us?" Delaney said. "They ain't ever going to let you just take this shuttle, little man, whether we're in it or not. It's the most valuable thing in the world to them. They'll do anything to get it back, in one piece—no matter what happens to us."

Zim smiled—his teeth were cracked and stained.

"You really believe that, do you, Tonto?" Zim asked. "Well, what would you say if I told you that there is a squadron of your warships in the waters to the south, ready and waiting to launch a cruise-missile attack. On you. On me. On that very valuable shuttle. Are you surprised to hear that?"

The answer was yes—both pilots were very surprised. But they tried not to show it.

"What's your point?" Norton asked Zim instead.

"My point is that maybe I should deal with you before

your military decides that killing us all and destroying the spacecraft is their easy way out."

Norton slung his gun over his shoulder.

"I guess we should make ourselves clear," he told Zim. "You can't deal with us, because we don't have any juice to deal. Your only real option is to let our guys just retrieve the shuttle—somehow—and we'll go our separate ways."

"Yeah, think of it," Delaney told Zim. "You'll live to terrorize again."

Zim laughed—and this time it sounded very cruel.

"Well, you see, that's where you are wrong, Mr. Jazz," he said. "Because I actually do have another option. Now believe me, there was no way I wanted this to become any more melodramatic than it already is. But, you leave me no choice."

He clapped his hands together; a baby would have generated more torque.

"I would say these negotiations are ended. . . ."

On those words, the ten men behind Zim raised their weapons.

But oddly, Norton was not looking at the gunmen. Instead, his eyes were drawn to Zim and specifically his hands. Zim was dressed like a woman, there was no other way to describe it. But for the first time Norton realized he was wearing two different gloves. One was sort of a church-lady's white glove. But the other was gray. And not so Sunday-looking. With the initials A.L. on it.

Norton was squinting so much his eyes began to hurt.

Was Zim wearing Amanda's other glove?

The shots rang out an instant later. There was no way either Norton or Delaney could have raised their weapons in time. Six bullets hit Delaney square in the chest. Five hit Norton in the stomach. They were both thrown back a dozen feet, landing in a crumpled heap against the palace's far wall.

Norton had never been shot before.

He had no idea what it felt like. He remembered looking down at his stomach and feeling as if he'd been hit with a concrete block. He looked over at Delaney, who was flat on his face, making a frightening gurgling sound. Norton could hear Zim laughing—his was just one of the many voices filling his head. Five shots to the stomach, Norton thought. There was no way he was going to survive this. . . .

More voices. His parents. His friends. His colleagues. It was as if they were all coming through a very staticky headphone. Many voices, speaking as one, but none of them distinctly.

So this is what it's like to die. . . .

A moment later, the floor beneath him began shaking. Then the air itself started to move. *Boom!* Norton's eardrums literally exploded, assaulted by the loudest noise he'd ever heard. Even in death he could not believe anything could sound so loud. The palace was nearly ripped apart by the violent concussion. Norton looked down at his hands. They were covered with blood.

Not from his stomach wound—but from his ears.

He put his hands to his face, and was surprised that he could still feel their touch. He took a deep breath and felt no more than the tight knot in his stomach. He looked down at his belly and saw no blood, no guts. Just five dull-colored pieces of lead, still burning into his uniform.

His flak jacket had worked as advertised. The boron plates had stopped all five bullets. He was still alive—at least for the moment.

But that horrible noise? What had that been?

The beginning of a cruise-missile attack?

Or something else?

Boom!

Once again, Norton felt a tremendous blast go right through him. The shaking became so violent inside the palace, he was sure it would disintegrate at any second. The lights began blinking madly. Norton's ears were bleeding heavily, but he could still hear hundreds of voices screaming in his head. And strangely enough, the loudest belonged to Captain Currier. His subject was revenge. *That* was why Norton had come here. He was shot, but he'd somehow survived. He was certain cruise missiles were dropping all over the plain outside—and that the next one might come through the front door at any moment.

Boom!

But he still wanted his pound of flesh.

And now was as good a time as any to get it.

An instant later, he was up and firing his weapon.

His first bullet went right between Zim's eyes. He was sure of this. His second and the third got caught somewhere in the man's enormous flab.

Norton could hardly see a thing. The lights above him were still blinking wildly, but they were staying off longer than staying on. He fired off two more bursts. One of them smashed into the big disco ball, shattering it into a million pieces. Then he slumped back to the floor and crawled over to Delaney.

His friend was still facedown, still making that awful gurgling sound. Norton rolled him over—and discovered the gurgling noise was actually Delaney laughing. He too was hurting from six direct hits in the chest; but each one of them had been stopped by his flak jacket. And so he was laughing, happy to be still alive.

"I'm glad you're enjoying yourself," Norton told him. "I

think I nailed the big flat slob, though. Too bad he won't
live to regret what he pulled up in the Paswar."

Delaney rolled over and retrieved his weapon. The lights
flickered on again—in that instant they could see a gaggle
of Black Squad goons staring back at them no more than
twenty feet away. The gunmen were astonished that Norton
and Delaney were still alive.

But the stupor didn't last long. The gunmen raised their
weapons and pulled their triggers. . . .

Then the lights went out again.

Norton and Delaney avoided the fusillade by rolling in
opposite directions. Norton tumbled over a divan and found
himself up against one of the phony plastic columns. The
lights came back on. Norton had his M-16 up and ready.
He sighted on the goon nearest to him and blew the man's
throat away. The lights went out again.

Norton scrambled away from the faux column, just seconds before it was disintegrated in a hail of gunfire. He
now hunkered down behind an overturned couch. The
lights came on again. Norton shot another goon, hitting him
twice in the heart. At the same instant, Norton saw Delaney
roll right across the floor in front of him, firing his M-16
wildly. With a move that would have rivaled any TV cowboy, he managed to blow apart the one last light hanging
from the palace ceiling.

The room was plunged into total darkness now—for
about two seconds. Then the emergency lights came on.

They were dozens of red bulbs buried inside the ceiling
and walls. They were like photo darkroom lights. Now the
big room was bathed in an eerie dull red.

Then the noise came again.

Boom!

Again the entire portable palace was shaken down to its
bolts. Norton's ears seemed to explode once again. If he

ever did get out of this one alive, he feared he'd be deaf
for the rest of his life. Wiping the blood from his ears again,
he lifted his rifle and began popping out the red bulbs. Then
he saw a hint of movement to his right. The two biggest
guys in Zim's entourage had been standing next to the main
entryway. Norton fired off a burst in that direction, and
caught one of them still flat-footed from the last tremendous
explosion.

Meanwhile, Norton saw Delaney roll again, this time to
his left, during which he was firing his M-16 at the guards
who were huddled behind the mountain of pillows. A storm
of tracer bullets came back in reply. Norton dove behind
another faux column and drilled another guard who'd been
stationed off to his right.

There was much screaming going on now as some of the
wounded guards slowly and painfully began to die. The gun
battle raged in spurts. The inside of the palace would be
crisscrossed with zinging bullets and lit by muzzle blasts
one second—then nothing for a few seconds more. Then it
would start up all over again. There were at least ten bad
guys left, but in the panic and confusion following the last
explosion, one had shot another, and suddenly they were
all shooting at anything that moved, including each other.

Norton stayed low during this brief spate of unintentional
internecine bloodletting.

Boom!

The portable palace shook once again; the walls began
flapping as if caught in an earthquake. Norton couldn't tell
if the cruise missiles were getting closer or if the sudden
explosions were just getting louder. Having never been in
the middle of a cruise-missile storm before, he had no idea
what it sounded like when the Tomahawk with your name
on it finally came down upon your head. But this latest
explosion seemed twice as loud, twice as earsplitting as the

first. Norton felt his eyes go out of focus, the noise was that brutal.

But it also gave him the opportunity to jam another clip into his M-16.

The bad guys were now regrouping. Two of them sent a stream of tracer fire over Norton's head. He lifted his rifle and blindly fired off three bursts of three in the general direction of the pillows. He heard two thuds and a gasp in reply. At the same moment he scrambled out from behind the faux column and dove behind a couch. A second later, the column was obliterated by the combined fire of the remaining guards.

Norton fired off another burst in the direction of the pillows, killing one goon and wounding another. At the same moment Delaney went rolling by him—*again*—adding his barrage to Norton's and greasing another guard.

Then Norton finally stopped to catch his breath. Incredibly, not even a minute had passed since the shooting began.

Boom!

The Tomahawks must be carrying concussion warheads, Norton caught himself thinking as the palace was rocked again by an earsplitting explosion. The follow-up roar was just as horrible. Despite being in the midst of this uneven gunfight, Norton dropped his weapon and covered his ears this time—he just couldn't take the full force of the trailing blast again.

Dazed by the tremendous clamor and bone-shaking vibrations, a guard wandered right in front of him. Norton steeled himself, took his fingers from his ears before the noise had entirely faded away, and picked up his gun again. He took the man out at the knees; he seemed too helpless a target to kill outright. No sooner had he done this when a stream of bullets hit the couch he was using for cover, one round coming so close, it actually shaved a piece off his earlobe.

That was when he spun around to see a huge guard standing over him, his AK-47 pointed right at his forehead. There wasn't enough time for Norton to lift his gun or even see his life flash before his eyes. And unfortunately, he was not covered head-to-toe with boron plating. The goon began squeezing his trigger. . . .

But then suddenly, half of the man's skull wasn't there. A stream of bullets had caught him square on the temple. He fell over in a heap. An instant later Delaney rolled by Norton yet again, shouting: "You owe me, buddy!"

The gunfire died down once more. The sounds of everyone reloading could be heard above the muffled cries and labored breathing of the dying. Norton figured there were six bad guys left. He was running out of ammo, and so was Delaney.

Boom!

This one caught Norton totally off guard. He fell over even before the palace floor began shaking. He hit his shoulder hard on a piece of broken couch, then collided with a thick chunk of something that nailed him right in the groin. He managed to roll right again, dragging himself up against one of the few fake plastic pillars that were still standing.

That was when he saw a guard crawling up the mountain of bloody pillows about fifteen feet away. The man was badly shot up, in obvious agony, yet he was moving with such determination, a grotesque smile plastered on his face.

What was so important at the top of the pillows that this guy was using his last ounce of strength to get it?

Then it hit him. Zim's remote control. Norton could see it lying next to the bloody mass he assumed was Zim himself. He felt his veins freeze. If the guy reached the remote,

he would detonate the explosives underneath the *Avenger*—
assuming the shuttle was still in one piece.

Damn, *another* complication.

Norton raised his weapon, pulled the trigger, and fired
two shots at the man. Then his gun went dry.

The guard was now about six feet from the remote. Norton frantically looked around for another weapon. If this
was a movie, the floor would have been strewn with the
weapons of dead bad guys. But not now.

With a deep gulp, Norton reached into his boot and took
out his enormous Bowie knife.

This would not be pretty.

He dashed across the room and landed right on top of
the guy. He was one of Zim's closest bodyguards, and thus
was a huge person. Norton first began beating him with the
butt of his empty M-16. But even though the man was
mortally wounded, he still had the strength to toss Norton
off like a rag doll.

Out of the corner of his eye, Norton saw Delaney roll
across the floor—again! The room was suddenly alive with
gunfire once more. A fire had started in the far corner. Now
smoke was filling the place as well.

Norton got back up and pounced on the bad guy again.
Again the huge man threw him off like a flea and resumed
his crawl toward the detonation controls. Norton was frantically looking about him for a gun—he so wanted to just
shoot this guy instead of stabbing him. It would be like
stabbing a side of beef. Besides, Norton had never stabbed
anyone to death before, and he really didn't want to start
now.

But there were no fucking guns anywhere. So he jumped
on the man again. By this time, the guard was just a foot
away from the remote control. He was reaching out for it.
Norton began slashing with his knife at the guard's arm,

but the man was wearing a heavy combat suit and the blade barely went through to his skin. All the while Norton was wrestling with him—and it was like wrestling with a bear. A huge, bleeding, pissed-off bear.

The man's fingers were within two inches of the remote now. And even though Norton was trying to hold him back with all his might, the guy was just too strong for him. So Norton went to his only option and it was a grisly one. He took a mighty slash at the man's fingers and cut off three of them at the knuckle.

The man opened his mouth to scream, but what came out instead was another tremendous *Boom!*

It was followed by such an earsplitting roar, Norton fell across the computer's keyboard, nearly detonating the explosives himself. Somehow he managed to yank out all the wires leading out of the computer. Then he crushed the remote with his bare hands. Then he rolled back down to the floor and covered his ears and felt the tremendous shock wave go through him again.

The next thing he knew, Delaney had rolled over to him, again firing all the way. They saw two streams of tracers coming right at them. They ducked—the fusillade went over their heads. Delaney threw something at Norton. It was a clip for his empty M-16. Norton jammed it into his rifle and began returning fire. Two yelps and a thud told him he'd beaten another bad guy to the punch.

And that was enough lucky shooting for him. He wanted to get out of this place fast.

Resisting the urge to crawl back up the pillows and check Zim's hand wear, he grabbed Delaney instead and began dragging him to the main door. His partner needed no prompting; Norton was just preventing him from rolling right out of the palace. Though the gunfire had died away inside the structure, they could hear lots of commotion outside.

Boom!

This blast knocked them both back to the floor. The mechanical scream that followed was tremendous. Much more of this and Norton was certain his eardrums would be destroyed forever.

The noise slowly subsided, and they crawled to the front door. But now what? They had to get out of the burning palace. But to where? Back to the shuttle? It was their only option, now that the "negotiations" had ended so badly. But Norton wasn't too happy about their chances of making it out in one piece. Cruise-missile attack notwithstanding, there were certainly more of Zim's gunmen waiting outside. The area had been thick with them when Norton and Delaney went into the palace—those that hadn't been blasted away were undoubtedly still around.

A scene from a movie flashed through Norton's mind. Two cowboys who had escaped by the skin of their teeth many times before were about to try it again. Facing hundreds of guns, they start to run, the gunfire erupts . . . and the movie goes into a freeze frame. And that's how it ends.

"You ready, Butch?" Delaney asked him. He'd been thinking of the same movie.

"After you, Sundance," Norton replied with grim humor.

Without a second's hesitation, Delaney kicked the door open and out he flew. Norton was right on his heels. Down the stairs and across the hard desert, they had their M-16's up and firing in every direction. It was about a hundred yards to the first line of cars, and then a zigzag run through them to the relatively safety of the shuttle—the one with all the explosives still around it. Norton guessed they wouldn't make it past the twenty-yard line.

But after running full tilt for ten seconds or so, guns blazing, they began to realize something.

No one was shooting back. . . .

It dawned on Delaney first. He stopped short, causing Norton to collide with him, dropping both to the ground.

There they stayed for a very long moment. But then it became apparent. The only bullets whizzing through the air were the ones they were firing.

What's more, the shuttle was still there, intact. And so were all the cars. And there were no deep burning craters that would have been apparent after a cruise-missile attack. In fact, the Sharpur-say was very peaceful.

Too peaceful.

They finally regained their footing and scrambled to the first line of cars. They checked the three or four closest to them. They were empty. Taking up a position behind one Benz four-door, they looked out on the plain.

The portable palace was totally engulfed in flames by now, as were the heavy trucks that had brought it into position.

But the hills beyond were quiet. The heavy guns were still in place. But there were no fighters to be seen anywhere.

"Okay, I give up," Delaney said. "Where'd everyone go?"

"Beats me," Norton replied, finally standing up and taking a good look around. "But there's only one way to find out. . . ."

Five minutes later they had climbed up Exxon One, avoiding the pathway and going up the hard way, straight up the rocky ledge. Gaining the top, they found the answer to one big question. The hill was quiet because everyone up here was dead. The bodies of dozens of fighters were strewn about. Some had been shot, but many more had been stabbed or had their throats slit. In most cases without a fight.

"Oh, man, this is brutal," Delaney said.

Norton had to agree with him. The top of the hill was stained with vast pools of blood. Whatever had happened up here had happened quickly, silently, while he and Delaney were battling their way out of the portable palace.

Still, there was no guarantee the hilltop wasn't going hot again, so it was not their intention to stay for very long. But they had to look for one more thing. They made their way down the path to the small clearing where they'd first seen the outline of the space shuttle drawn in the wet sand. The likeness was still there, but another had been added. This gave them a clue as to what demons had descended on the hill.

Next to the space shuttle someone had drawn the outline of a banana . . . with rotor blades attached.

"Wow, the Kyrgyzstanis saved our hides *again*," Delaney breathed. "It looks like they went through here like shit through a goose. No doubt after bustling major ass just to get up here."

"Twenty-four of them against two or three hundred up here?" Norton said, searching the sky for any sign of the antique Flying Bananas, but finding none. "Damn, I'm sure glad they're on our side. . . ."

Suddenly they were rocked by another *boom!* It knocked both of them to the ground. The tremendous scream soon followed—but this time Norton kept both his eyes and ears open.

And that was when he finally saw what was causing all the noise. It wasn't cruise-missile blasts at all.

It was an SR-71 Blackbird spy plane rocketing over the plain at tremendous speed—and no more than five hundred feet off the ground. Neither Norton or Delaney had ever seen anything so big move so fast, at such a low altitude.

"Well, I guess your idea worked," Norton yelled to Delaney after the noise began to die away. "They found us!"

"Is this where the happy ending comes in?" Delaney asked.

They watched as the SR-71 climbed, turned, and came back again. But instead of screaming by at five hundred feet and bouncing a sonic boom off the flat terrain like a huge bowling ball, the airplane appeared to be slowing down.

"Are they trying to land that thing?" Delaney exclaimed "Out here?"

"I didn't think those things *ever* landed," Norton said.

But sure enough, the spy plane had drained away a lot of its speed, and now had its gear deployed. It was indeed coming in for a landing.

"*This* is the rescue plane they send?" Delaney cried. "How the hell are we all going to fit in that!"

27

The storm had been the worst piece of weather either Jimmy Gillis or Marty Ricco had ever flown through.

They first encountered it as they were nearing the northern reaches of the Bay of Bengal. Its clouds reached up higher than the jumbo was safe to fly, and it was wider than the amount of gas they had on board to go around it.

So they had to fly through it. It was fifty-five minutes of sheer terror. Lightning strikes, horrendous thunderclaps, turbulence that had them bouncing all over the sky, sometimes losing as much as three thousand feet on a single jolt.

Through all this the Sky Crane was grunting and groaning in the back. The big chopper wasn't tied down very well. It was essentially attached to skids on a set of loading rails. The rails themselves were held in place only by handlocked brakes. With each sickening thud from the rear bay, Gillis and Ricco thought the next might be the last. If it came undone, and they had several tons of loose helicopter banging against the interior wall, in such bad conditions . . .

well, their life expectancy under such circumstances would probably be very low.

So it was with great relief that they finally broke through the typhoon and found themselves at the beginning of an incredibly clear, bright sunny morning. Both Gillis and Ricco said silent prayers—not the first of their careers— then celebrated their new lease on life by sharing a pot of truly awful coffee.

They now found themselves somewhere over India. The bad weather seemed to have pushed them all over Southwest Asia. But even though they were way off course, they were nevertheless closing in on their goal of Diego Garcia, the American forward base located in the Indian Ocean.

They could only wonder what would happen once they reached the isolated American base. Many a special operation had been launched from this pinprick in the sea, so a fake airliner touching down would not even turn a dozen heads. But what orders would be waiting for them there? Ricco's guess was that they'd be told to turn around, and fly all the way back to Honolulu. Gillis predicted they would sit on the ground for days on end, doing nothing.

Neither man dared to speculate that their orders might simply tell them they could go home and just forget the whole thing.

They were both too smart to wish for that.

It was somewhere over northeast India, with the storm more than twenty minutes behind them, that Ricco's headphones came alive.

At first he thought it was New Delhi air traffic control, rerouting them once again. But the voice in Ricco's headphones sounded very distant, almost echoing, with a vaguely familiar quality to it. There was a chance he'd heard it before.

The person was slowly and methodically reading out a course change and a new heading for the jumbo. They then realized they were finally being diverted from their long, looping flight path to Diego Garcia, just as the beautiful Ginger had told them they might be.

The new orders were simple: They were to turn immediately to the northwest and increase power. Their new destination was a piece of central Pakistan that was but a few minutes away.

"Oh, lovely," Gillis commented once the voice had disconnected and the instructions were punched into their flight computer. "I've always wanted to see what Pakistan was like this time of year. . . ."

They flew for another ten minutes before reaching the coordinates.

But on arrival they found a somewhat confusing scene below them. They had come upon a long, narrow plain, one bordered by hills to the south and huge white mountains to the north. Just about at the center of this plain they could see dozens of smoke plumes being blown in the early morning wind. Several fires were raging below as well.

And in the middle of it all was a space shuttle.

"This must be the place," Gillis deadpanned.

The closer they got, the more apparent it became that a battle had just been fought here—and possibly another one was to come. By using their electronic binoculars, they could see a huge military column heading for the area from the west. There were at least twenty-five vehicles in the convoy, many towing large mobile guns. Oddly, the trucks were being led by a gold limousine, possibly a Mercedes. The column was about ten miles away.

Then, about fifteen miles or so to the north, near the foot of the mountains, they could see a half-dozen gray helicopters on the ground, their rotors turning, ready for flight.

"Are you thinking what I'm thinking?" Gillis asked Ricco.

"You mean like we've been here before?" Ricco replied.

It was true. The terrain, the unusual troop movements, the totally weird atmosphere. It was as if they were back inside the top-secret Nevada Weapons Range.

"Well, this is obviously where we are supposed to be," Gillis said. "I suggest we land and get this show on the road."

Five minutes later, the huge jumbo jet had come in for a bumpy landing on the Sharpur-say. Fighting smoke, dust, and high winds, Gillis and Ricco taxied up to a point about fifty yards from the rear of the shuttle.

The two pilots climbed out of the airplane and walked over to the shuttle. A very strange scene was waiting for them.

Sitting on the bottom steps of the stairway leading into the shuttle were four men in dirty, sweaty spacesuits. Each one had his head in his hands or was staring at the ground. Gillis and Ricco didn't recognize any of them.

At the top of the stairway, however, they saw three very familiar faces: it was Norton, Delaney, and Smitz.

Now this was freaky. The five of them had flown the ArcLight mission, as well as the operation to recover the Russian aircraft carrier. And while they couldn't all be called close friends—it was fair to say that Gillis and Ricco were no big fans of Norton and Delaney—they *were* colleagues and had gone to hell and back together. Twice.

"Déjà vu all over again," Ricco said to Gillis, looking at the three men.

"Or maybe we're just in a bad dream and we keep making the same mistakes over and over again," Gillis replied.

They stepped around the bummed-out astronauts and climbed up the stairway. Their three colleagues didn't seem very surprised or happy to see them.

Smitz had his ear to his cell phone, and was especially agitated. He looked up at the National Guard pilots.

"To what extent have you two been briefed?" he asked them bluntly.

"Zero percent," Ricco replied. "Other than the fact that there's a shuttle involved, we know nothing."

"That's just fucking great," Delaney mumbled. "Two more screaming mee-mees to put up with when the end comes."

"Listen, we've got a problem here," Smitz said to Gillis and Ricco. "Our friends at Langley are about to grease this place . . . with cruise missiles. In fact, the missiles are already on the way."

Gillis and Ricco just stared back at him. "Grease it?" Gillis asked. "Why? Isn't this the shuttle everyone's been looking for?"

"Yeah, but we found it too late," Smitz replied, looking at his watch again. "Exactly thirty-two minutes too late to be precise . . . Look, it's a long fucking story, but I've got a Blackbird flying about eight miles high, right above us. He can see everything, he can hear everything, and—"

"Let me get this straight," Ricco interrupted him. "You're saying a missile strike is on the way?"

Smitz nodded angrily. "And those missiles will be here in a matter of minutes," he confirmed.

"Well, whatever the reason is, this is a no-brainer," Gillis told them. "Let's get on the jumbo and get the hell out of here. I mean, we've been driving that can around like it's an old Chivvy. We can be off the ground in under five minutes."

Smitz frowned. "Well, there is one complication. . . ."

At that point Norton moved one way and Delaney another, and for the first time Gillis and Ricco saw someone else was standing in the shuttle's doorway.

It was the guy they knew as Angel. He was holding a gun on them. A *very* strange-looking gun.

"Whoa! Why the dramatics here, pal?" Ricco asked him. "We're all on the same side, aren't we?"

"Now that's a good question," Delaney said.

Gillis was getting pissed. "Look, what the fuck is going on here?" he asked. "You say there's a missile strike on the way. We're saying we can get off the ground in less than five minutes. And there's plenty of room for everyone . . . even Delaney."

"We're not going anywhere without the cargo," Angel replied. "That's the way it's got to be."

Gillis was still confused. "Cargo? What cargo?"

"I'm talking about what's inside the holding bay of this shuttle," Angel answered. "It is more important than anything else right now. Anything . . ."

The two National Guard pilots were simply bewildered.

"It's not a Lincoln Continental, is it?" Ricco asked.

Angel went on: "Look—why did you two come all this way? Not to save us, right? It was to retrieve a very valuable piece of equipment. That piece of equipment is in the cargo bay of this shuttle. Now, I'm just suggesting that we allow you to complete your mission."

"Yeah, sure," Ricco began with false diplomacy, his voice rising with just about every word. "But there's a problem with that, Clyde. You see, apparently a bunch of cruise missiles are on their way here. And apparently they're not that far away. And just to add a bit more to the mix, we saw an army column coming up from the west, and some real nasty helicopters just to the north. So if we all really want to dodge this very big bullet, the best thing for us all to do is get our asses inside the jumbo and get the fuck out of here."

Angel stayed cold and calm.

"It's already too late for that," he said. "Those missiles are so close, in the time it would take to get aboard the jumbo and take off, we'll all be dead."

They just stared up at him. "How do you know?" Ricco asked him. "You got antennas in your head?"

"He's right," Smitz confirmed after a long stream of curse words. "The Blackbird says we're looking at first impacts less than three minutes now."

"Well, it's official," Norton said. "We're screwed in blue. Even if we started running now, there's no way we could get far enough away."

Delaney turned back to Angel.

"Still want us to hang around and unpack your toy, pal?" he asked him bitterly.

"I do," the man in the white flight suit replied. "We have to."

Delaney just shook his head. "Knowing how the CIA works, the first cruise missile is probably aimed right at this shuttle—with twenty more behind it, just to make sure. And there's no calling them back. So what you want us to do just makes no sense."

Angel nodded.

"I know," he said. "But trust me, it will."

He put the gun away.

"I promised you that if you helped us, I'd tell you what we are carrying in the back," he said. "Well, now I will. It's an aircraft. The same one I've been flying around in, watching over you guys for the past two years."

"Well, we figured that," Delaney spat back at him.

Angel ignored him and went on: "Now, I can't tell you exactly what this aircraft is, or what it can do, or where the technology even came from. But I *will* tell you I was taking it up for a routine systems check—and, well, something went wrong. The next thing I knew, the acceleration valves were stuck on maximum, my inertia dampener went off line, and I wound up in orbit.

"The call went out. And my friends here in the *Avenger* came to my rescue. Just in the nick of time, I might add. My aircraft has some post-atmospheric capability—but not that much. . . ."

During all this, Norton and Delaney were looking at each other and mouthing all the strange words they were hearing.

Acceleration valves? Inertia dampeners?

"Suffice to say," Angel continued, "it can do some pretty incredible things and it has the price tag to prove it. So, there's no way anyone would allow it to fall into the hands of someone like Zim—or anyone else, friend or foe. First page, first sentence of the flight regulations for my aircraft says, if it ever falls into a nonsecure situation, then it will be destroyed. Whether I'm in it or not. That regulation is simply being acted on—we can't really blame the people who've launched the cruise missiles on us. They're just doing their job—like we all are."

"So all this time, the search for the shuttle was just so the CIA could destroy it?" Delaney asked.

"That's correct," Angel replied. "Along with a last-minute safety-valve effort; that's why Gillis and Ricco are here."

"Well, they arrived just a bit too late for that," Norton said, gloomily searching the sky to the southwest and wondering if he would be able to see the first wave of cruise missiles coming in.

But then an odd look came to Angel's face. "Don't be so sure of that," he said.

Smitz broke into the conversation. He was in touch with

the SR-71 pilot still circling overhead. He had three pieces of news, all of them bad.

"The missiles are three minutes away," he said. "And we've also got a half-dozen Hokums coming at us from the north, and indeed, an army column is setting up big guns to the west."

"At least we won't get blasted into Kingdom Come all by ourselves," Delaney said.

"If we work quickly," Angel replied. "It might not happen at all."

As Gillis and Ricco quickly left to pull the Sky Crane from the jumbo jet, Norton, Delaney, and two of the astronauts scrambled up to the top of the shuttle.

Because the shuttle did not have any electricity running through it for fear of setting off the explosives underneath, they had to open the cargo bay doors manually. Supposedly this would not be difficult, as the doors were equipped with spring motors. If they didn't have enough power to operate, they could be opened with just a little muscle power. The problem was, this backup system was built into the shuttle in case something went wrong with the doors in space.

It was different on Earth.

Norton and Delaney got on one side of the door seam, two of the astronauts on the other. The opening between the two doors was barely wide enough to get their finger-nails into.

They got as best a grip as they could, and then pulled with all their might.

Nothing happened. The doors didn't budge.

Norton checked his watch. By his calculations, there was just one minute and forty-five seconds left before the first missile was due to hit. . . .

"Jezzuz, pull again!" he screamed.

They yanked the doors again. Still nothing.

"How about four guys on one side?" Delaney suggested. He and Norton jumped over to the other side, and began yanking the left side door with the two astronauts.

It wouldn't budge.

They tried again.

Nothing . . .

Norton checked his watch.

One minute, forty seconds . . .

He felt like his head was about to explode. With rage. Anger. Frustration. Even if they got the doors open, they still had to corral the secret aircraft and attach it to the Sky Crane's sling. Then they'd have to lift it out of the shuttle and up under the chopper's belly. Then the Sky Crane would have to carefully move back over to the jumbo. Then it would have to land. Then the copter would have to be pushed up into the jumbo jet. Then the jumbo would have to take off.

"We just don't have the time to do this. . . ." Norton said to Delaney as they tried to yank on the doors again.

"Put that glove away and it might go faster," Delaney replied.

Now airborne, the Sky Crane was coming into a hover above the shuttle. Its downwash hit them like a small hurricane.

"Pull again!" Norton screamed.

They pulled again. Absolutely nothing.

One minute, thirty-five seconds . . .

"Isn't there any way to get some power into this thing?" Norton yelled down to the flight deck. The lead astronaut was stationed here with Smitz; both were listening to the Blackbird pilot's gloomy updates.

"We can try," the astronaut yelled back. "But just one spark and we all go up!"

"We're all going up in a minute anyway!" Norton told him. "So do it!"

The astronaut ducked back into the hatchway. Norton could hear him throwing switches. Then they all heard the distinct sound of electrical sparks crackling. A burnt rubber smell enveloped the shuttle.

One astronaut was on the ground next to the stairway. He began waving his arms madly.

"Kill the juice!" he screamed. *"Kill the juice!"*

He was pointing frantically to the crumpled landing gear. The shorn wires inside its wheel fairing were sizzling hot.

But at the same time, the whine from the cargo bay door motors was also heard from below. The doors began to move—for about one inch. But then they jammed again when the electricity went down.

Norton looked at his watch.

One minute, twenty seconds . . .

"Juice it again!" he yelled.

"Wait!" the astronaut on the ground yelled. "You've got a shitload of electrical sparks in full blow not two feet away from a stack of dynamite!"

"Does anyone have a gun?" Norton asked those on top of the shuttle with him.

"I do," Delaney replied.

"Then shoot that guy, will you?"

The astronaut below got the idea. He signaled to the astronaut in the cockpit. This man did as Norton requested. He turned the electricity on again. The wires crackled. The smell returned. The door came up another inch—then jammed again.

One minute, fifteen seconds to go.

"Juice it again!" Norton yelled.

The astronaut complied. The door opened another inch. Then jammed once more.

One minute, ten seconds . . .

"Okay, when he juices it again, we all pull. . . ."

The astronaut juiced the shuttle again, everyone yanked— and the doors came flying open.

The four men fell away in four different directions. Norton nearly toppled completely off the shuttle, a fall that would have broken his back. As it was he was thrown hard onto the wing.

He regained his footing to see the doors had fully deployed. He could see Delaney gazing down into the cargo bay. The look on his face was absolutely frightening. A strange glow was emanating from below and reflecting off his partner's uniform. The color was hard to describe, but it was not unlike the bizarre hues of the Paswar. One moment blue, the next yellow, the next an eerie green.

Norton climbed back up to the cargo bay, using the bent back door to boost himself up.

Then he looked into the bay for himself—and felt his heart begin beating very fast.

"Mama-loosha . . ." he said. "Look at that. . . ."

One minute to go . . .

The Sky Crane was now in position over the shuttle.

Gillis was fighting the controls. The wind was furious— it took all the strength he could muster to keep the aircraft steady in the gale.

It was obvious now that the training they had gone through in the top-secret Nevada range had been intended for retrieving the shuttle cargo from the bottom of the Paswar crater, and not on a very windy open desert plain. As a result, the huge chopper did not want to stay steady.

"Hurry, Marty!" he yelled back to Ricco. "I don't know

how long I can maintain this hover . . . it's your show. . . ."

Ricco, meanwhile, was staring at the panel of buttons and switches that ran the Sky Crane's lifting sling. He'd never worked the controls before.

He started pushing things and pulling things, and after a few seconds, the loading sling dropped from the center of the chopper's open bay. But it only fell halfway. It was caught up on itself. He tried jiggling the vertical-control lever. It only made the situation worse.

"This thing didn't enjoy the ride over!" he yelled forward to Gillis.

They had worried about something breaking on the chopper during the long, bumpy flight from Nevada. Something in the engine. Or the electronics. Or maybe a snapped rotor blade. Never did they think it would be the lifting-sling chains that would get screwed up. They were probably the simplest things on the aircraft.

Ricco jiggled the release lever some more, but he knew it would have no effect. The chains holding the sling looked like a ball of spaghetti.

Suddenly a major gust of wind hit the Sky Crane. It was so forceful, it knocked Ricco on his ass. He heard Gillis grunt twice as he fought with the controls. But once the chopper was righted again, Ricco saw one of the chain strands drop.

"Can you do that again?" he yelled up to Gillis.

Before there was a reply, the chopper was again buffeted by a strong wind. Again, Ricco was tossed to the floor. Again, one of the chain links unraveled itself.

This might take a while, Ricco caught himself thinking.

Then he looked down at the men standing precariously atop the battered space shuttle. That was when Ricco saw the object in the cargo bay for the first time.

"Whoa, what the fuck is that?"

Gillis saw it too. "It really ain't a Lincoln, is it!"

It was shaped like a metallic pancake, broad yet triangular, with winglets on two tips and two tiny cockpit windows.

From Ricco's point of view, the strange thing was that it seemed like he was seeing two things at once. He was looking down at the aircraft, but he was also looking at what he could only describe as a collection of thin blue mist. It was not part of the aircraft inside the cargo bay, but then again, it was. Not quite a hologram, but damn close. He stared at it for a few moments, totally mesmerized.

Then his eyes began to hurt.

Thirty seconds . . .

"There's just no way we're going to make this!" one of the astronauts yelled.

Norton and Delaney were now down inside the cargo bay, waiting for the loading sling to fall into position. Both men were in awe of the strange aircraft, at the same time realizing that in less than a minute, they would both be blown to smithereens.

Suddenly they heard Sky Crane's engines start to cough. They looked up and saw the aircraft was coming down right on top of them. The huge copter filled Norton's eyes—he shut them, expecting to be flattened any moment. Yet, when he opened them again, the helicopter had somehow regained its proper altitude.

An instant later the chain sling hit him on the head. Luckily, his oversized Fritz helmet took most of the blow. Still, it seemed like he'd been whacked with a sledgehammer. While he was trying to regain his vision, one of the astronauts up top yelled: "Jessuz, look!"

Norton stuck his head out of the cargo bay and looked to the north. Six helicopters were rising out of the mountains. They were Hokums and coming on quick. Even worse, off to the west, he could see soldiers massing and big guns being deployed.

"One way or another," Delaney said, standing beside him, "we are royally fucked. . . ."

Twenty seconds . . .

As hopeless as it seemed, they returned to their task inside the cargo bay. But now there was another problem. When they had first looked down at the object from above, it had seemed as if it was too large for the cargo bay and that its wings were too wide to get back out.

But now that they were inside the bay and actually trying to tie the aircraft to the Sky Crane's loading lines, it appeared that the vehicle was actually a lot smaller. There was no rational explanation for the weird effect. But it was making it almost impossible for them to get the sling around it.

Fifteen seconds . . .

Angel had climbed inside the weird aircraft by now, and with a jolt from the shuttle's batteries, started his propulsion unit. Then it really got weird. The aircraft began glowing very brightly now. The faint blue mist turned into a bright blue halo of electricity surrounding it.

Ten seconds . . .

Norton looked up. The Hokums were right on top of them, frozen in the sky. An artillery shell seemed to be hanging right over his head.

He looked at his watch.

Five seconds . . .

That was when Angel intensified power. The wind died down. The blue glow intensified. Norton felt a *zap!* go right through his body.

So this *is what it feels like to die. . . .*

He looked over at Delaney, who was staring back at him,

a very strange look on his face. It appeared as if his friend was suddenly clean-shaven. Norton looked down at his hands to see the strange aircraft was already hooked up in the loading sling and Ricco and Gillis were lifting it out of the cargo bay.

He looked at his watch again.

It had stopped.

He pointed to Delaney's watch. His partner held it up to Norton's eyes to see.

It had stopped too. . . .

Aboard the Destroyer Gates

"Okay, the *Virginia* says we've got hits. So does the *Neponset*. . . ."

As soon as the destroyer's weapons team leader heard these words in his headphones, he began pushing buttons and querying his computer. "I copy, Comm. We are awaiting confirmation of live video access."

Captain Koosman put his glasses on and studied the computer-generated battle-management map that dominated his ship's combat room. Little red indicators were popping up all over the section of the screen designated "IP-Alpha." This was the battle-management computer's way of telling them that the first Tomahawks launched by the shadow force had reached their target and were in the process of pulverizing it.

"How long until we get a live read?" Koosman asked his weapons team leader. The officer began pushing more buttons.

"I'm downloading a live feed from an SR-71 overflying the area now," he reported. "Pilot reports a lot of debris in the air already. Missiles are still arriving over the target. All detonations look good."

Koosman leaned back in his seat.

"Seventy-four Tommies . . . with fake-nuke warheads . . . on a quarter-mile-square IP," he said. "They'll be lucky if they don't strike oil. . . ."

"I'm glad I'm not the one who has to make the call to the Pakistani Embassy," the weapons officer said to him in an aside.

Koosman just shrugged. "Probably nothing a few hundred million in foreign aid won't cure."

An image started coming across their battle-management screen. It was the real-time video of the target area.

"Okay, here's the feed from the SR-71," the weapons officer announced.

The seven men of the weapons team, plus Koosman, gathered around the screen. As one, the men let out a gasp.

The impact point now looked like part of the moon. Craters upon craters upon craters. With missiles still exploding over it everywhere.

"Well, they wanted dust," Koosman said. "And it's dust they got. . . ."

Aboard the *Bataan*

Captain Currier found Chou Koo sitting alone in the officers' mess hall.

The Marine captain was staring into a cup of coffee that had gone cold long ago. He looked like he hadn't slept in many weeks, which was close to the truth. Every few seconds, his body would shake, from head to toe, just for a moment. He was feeling the reverberations of dozens of cruise-missile impacts more than five hundred miles away.

Currier sat down next to him.

"I know you don't need any more bad news," he told Chou. "But I'm afraid I have some. . . ."

Chou barely looked up. His body shook again.

"Your pals, Delaney and Norton . . ."

Currier didn't have to say any more. Chou knew what he was talking about. He put his head in his hands.

"God, this thing has been a disaster from the start," the Marine officer said, his body shaking again. "I just wish I was up there with them. That's the least I could have done."

"And you would have wound up just as dead as they are," Currier told him. "Look, man, you're alive. They're not. Sure, things went wrong—but you're still here. There's no shame in that."

Chou laughed grimly.

"You sure of that, Skipper?"

Currier got up to go.

"I have one small piece of good news too," he said. "Our friends, the Kyrgyzstanis, are well on their way back to their home base. It looks like they'll make it in one piece, though there are indications they took a detour along the way. They were good guys—even if no one knows how to spell the name of their country."

"Yeah, they're some of the best soldiers I've ever seen," Chou replied, then added after a pause, "I wonder if they have any openings. . . ."

28

Nevada Special Weapons Testing Range

As he usually did this time every day, Lieutenant Moon was sitting atop the mesa that hid the secret air base and hangar, drinking coffee from a thermos.

This was his favorite place in the entire secret weapons range. It had a great view. It was peaceful. It was a good place to be alone and think.

It was the nature of his job as den mother to transiting special-ops newbies that some of the people he met never came back. And though he considered himself a professional in a highly unusual assignment, it was difficult not to take some of these things to heart.

Just an hour before, he'd received word that Jimmy Gillis and Marty Ricco had been killed. In the line of duty, doing what they'd been sent overseas by the president himself to do.

This one was tough to take. Moon knew both pilots were

family men, with wives and kids and jobs and mortgages. True, they'd been cranky during their stay inside the top-secret weapons range. But they were also very likable guys; good people you'd want to share a beer with. And great pilots.

But now they were gone.

It was usually quiet on the range this time of day. The daylight exercises were all over with and the nighttime operations had not yet begun.

That was why hearing the sound of a jet approaching seemed so unusual. Moon drained his coffee cup, folded his chair, and closed up his thermos.

The sound got louder.

He knew it was a good-sized airplane making the noise, and it seemed to be coming his way. This was odd. He wasn't scheduled to receive any visitors today. And his bosses rarely brought someone in without letting him know first.

He retrieved his binoculars from his small copter and began scanning the western horizon. His instinct told him that this was not a military flight. The sound was all wrong. Perhaps a commercial airliner had wandered into the restricted airspace above the range. It was not unknown for flights from Las Vegas to Reno to drift a bit on occasion.

Finally he saw it. An airplane was coming right out of the setting sun, growing bigger by the second. And Moon had been right. This was not a military airplane, or an off-course commuter flight.

This was something else.

"Son of a bitch, " he whispered.

It was a jumbo jet. Big and white, with the words South-west Asia Airlines splashed on its sides.

Moon ran to his copter and hastily began starting its engine.

"I really hope there's someone alive aboard that plane," he whispered to himself. "I really do. . . ."

The jumbo jet had landed by the time Moon reached the ground.

The big plane rolled to a halt in front of the hidden hangar, and was immediately surrounded by several dozen soldiers in gray uniforms.

Moon reached its side hatchway just as it swung open. A man he didn't know literally fell out of the doorway, face-first, landing hard on the ground three feet below.

Moon was quickly at his side and rolled him over. But the man wasn't injured. He was drunk. His uniform name tag identified him as "Delaney, R."

Next out the door was Gene Smitz. He was drunk too. Somehow he helped Delaney to his feet, and both of them snapped very unsteady salutes, before collapsing into gales of intoxicated laughter. Then Gillis and Ricco climbed out of the airplane, pushed the drunks aside, and rushed to shake hands with Moon.

"Mission accomplished," Ricco said to him with a crisp, sober salute. "Can we go home now?"

Moon was so shocked, he could barely speak. The intel briefing paper he'd read stated without equivocation that the shuttle had been pulverized—with all hands on board. The report had implied that the recovery team had not been able to evacuate the area before the cruise missiles arrived.

Yet here they were.

"Jessuz, do you have the *Aurora* in the back?" Moon asked the two National Guard pilots.

"*Aurora? Avenger?*" Gillis asked. "Which is which?"

"You mean the flying saucer?" Ricco asked him. "Yeah,

we got it. Like we said: mission accomplished."

Moon still couldn't believe it. This really *was* a case of the dead coming back to life. Now the four astronauts climbed out of the airplane, followed by Norton. The astronauts were as loaded as Delaney and Smitz, and could barely make it down the ladder.

"Excuse us, we stopped for beer in Hawaii," one astronaut told Moon.

Moon turned back to Gillis and Ricco. "Did he just say you stopped *for beer* in Hawaii?"

Ricco shrugged. "Well, we had to get fuel too," he explained apologetically. "That guy Angel arranged it all. . . ."

Moon just stared back at them. They were a mess, a rabble. But somehow these men had saved the nation's most valuable, most highly secret weapons system from the hands of the world's most demented terrorist.

But how?

"Don't ask me," Ricco said, anticipating his question.

"No comment," Gillis agreed.

They opened the 747's loading ramp, and Moon saw it for himself. The *Aurora* was tucked up underneath the Sky Crane, just barely fitting between the chopper's long gangly legs. It was still glowing a light shade of blue. Moon immediately took his watch off and put it in his pocket.

Angel walked down the ramp and greeted Moon. They'd known each other for years.

"I'll copy you for my report," Angel said, also anticipating the question of why they were all alive, and here in Nevada, with the world's most classified secret still intact. "But I warn you, it will be *so* many pages, you might want to wait for the movie."

At this point several gray-uniformed officers appeared from the darkness of the hidden hangar. They had a brief conversation with Moon and Angel. Then they walked over to Smitz.

"Can you come with us please, sir?" one of the officers asked the CIA agent.

Smitz laughed in their faces. "Where we going? You got a bar out here somewhere?"

"Please, sir."

The officer's voice was rather stern, almost chilling. Suddenly Smitz wasn't as drunk as he was before.

Angel stepped up. "It's probably best you go with them," he said.

With that the soldiers flanked Smitz and led him into the giant dark maw of the hidden hangar.

He was put on an elevator at the rear of the hangar.

His buzz was fading and reality was now flooding in. Where the hell was he anyhow? And why was he the only one that had been led away by the soldiers? They were huge, nonspeaking, and wearing Confederate Gray uniforms. *What was up with that?* Still unsteady on his feet, he heard a million voices floating around his head. One seemed to whisper: "You know *way* too much. . . ."

The elevator went down fast and deep. Smitz counted fifteen levels before it finally squeaked to a stop. The doors opened and Smitz found himself looking into a vast chamber. It was almost all wood. Big table in the middle. Huge TV screen on one wall.

And seven old guys looking out at him, smoking cigarettes and sipping coffee.

Smitz couldn't help letting out one last drunken laugh.

"Hey, this place looks a lot bigger on TV. . . ." he said.

The soldiers pushed him to the head of the table and then took a few steps back. Smitz studied the face of each man. They were a lot older than they'd appeared on TV, nor did they look as "movie-ish." In fact, if the circumstances were different, they could have passed for seven old cowpokes sitting around a table at a diner bullshitting and drinking coffee.

"We have a few things to say to you," the man he knew only as the Voice told him, his tone sounding softer, older. "First of all, you did an outstanding job out there. Obviously you have great stamina."

Smitz burped. "Check with me in a couple hours on that one."

The Voice hit a button on the table in front of him, and the huge TV screen flickered to life. "You might be interested in this," he said.

The image came together, and Smitz realized he was looking at a picture of the missing soda-pop blimp resting on the side of a snowcapped mountain. There was little doubt the peak had literally punctured the balloon.

"We found it about a hundred miles west of Paswar," the Voice explained. "They're still looking for the crew, but as you can see the weather isn't helping them any."

It was true. The snow was falling so hard on the mountain, it was quickly covering up all traces of the deflated airship.

"Well, the person who finds that in about a thousand years will get a hell of a jolt," Smitz said.

"Actually it will be eleven hundred and sixty-three years," the Voice said. "But that's another story."

Smitz looked at the guy strangely. *What did he mean by that?*

"The second thing we have to say might not please you very much," the Voice went on.

Suddenly Smitz was all ears. He really didn't like the sound of that.

"You've become privy to many, many things in the last

few days," the Voice told him soberly. "Things we cannot afford just anyone knowing about. We don't have the time or the inclination to tell you now exactly what this setup here is all about. The short version is we think of ourselves as a safety valve. We step in when we see our cousins at Langley about to fuck something up, or when it looks like something very important is going down the drain. Witness the ArcLight and the Russian carrier missions.

"But this last mission—well, there were some pretty big secrets spilled here. Aside from the fact that you've now seen this weapons range and what's inside this mountain, you've also met the astronauts. Those guys are so classified they're not allowed to give out their names—even to each other. And you saw the *Aurora* itself. You know how it got stuck in orbit and how we sent the *Avenger* up after it and how its propulsion unit can, shall we say, *distort* a few things? And of course, if what we think happened over there actually *did* take place to get you out alive—well, the truth is, you know *way* too much. Almost as much as we do. And that is just not acceptable. Not only does it make you a security risk, it makes you a national security *threat.*"

Smitz felt the hair go up on the back of his head. Suddenly it became very clear what the men were talking about.

"Jesus, you really *are* going to kill me. . . ."

The men all stared back at him—and then laughed.

"Kill you?" the Voice said. "Boy, you really *have* been seeing too many spy movies. We're not going to kill you—quite the opposite."

They all looked down to the far end of the chamber. Suddenly an overhead light snapped on and illuminated an empty chair at the end of the table.

"You know so much, we have no choice but to have you join our little club."

Smitz was stunned. Really? He was graduating from being a Spook to a true Ghost?

"Just one more question?" the Voice asked.

"Yes?" Smitz replied, still stunned.

"Do you know how to make a good cup of coffee? Because we all really stink at it."

It was now early evening.

The meal was steak sandwiches and champagne. The location was the mesa top where Moon usually took his coffee. The occasion was a Welcome Back from the Dead dinner.

He had transported nine chairs to the top of the butte, along with the food and booze and the rest of the recovery team. The view this time of day was spectacular.

The astronauts were especially loving the feast. Gillis and Ricco were also chowing down with vigor. Delaney, however, was a bit subdued.

Moon lowered his voice between bites.

"I know I probably shouldn't ask this, but—"

"Don't bother," Delaney said, stopping him in midsentence. "I can't tell you what happened because I don't know myself. If you want the details, you'll have to ask your pal Angel."

Moon took a huge bite of his sandwich. "Well, I'll have to tell you one thing," he said. "You guys are golden now. You retrieved a trillion-dollar piece of equipment—something that was so freaking top secret, it has its own classification. You'll be able to write your own ticket after this. No more stupid, bullshit missions. Maybe no more missions at all. You've got to be happy about that. . . ."

Delaney looked up at Moon for a long moment. Then he pointed to Norton, who was sitting apart from the rest of them, not eating, not drinking, just staring off into the west and turning a well-worn glove over and over in his hands.

"Does that guy look happy to you?" he asked.